THE SECRET
OF
EARNIE'S ISLAND

Thomas H. Mathis

A Novel

simply francis publishing company

North Carolina

Library of Congress Control Number: 2022921213
ISBN: 978-1-63062-044-8 (paperback)
ISBN: 978-1-63062-045-5 (e-book)
Printed in the United States of America
Cover and Interior Design: Christy King Meares

For information about this title or to order books and/or electronic media, contact the publisher:

simply francis publishing company
P.O. Box 329, Wrightsville Beach, NC 28480
www.simplyfrancispublishing.com
simplyfrancispublishing@gmail.com

DEDICATION

To my dear friend, Earnie.

TABLE OF CONTENTS

CHAPTER 1

Harrison awoke in a sheer panic, at first not knowing where he was. Shivering, fear completely froze his body as he slowly opened his eyes. The fingernail moon above provided faint light, allowing him only to see a few inches. Anything beyond that was a total blur. All he could see was sand.

Lying on his left side, he lifted his head a few inches, but the movement produced such enormous pain, he laid his head back down. The throbbing in his head made him nauseous. The vice grip feeling in his chest got tighter. His breathing was shallow and short like a dog panting after a long run.

With sand caked to the left side of his face and clinging to his eyelashes, he tried to bring his right hand toward his face to rub away the grit. Stunned, he realized his hands were tied together. Using the back of his hand, he gently removed the sand from his face.

Cold and shivering, his attempt to curl into a ball to generate some body heat failed. His right leg was dead weight. He tried again but the pain from his leg made it impossible.

As his breathing became heavier and more erratic, he could not stop the shivering. He felt himself drifting into a semi-conscious state. That frightened him even more. Raising his head again, the neurons in his visual cortex fired off bursts of light, and he could not see anything clearly. He rolled gently to his right and laid there on his back waiting for the streaks and specks of light in his vision to clear before trying to open his eyes again.

When Harrison finally opened his eyes, the ghostly moon was barely visible through the canopy of low-hanging trees. He tried to gather his thoughts. His entire body was riddled with pain, especially the constant throbbing in his right leg. The only sound he could make out was the constant croaking of tree frogs calling for rain. He dared not raise his head again, so he just lay there, not moving a muscle. Any attempt to comprehend his strange predicament proved futile. He couldn't remember his name.

"My God where am I? What has happened to me?"

Harrison prayed that he would have his answer soon as fear mounted in his mind. The shivering increased almost as if he was experiencing a full-blown convulsion. Strange scenes of violence kept flashing through his mind, but he could not put anything into a logical order. A young girl in a red dress, a door with the words CIMM on it, a huge rat in a black limousine, a garden hose all crazy mixed-up thoughts and images entered his mind. It made no sense at all. He closed his eyes and prayed again.

As the pale light of the moon started to fade into a wisp of hazy orange with a tint of blue far off in the distance, he knew his prayer was answered. He welcomed the early signs of a new day rising. Soon he would be able to see his environment and finally grasp his circumstances. It didn't take long before he could see his immediate surroundings. When he lifted his head up a few inches, he did not recognize anything around him. There just wasn't enough light yet, so he closed his eyes and rested his head on the sand.

Harrison drifted off to sleep for a few minutes. Suddenly someone grabbed him by the shoulders and lifted him straight up. He stood face-to-face with a monster of a man who glared at him. Harrison was looking into the eyes of the devil himself. The fear he had experienced earlier turned into raging anger. Like those who had a near-death experience and had their whole life flash before them, the events of the past few days came flooding back. His predicament became crystal clear.

He wasn't sure exactly what day it was, but that didn't matter. His memory was recovering. The scenes of the last forty-eight hours unfolded as if watching a movie. This wasn't some sort of horrifying nightmare. It was reality. He clearly recognized the man standing before him. Harrison's earlier anger turned to paralyzing fear. It was this man who beat him so severely. He was the reason for all the pain.

As Harrison gazed back into Jaxson's eyes, his increasing cognitive faculties allowed him to recall and relive, bit by bit, the events of the last few days. His first vivid memory was a beautiful green fairway on a golf course. How did he get from a golf course to standing in front of a man who scared the hell out of him?

CHAPTER 2

It all began with a gorgeous spring morning at Harrison's home in Middle Sound. Only ten minutes outside downtown Wilmington, North Carolina, Middle Sound is a close-knit coastal community nestled between US Highway 17 and the Intracoastal Waterway. Home to a rural population of under four thousand residents, Middle Sound is a hidden gem along the southeast coast of North Carolina.

The temperature was slightly above sixty degrees with no humidity, and the sweet smell of wisteria wafted in the air. After a light shower the night before, the dogwood petals and azalea flowers were glistening in the early morning light. The flowers were nearing their peak, ready to display their full beauty for the upcoming annual Azalea Festival.

The highly advertised book signing for Harrison Thomas's debut novel was scheduled to start at two-thirty that Saturday afternoon. His publisher, Rex Calder and Associates originally wanted the event to take place along the riverfront in downtown Wilmington, but Harrison argued for an alternative location closer to home. He felt the ideal location would be the Barnes and Noble bookstore located in Mayfaire Town Center, a high-end shopping center with brand-name retailers, eateries, a multiplex, and several supermarkets. The publisher relented.

The residents of Middle Sound were thrilled to know that one of their own had written such a successful novel which achieved national recognition. The wonderful descriptions of their coastal community were well-received. For many, a signed copy of the book would be cherished for years.

The novel was a heartwarming story about an elderly man, who was dying of cancer, spending his last summer with his beloved grandson in and around Middle Sound. In chapter after chapter, the old man described in detail his past failures and wrongdoings, trying to educate his grandson not to do the same.

One of the most exciting and thrilling chapters in the book was when the old man unearthed a clump of rare Spanish gold coins while metal detecting one morning on a nearby barrier island with his grandson. The novel related the tender inspirational experiences shared between a dying man and his only grandson. Each chapter disclosed the principles and the practices the old man wanted his young grandson to abide by once he was gone. The story concluded with the grandson inheriting all the gold, making him a rich man.

There were rumors of a movie deal, and social media was buzzing for weeks since Wilmington was home to the EUE Screen Gems Studios, originally established by Dino DeLaurentis back in 1985. With a multitude of tourists already in town for the Azalea Festival, Rex Calder's publishing staff anticipated a large turnout for the book signing. They placed ads in the *Wilmington Star News* and the *Wrightsville Beach Magazine,* along with multiple Facebook ads.

As he had done for decades, Harrison woke up at four-thirty a.m. sharp. He did not need an alarm clock, as his internal clock had been set many years ago from getting up early to attend swim practice. From the tender age of five until now, he shot out of bed each morning at four-thirty. Today was no different and his first objective of the day was to make himself a strong cup of coffee, black with no sugar. His swimming days were long gone, and being only five foot ten inches tall, weighing slightly over two hundred pounds, he needed to watch his weight. That young swimmer's physique of one hundred and forty-five pounds with a ripped six pack stomach had vanished. At seventy-years-old, all he had now was a shed covering his toolbox.

Harrison had been invited to play a round of golf that morning with his dear friend Robert Glover at the Castle Bay course in Hampstead. Tee-off time was seven-thirty. That would give him plenty of time to play and still make it on time for the book signing.

Robert was eager to see Harrison's talent since he heard that his buddy had made, not only one, but two holes-in-ones back in 1991. Robert trounced his butt, posting an amazing five under par, sixty-seven while Harrison shot a pathetic ninety-eight.

When he returned from playing golf, he placed his golf clubs in the back of the master bedroom closet, vowing to never bring the sticks back out again. The next few hours were spent with ice packs on his lower back while resting in his favorite recliner in the living room.

Ms. Kelly, Harrison's wife of twenty-nine years, left the house around one-thirty that afternoon to meet family and friends to help set up the event. Harrison stayed at home to prepare his speech. He was not used to speaking in public, and in fact he was deathly afraid of it. His nerves were on edge. Walking around the house with wads of toilet paper crammed into his armpits, he needed to calm down and stop the unsightly hyperhidrosis that was drenching his T-shirt. Bounty was not doing its job, and he thought about going out to his work shed and painting his armpits with shellac.

Harrison stood in front of his closet, trying to decide which shirt to wear. Black would be a good choice to hide the ugly under-arm sweat rings, and would coordinate with his graying hair, what little he had left. He had a multitude of baseball caps to match his black shirt, but overall, he just wasn't sold on black. He thought his attire needed to be more vibrant, colorful and bold. He decided to wear his bright orange fishing shirt.

Ms. Kelly arrived at Mayfaire Town Center only to find a packed parking lot in front of the bookstore. She circled around and parked in the last space in the back parking lot. When she entered the bookstore, she was shocked to see so many people. She glanced around and spotted her seventeen-year-old grandson Bryson, just beaming with pride. After all, it was his idea for his Paw Paw to write a book.

Bryson had spent every other weekend with his Paw Paw and his Grandmama Kelly since he was in diapers. He loved to listen to all the wild and crazy stories his Paw Paw told about his younger days.

The stories Harrison told about his time at East Carolina University were educational in nature, and a tad boring. However, the juicy stories of his bachelor life at Wrightsville Beach captivated Bryson for hours. Those tales were filled with adventure and sheer excitement, especially when the stories were about women.

Over the years, Ms. Kelly had heard them all. If Harrison had a few too many cocktails and the stories became too exaggerated, she would give him a glare that could stop a tank and send him off mumbling to himself.

Harrison loved to read, and often took Bryson to the local bookstores. He tried his best to get Bryson to read as well. He once bought him Ernest Hemmingway's, *The Old Man and The Sea,* thinking a short novel would be an easy read for him, but the book just collected dust.

7

During their last visit to his favorite bookstore, Harrison purchased a novel by Dane Bahr titled *The Houseboat* strictly because of the intriguing cover. Leaving the store and walking across the parking lot, Bryson turned to his Paw Paw and said, "Hey, you should write a book. The way you tell stories, it should be easy for you."

Over the next hour or so, the two conjured up possible story lines and characters. Bryson wanted the main character to be his own Paw Paw. Searching for a topic, they decided to focus on metal detecting and the story was born. The novel would be about Paw Paw finding buried treasure with his metal detector on a tiny remote island adjacent to the Intracoastal Waterway. This tiny island was a favorite weekend camping site that Bryson and his Grandmama Kelly had visited for the past couple of summers. Grandmama Kelly's friend, as well as Harrison's best friend, Earnie Cafaro, found it one day while out clamming. From that day on, everybody called it Earnie's Island.

"Maybe we can call the book *Earnie's Island*. How does that sound?"

"It is perfect, Paw Paw. Everybody knows that pirates used to roam around these areas. There is even an island somewhere around here named Money Island, isn't there? And didn't Blackbeard supposedly anchor his ship at Topsail Sound?"

"Didn't you once tell me that your friend Gene found a Spanish doubloon on Shell Island with his detector right after a big storm? Everybody would believe the story, wouldn't they?"

"Ya know, maybe you're right. I'll think about it," Harrison said. "I'm seventy-years-old now, so it might be too late. I don't know if I have the mental fortitude to do this."

After dropping Bryson off at home, Harrison's mind was moving a thousand miles an hour. He hurried home to get in front of his computer. He wanted to dive into Google and do as much research as he could about the pirates of long ago who traveled along the North Carolina coast. How was he going to write a story that was even believable? He had spent hours and hours, if not days, metal-detecting the coastal areas and never found any pirate gold. Nor did he hear of anyone finding any significant treasure except down in Florida.

By eleven o'clock that evening, Harrison had written a rough outline for the story. There were fifteen characters along with ten scenes all taking place within a short distance from his house. Excited, he transferred his notes into the computer. He had a grandiose plan to write a chapter a day to complete his novel in a month. Somewhere around two o'clock in the morning, he finished chapter one, saved it on his computer and went to bed. It took nearly an hour for his mind to stop swirling with ideas for his book.

Rising early the next morning, Harrison rushed to his computer and read his first chapter. He was so disappointed with what he read; he deleted all of it. It was a jumbled mess that made no sense at all, and he learned his first lesson in writing - don't attempt such a task late at night. He decided to write when he was wide awake - five o'clock in the morning till eight o'clock.

The first draft of the novel was completed in less than two months. The plan to write in the early morning hours paid off, as the words seemed to flow freely through his fingertips. The first manuscript he sent out was rejected by a large publishing company up north. They wouldn't even look at it unless he had a so-called agent. He wondered if they had even read the first page. The second manuscript was formatted correctly and sent to a well-known agent in New York City. That too was rejected, in brutal fashion. Written across the front page of the returned manuscript in bold red ink were the words....*my third-grade daughter could write a better story than this garbage.*

Although the rejection hurt, with the encouragement of Bryson and his older sister Andrea, he sat down and drafted his third manuscript. The task of writing a book was not as easy as he originally thought it would be. He gained a lot of respect for all the authors of books he had read in the past.

Once the third manuscript was completed, Harrison decided not to send it to the big publishing companies. He needed an agent but wasn't sure how to go about getting one. An idea came to him. He needed to find someone local, and he knew exactly where to turn, Bryson's other grandma, Ms. Molly.

Ms. Molly was a gun-toting former FBI agent from Wisconsin who retired to North Carolina to write a book about her adventures with the FBI. Since her book was published locally a few years ago, this was the person he needed to talk to.

Molly received Harrison's manuscript in the mail and called him three weeks later, to set up a meeting. She suggested they meet at the local shooting range that was close to Harrison's house. Molly greeted Harrison with open arms, and to his surprise she liked the story. She felt it lacked what she called atmosphere. She had taken the liberty of making notes on each page. She listed some possible re-writes along with tips on character development.

"I really like your story. It has a lot of tension, it moves along well, and your voice is engaging. It's got potential but needs a lot of work to be successful. For one thing, it is too short. Take my notes and my suggested re-writes and write another draft. Send it back to me when you're finished."

"What do you mean that it is too short? I think there are some thirty-four thousand words in my story. Isn't that enough?

Ernest Hemingway's *The Old Man and The Sea* was only some twenty-six or twenty-seven thousand words, wasn't it?

"Look sweetie, you're no Ernest Hemingway. Get your head out of your ass, use your imagination, and get to work. Keep the pen moving."

CHAPTER 3

Three weeks later, after reviewing Harrison's latest draft, she picked him up and they went to see her publisher, Rex Calder. His office was located on the fifth floor in the historic Murchison Building on North Front Street in downtown Wilmington.

Entering through a massive double door, they walked across the small marble foyer leading to the elevator. The door opened and much to Harrison's amazement, they were greeted by an elevator conductor. When they entered the elevator, it sagged downward momentarily. Harrison's knees slightly buckled. Molly chuckled.

"Floor please?"

"Five."

Harrison was a tad reluctant to ride in the antiquated elevator. He overrode his fears because he felt that a face-to-face meeting would yield better results than just sending a manuscript to some pencil-necked wordmonger.

The clickety-clack ride in the two-person elevator took forever. The doors opened directly opposite Mr. Calder's office. On the glass door, it read, Rex Calder CIMM.

He knocked on the door and waited, staring at the lettering CIMM.

"Come on in," a meek voice sounded in the distance.

Harrison opened the door letting Ms. Molly enter first.

"Oh, good golly, Miss Molly, how are you?" bellowed out a short man standing about four-foot-eight. "Give me a hug sweetie."

The one-hundred and fifty square foot office was something straight out of a Humphrey Bogart movie. A large wooden desk, with a high-backed leather chair sat in the middle of the floor. He had not seen an asbestos green-and-white tiled floor in decades. The floor was scattered with paperback books, newspapers, and an assortment of magazines covering subjects from golf to ladies' lingerie. In the corner, stood a grey metal filing cabinet that had seen better days. On top of the cabinet was one green book, Chapter 66 of the North Carolina General Statutes, which was covered in dust.

The old marble windowsill had a clay pot with dead strands of some plant life that must have died a century ago. Harrison couldn't believe his eyes when he spotted on the corner of Calder's desk, not one, but two rotary-dial-telephones. Dumbfounded, he didn't even notice Calder standing in front of him with his hand extended.

"So, you're the one that Molly here has been telling me about, huh?" Calder asked in his thick Long Island accent.

Although short in stature, his handshake was strong and powerful for a man in his mid-fifties.

"Ah, yeah I guess so," said Harrison stumbling over his words. "Molly said you helped publish her book, and here I am, needing your help, Mr. Calder."

"Yo, no problem boss, I've got you covered, and call me Rex, okay?" said Calder as he sat down at his desk leaning back in his leather chair lighting up a fat cigar.

"Did you bring me a copy of your manuscript?"

"I have it on this flash drive," Harrison said handing the cartridge to Rex, not knowing if he even owned a computer to view the contents.

"Give me about two weeks to read it, and I'll get back in touch with ya, okay?"

"Before we go, I need your opinion on the cover design I have in mind. Can you help me with that also?" Harrison asked.

"Okay, what do you have in mind?"

Harrison handed Rex a folder with several examples.

"Look, whenever I go to a bookstore to buy a book, I always head to the area where the books are laid out and displayed on a table so I can see the covers. For me, if I see a cover that captivates my attention, regardless of the title, most of the time I'll buy that one. I like those covers that have a drawing, a picture or even one that has a photograph on it. It seems like I will buy a book just because it is visually striking to me."

"Oh, absolutely, I totally agree. Can I keep these to review with my graphics people?"

"Sure, thanks."

As they got up to leave the office, Rex approached Molly with his arms outstretched, asking for a goodbye hug. What a sleazeball Harrison thought. With Molly being a tall, buxom woman, standing at least six feet four, a hug from Rex appeared to be a tad inappropriate.

Harrison took the fire exit stairs, letting Molly take her life in her hands in the clunky elevator.

The rain had stopped when Molly and Harrison left the building heading for the parking deck. Passing by a local ice cream store, they decided to treat themselves to some homemade ice cream. Molly indulged herself with a single scoop of mint chocolate chip. Harrison, being bold, elected to have a single scoop of something he never had, Blue Moon.

They were enjoying their ice cream seated at one the curbside tables, when Harrison noticed Rex approaching. Rex stopped behind Molly's chair.

"Hey, glad I caught you here, I forgot to ask you something."

"What is it you need to know?" Harrison asked, annoyed at the nasty smell of the cigar.

"Do you have an attorney by any chance?"

"No, not really. Do I need one?"

"Yo, don't worry about it, I know a guy."

"Really, and I will assume his name is Tom Hagen?" Harrison said jokingly with his best imitation of an Italian mobster's accent.

At first there was dead silence, and Harrison wondered if he had spoken out of line referring to the consigliere in *The Godfather*. Molly looked at Rex and they laughed hysterically. He spit out his cigar and it landed on the table, burning a small hole in the tablecloth. Molly choked for a second, then spewed out chunks of mint onto the sidewalk.

"Oh, I really like this guy. He's got a great sense of humor, doesn't he?"

Staring at Rex, Harrison couldn't help but notice that he was the spitting image of Thayer David, the actor who played the part of the boxing promoter in the 1976 film *Rocky*. He also had that same resonant voice as Thayer. His black hair was combed straight back, revealing a receding hairline. Most likely it was all held in place by a couple dabs of Brylcreem.

If Rex had been wearing a bow tie instead of his black necktie, he could have easily passed for Marlon Brando in *The Godfather* movie as well. Harrison was wondering if Rex's attire was required by those that held such a distinguishing title of CIMM.

"Hey Rex, before you leave, I need to ask you something."

"Yeah, what's that?"

"I've seen a lot of different business cards in my day with labels like PhD, BA, or AIA, but I've never seen the CIMM title you've got. What the hell does that stand for?"

"Yo bro, I am a Consultant in Many Matters."

Harrison slapped the table and Molly leaned her head back and both just broke up in laughter. They watched Rex hurry off leaving a trail of blue smoke behind him.

"I'm beginning to like that guy," Harrison said to Ms. Molly.

"He's a rare breed, no doubt, but he really does know the publishing business. Be prepared for a brutal critique of your work. Your ego may get bruised some but keep going with his guidance."

Three weeks later, Rex called Harrison and extended an invitation to attend a small gathering of friends that his wife, Sofia, was putting together to celebrate her nephew's twenty-fifth birthday.

"Yo, dude, I want you and Molly to come over to the house this coming Wednesday afternoon around three o'clock, and we'll discuss your book. I really like what you have written, and I've got some ideas we need to discuss. I'll text you and Molly the address, and I'll let the gate know you are coming."

"Okay, thanks, I'll be there. But I've got one question for you."

"Yeah, what's that?"

"Is your wife's nephew named Luca Brasi?"

The two men roared in laughter and at that moment, they both knew a solid and trustworthy relationship was being forged.

For the next several weeks, Harrison spent hours at Rex's gorgeous residence, re-writing his story. Rex pushed his new author hard, at times bruising his ego, but progress was being made with each visit. After each session, they would sit back with a glass of Rex's favorite scotch and talk about their lives.

Rex and his wife Sofia were retired attorneys who had been on retainer to several major book publishers in New York City during the eighties and nineties. The insane pace of the city, along with the ridiculous politics of the business drove them to North Carolina. This brought them close to their only daughter who was attending college at UNCW. They still maintained a fully-staffed office on 17th and Broadway in New York City, communicating with their staff via videoconferencing on a regular basis.

Using his contacts in New York City, Rex was able to solicit the help of talented writers and editors to help Harrison fine-tune his novel. He so strongly believed in Harrison's story that he took Harrison directly under his wing by flying him to New York City to meet with the staff. Two weeks before Labor Day the book was published with an eye-catching cover using one of Harrison's photographs.

The Secret of Earnie's Island by Harrison Thomas hit the North Carolina best seller's list within two months, coming in at number three. The paperback edition flew off the bookshelves in North Carolina during the early months of 2021. It easily captivated the attention of local coastal residents, since there was a long history of pirates prowling all along the coast, with the likes of Captain William Kidd, Stede Bonnet and the most famous pirate of all, Blackbeard. To the surprise of everyone, it flew to number twenty-six on the New York Times bestseller list.

For referencing their product in the book, the Fisher company sent Harrison a brand-new metal detector. A well-known sportswear company sent him an ensemble of fishing shirts for the same reason. The arrival of three different styles of the fishing sunglasses was yet another gift for mentioning their name in the book.

The checks were steadily rolling in from regional book sales, when Rex called Harrison telling him to come to the office right away. His voice was filled with excitement and urgency, but he hung up before Harrison had a chance to ask him why he needed to be there on such short notice.

Both Rex and Harrison had received a call from the advertising director of the Fisher Metal Detector Company a week earlier requesting an interview with Harrison. Unbeknownst to Harrison, Rex a month earlier, had sent a copy of the book to Dr. Gary Wilson, the advertising director located in El Paso, Texas, on a hunch they would like the fact Harrison mentioned their brand in the book and not that of their direct competitor.

If that meeting got cancelled, Harrison was going to be deeply disappointed. Dr. Wilson had indicated to Harrison and Rex that they wanted to insert a photograph of Harrison holding a CZ-21 detector in their upcoming fall catalog along with a brief tag advertising Harrison's book. It was intended to be a joint advertising venture that would benefit both parties. Rex knew the exposure the book would get through Fisher's nationwide mailing list would be enormous and wouldn't cost him a dime.

Knowing the traffic on Market Street would be snarled by numerous construction projects, Harrison took his time to reach Rex's office. Approaching the front entrance to the Murchison building, he noticed a limousine parked out front with the chauffeur, cap and all, standing at attention next to the limo. It was an impressive sight as he drove by looking for a parking space. Harrison found a space two blocks away, parked his truck, and headed for the office. Ten minutes later he was riding the old relic of an elevator to the fifth floor.

"Come on in, sit down. I want you to meet someone," Rex instructed.

Before Harrison could sit down, the exquisitely dressed gentleman standing next to Rex reached out and handed Harrison a gold foil business card. He handed a large yellow manilla envelope to Rex. Harrison could not believe his eyes. The card he was holding was none other than the Executive Director of the largest publishing company in the country, Sir Jeremy Middleton.

A tall thin man, standing nearly six feet five inches tall, Sir Middleton wore a double-breasted blue suit and a light blue silk shirt. His Italian leather shoes were so shiny that Harrison could see his own reflection. Not a strand of his thick red hair was out of place. Harrison couldn't help but notice that the man's fingernails were expertly manicured.

Harrison collapsed into the olive-green office chair. Before he could even speak a word, Sir Middleton bent down and handed him a white legal-sized envelope. As impressive as the figure was standing in front of him, he noticed that the patch of hair protruding from the blue shirt was peppered with gray, and he figured that Sir Middleton was desperately trying to hide the onset of middle age, as his red hair showed no signs of gray at all.

It was rumored that Sir Middleton was once a major stockholder in the Blockbuster video stores, pouring millions into the startup venture with his friend and founder Patrick Cook. Middleton foresaw the end and sold all his holdings before the inevitable collapse of the company. Supposedly, in the early months of 1997, as a silent partner, he invested his Blockbuster profits with his other two friends Reed Hastings and Marc Randolph who were in the early stages of developing Netflix, which eventually became a company worth seven-billion-dollars.

Sir Middleton was a voracious reader, reading novels from authors all around the globe. Because of that, he came up with the idea of creating film "series" based on the novels he-liked. He had a knack for finding stories that the film producers of Netflix could produce in a short period of time and thereby make an enormous profit. His idea spread worldwide, with huge success, especially in the India Bollywood market, and with the South Korean Hallywood market. Soon Hollywood executives and producers in California came to his doorstep begging for his advice. Not wanting to miss a profitable venture, Middleton established his own publishing company with deep ties to his Hollywood connections.

"We are buying the rights to your book from Mr. Calder, and there is a check in that envelope that we hope will persuade you to sign a contract with us," Sir Middleton explained.

"Excuse me?" Harrison blurted out, totally confused.

"We are going to take your book national. We, with all expenses paid, expect you to attend twenty or maybe thirty book signing events on the east and west coasts during the next year. How does that sound?" Sir Jeremy said, raising his eyebrows.

"What?" Harrison asked, glancing towards Rex with a perplexed look on his face.

"Go ahead, open the envelope."

Harrison at first fumbled with the envelope, but soon the green-colored check came into view. $178,000.00. Out of nowhere, a female photographer appeared and took a barrage of photos. As fast as she appeared, she was gone. One photo was placed in the local newspaper the next day, with a headline...*Local Author to go National.* The description below the photograph was a hodgepodge of nonsense that no one would really pay any attention to.

After a short brisk handshake, Sir Middleton left the office and was ushered away in his black limo, leaving Harrison standing there in a stupor. Rex handed Harrison a large manilla envelope and instructed him to sit down. Harrison remained standing, dumbfounded, staring out the window.

"Good God, man, it's not like he is the King of England. Have a seat and relax," Rex said pointing to the chair. "And don't get too excited. If you sign the contract in that envelope, they will own you and will run your life for the next two years. Think of it this way: One hundred and seventy-eight thousand dollars divided by two equals what, eighty-nine thousand dollars a year, right? Big deal, huh? Out of that, you'll need to hire an attorney and get yourself an agent. That my friend costs money, plus the outrageous taxes you'll have to pay since it is regular income. You might end up with maybe forty-five grand a year tops."

Rex leaned back in his chair, and looked Harrison square in his eyes and said, "Hey bud, fame and fortune has a price, be careful what you do."

"Dang, I feel like a shrimp in a bucket of grits."

Both men broke out in laughter. Rex suggested they go get some lunch, but Harrison was late for another appointment and declined.

"Look, for now just sit tight and don't you dare cash that check," Rex instructed as Harrison bolted out of his office.

CHAPTER 4

Harrison hurried out of Rex Calder's office. Choosing not to use the elevator, he side-skipped down the marble steps two at a time. He cursed the snarled traffic, as he needed to get to the airport in fifteen minutes.

Earnie's seventeen-year-old son Wyatt was taking his first solo flight in a Cessna 152 plane hangared at the Wilmington International Airport. Harrison had promised Wyatt he would attend. The shortest route was traveling along 23rd Street North. If all the lights were green, he would make it on time. Harrison, who normally heeded posted speed limits pushed his Ford pickup truck twenty miles an hour over the speed limit. He even ran a red light.

Two miles from the airport entrance, Harrison encountered a long funeral procession. Traffic was at a standstill. Harrison pulled over directly across the street from the film studios. The funeral procession, at first obscured his vision into the studio parking lot. Once it started moving, he glanced over and could swear he saw Sir Middleton's limousine parked out front. No doubt it was Sir Middleton's limousine, as the chauffeur he had seen earlier was in clear view.

"That's strange. What the hell is he doing there?" Harrison mumbled under his breath. "I need to call Rex."

When he did not answer, Harrison figured he was on his way to the bank to cash his own check from Middleton Publishing.

Harrison's cell phone rang two minutes later, the screen showing it was Rex.

"Sorry, I stepped out to get a sandwich. What's up?"

"I'm here on 23rd Street, stopped because of a funeral procession, and in the main parking lot I can see Middleton's limo. What's up with that?"

"What parking lot are you talking about?"

"The film studio here on 23rd Street."

"That sly fox, I'll be darned. Did you cash that check yet?"

"No, I am on my way to the airport to see a friend."

"Good, don't you dare cash that check. Don't you see what he is doing?"

"Look man, I don't have a clue of what's going on."

Harrison was getting agitated and wanted answers.

"Come back to the office right now and let's read that contract together before you do anything else."

Knowing he was about to break a promise left Harrison with a heavy heart. Earnie, a decorated veteran Army pilot, was already on site, anxiously awaiting Harrison's arrival. Both had encouraged Wyatt to take flying lessons to follow in his dad's footsteps. Wyatt was overjoyed knowing that Harrison would be there to witness his first solo flight.

Once Wyatt started his lessons, Earnie bought him a new high-powered computer to run the 2020 Microsoft Flight Simulator. Harrison and Wyatt spent hours together flying simulations and practicing different maneuvers. After they completed one of their sessions, Wyatt asked Harrison if he was coming to see his first solo.

"I wouldn't miss it for all the tea in China, buddy."

Now he had to break that promise. He hoped that Wyatt would understand and acknowledge that he too was on a solo flight as well.

Reluctantly, Harrison turned around and followed the funeral procession back down 23rd Street, turning right onto Market Street at a snail's pace. He thought he would never get to his destination at this rate, and thankfully the procession turned left onto 17th Street heading south. This left him an unobstructed route straight to Rex's office.

Irritated at the whole situation, Harrison glared at Rex as he opened the manila envelope containing the contract. Rex removed the staple and placed the document on the copier. Thirty seconds later, they each had a copy to read.

"Have a seat my friend," Rex spoke pointing to a chair while handing a copy of the contract to Harrison.

Harrison took the contract but remained standing.

"Well, it's time to put my CIMM degree to work, huh?" Rex spoke first, lighting a half-smoked cigar.

"Jesus Christ, do you see paragraph four on page thirty-six?" Rex blurted out. "Just as I thought."

"Page thirty-six, my God man, I'm just on page two and don't understand any of this mumbo jumbo stuff. What does it mean?"

"Oh, sorry. I learned long ago to skip most of the text and get to the meat of a contract which is usually on the back pages," Rex explained.

"You're screwed, that's what it means. You need a lawyer big time. I seriously recommend the Baker and Baker law firm. I had a feeling about this, so I've already called them. They are available for a consultation today if you have time. Their office is just a few blocks from here, a short walk, so let's go see them. Oh, and by the way, do you have $1,000 on you?"

"On me right now? Hell no, why do I need $1,000?"

"You might decide to retain their services today, and it costs $1,000."

"They wanted $2,000, but I told them we'd cut them in on any future deals."

"What, I have to pay someone up front without knowing if I'll get anything? That's total garbage," Harrison growled. "And what's this about a future deal?"

"Quit your bitching, okay? You're in for a surprise."

On the way to the law offices, Rex explained exactly what the contents of the contract contained. Hidden in the fine print, Middleton's publishing company had the rights to sell the story to basically anyone without Harrison's knowledge or consent. He would not receive a single dime for such future transactions.

In other words, Sir Jeremy obviously had already contacted the film studio negotiating a deal to sell the story, probably to Netflix or maybe even HBO. He was using the $178,000 check as bait. Once that check got cashed, that would be all Harrison would receive. All his rights would be gone, and he would never see the big bucks that would be generated by the film studio to be shared by them and Sir Jeremy only, leaving Harrison in the cold.

For a short man, Rex walked at a feverish pace, at times getting several yards in front of Harrison where he had to turn around to converse with him. Rex was obviously upset with his arms flapping up and down, slapping the side of his trousers for emphasis.

On their way they stopped by the First Citizens Bank and Harrison reluctantly withdrew $1,000. He knew he would have to explain the withdrawal to his wife Kelly, and it would not be pretty. He already pictured it in his mind. Even if he was standing tall in front of her, Ms. Kelly with a stern look in her eyes could whittle Harrison down to a stump in an instant. He dreaded the encounter once he got home. He could hear her now.

"You're such an idiot. Why would you give those licenses to steal scumbags' money up front? You should have given them $250 and told them they would get the rest if you were satisfied with their plan of attack."

The newly renovated law office occupied the entire second floor of an old historic building which was once part of the original Cotton Exchange complex. A twelve-foot-wide staircase, covered with rich burgundy carpet, led Harrison and Rex into a magnificent office layout resembling something that Frank Llyod Wright would have designed. Huge overhead skylights illuminated a variety of elegant potted plants that reminded Harrison of the Longwood Gardens Conservatory in Kennett Square, Pennsylvania. The aroma of the plants was enchanting.

The conference room featured an oval table made of three-inch-thick glass. Twenty chairs ringed the table. Directly across from the conference room, Harrison saw two men sitting across from each other in a spacious office.

Harrison stood frozen, taking in the sheer magnitude of the elegant décor before him. It brought back fond memories.

"Good God, Rex, this place is unbelievable."

"I told ya you'd be surprised."

"Mr. Calder and Mr. Thomas, I presume, for your two o'clock appointment? I'm Vanessa, the office manager. Welcome gentlemen, please follow me."

Frozen again, Harrison with his eyes wide open was not able to speak. Standing before him was a young, tanned woman in her late twenties with an absolutely stunning figure. Her high hemmed, skintight ruby red dress accentuated her lovely figure.

She walked down the hallway, teasing the two by gently swinging her hips. She stopped just short of an opening to the main office, turned sideways revealing her figure, and with her toned arm extended, she ushered Rex and Harrison into the conference room.

"Gentlemen, I see you've met our office manager Vanessa?" said Chris Baker with his eyebrows raised. Harrison couldn't even speak and just nodded. Scott Baker, the younger brother, noticed and snickered to himself.

"Please have a seat gentleman, and let's get started."

"How ya boys doing? It's been a while," Rex inquired.

"Hanging in there like a hair on a biscuit," Chris stated.

With a beautiful view of the Cape Fear River, Rex and Harrison sat across from the two attorneys. With one click, Chris raised two large monitors through slots in the glass.

Harrison expected to see two eloquently dressed gentlemen when he entered the office, but much to his surprise, the brothers were wearing shorts, flip-flops, and fishing shirts.

Harrison scanned neatly hung diplomas, indicating that they had graduated from the law school at the University of North Carolina at Chapel Hill. Although Harrison was a Duke fan, the brothers' attire put his mind at ease.

Handing the contract to Chris, the older brother, Rex took the lead and brought the brothers up to speed. Scott wanted his own copy of the contract and buzzed for Vanessa.

"No need for that. I'll take mine to her and you guys keep talking," Harrison said, already halfway out of the room. The contract was some thirty or forty pages and Harrison hoped the copy machine was so out of date it would take Vanessa hours to copy. He was not disappointed and returned to the brothers' office some fifteen minutes later. They all looked at Harrison and snickered.

To Harrison's amazement, the brothers had read his novel, and they thoroughly enjoyed it. They agreed that the big money was in fact through the potential movie deal, and they wanted to rewrite the contract structured around that potential and protect Harrison in other aspects as well. They explained they had tackled one of Sir Middleton's contracts in the past.

"Come back in four days and we'll have a new contract for you to review. In the meantime, don't even think about cashing that check. For safe keeping, leave it with Vanessa."

In a flash, Harrison was up and heading for the door. He could hear snickering behind him. He stopped short of leaving the office and turned back towards the two brothers.

"I'm sorry, but I have to ask you something."

"What's that?" Chris asked, while hitting the button to retract the two monitors.

"How can you guys get anything done with that . . . you know . . . Vanessa walking around like that?"

"Ha, she's our niece," Scott answered laughing. "You ought to see her girlfriend. If you think Vanessa is hot, her girlfriend Lila is smoking hot."

"Wait a minute, you're telling me she has a girlfriend?"

"Yeah, one hundred percent," chimed in Scott Baker.

"Well, I'll be damned," Rex blurted out.

"Ah, there's more. She also has a boyfriend as well," Chris added.

"Sounds like she has the best of both worlds. Can't object to that. Man, times sure have changed, haven't they?"

Harrison's last comment set off an hour-long discussion about their escapades when they themselves were much younger.

Much to Harrison's surprise, both lawyers frequented the same bars and hangouts down at Wrightsville Beach during its heyday. Wild stories went back and forth as they recalled the old hot spots like The Wits End, Red Dog's, and the King Neptune. With the testosterone flying around the room, each one tried to outdo the other with their stories. Before long, they realized they knew a lot of the same people. Harrison was convinced he was in good hands. He elected to retain their services that very day.

Vanessa popped in letting the two attorneys know they had another client waiting. With that, Harrison and Rex stood up to excuse themselves.

"We'll call you when we've rewritten the contract in your favor. In the meantime, if Sir Jeremy or anyone from his office should call, just ignore it and don't even answer your phone. Let it go to voicemail and make sure to save that conversation so we can listen to it," instructed Scott Baker.

"And please leave the retainer payment with Ms. Vanessa."

Standing over Vanessa, Harrison handed her the check with instructions to file it in a safe place. She was keenly aware of Harrison's wandering eyes, so she took the check, stuffed it in her blouse and gave Harrison a warm smile.

Leaving the office, neither Harrison nor Rex could talk about anything else other than the voluptuous Vanessa.

"Do ya think they're real?" Rex asked.

"Who the hell cares? They're perfect."

"Geez, her dress was so tight, I thought she would pop out of it."

"My God, that girl is a sight for sore eyes, isn't she?"

"Yeah, let's try to focus on the contract."

With that, both men broke out in laughter, since they knew it would take a while to stop thinking about the lovely physical attributes of Ms. Vanessa.

"How much do you think it is going to cost me for them boys to rewrite a contract?"

"Look, I've been through this before. I am sure that Sir red top had no intention of taking you on his supposed book tour with all expenses paid nonsense. Nope, he saw potential of a movie making well over that check he handed you earlier."

"I don't care about that, I want to know how much this is going to cost me."

"Relax bud, let's get back to my office and I'll look up an old invoice from them."

Rex took the elevator while Harrison chose the safer route using the stairs. Exhausted from the day's events, Harrison just wanted to get home and pour himself a big fat white Russian and ease his mind.

"Alright, here we go. The last contract from Baker and Baker for my client was five thousand bucks."

"Jesus Christ, are you kidding me? I've already spent a thousand, and now I have to come up with another four thousand. Screw this crap. I'm going home."

"Look, trust me. These guys are so good, they could talk a hound dog off a meat truck. You are in good hands. Take their advice."

CHAPTER 5

The local hangout was busier than usual. The stand-alone, five thousand square foot building, home to the Diamonds Grille and Billiards Pub, was a hidden gem within the Middle Sound community. The locals flocked to it for its delicious food and drinks. The simple décor consisted of a forty-foot horseshoe bar, twenty pool tables, and half a dozen dart boards with tables and chairs facing a dozen big screen TVs. Without overhead lighting, the glare from the TV screens, coupled with the low hanging pool table lamps, provided just enough light and ambiance for the patrons. The crowd that gathered there was an eclectic mix of society, young and old.

During weekdays, local contractors flooded the bar at lunchtime to feast on the best cheeseburgers in town at a bargain price of just six dollars. Even kids, at least sixteen years old, were allowed inside until eight o'clock in the evening, much to the delight of parents wanting a family night out for dinner. The pool tables, with their classic emerald green tabletops, were always active and since there were multiple size tables scattered throughout, everybody could play no matter what their skill level was.

On the Friday evening before the book signing, Diamonds was packed to capacity with a hundred excited patrons. A few days before, Harrison's wife Kelly, used the Facebook link called "In the Loop" to spread the word that her husband would be at Diamonds between five o'clock and eight o'clock. She encouraged everyone to attend to wish him well. The turnout was more than Kelly expected, and she was delighted to see the joy on her husband's face as he greeted so many friends.

No one even noticed the two burly men sitting at the far end of the bar that evening, tucked away in a corner next to the jukebox.

Luke Jefferson and Jaxson Cook sat in the shadows at the end of the bar deep in conversation. They glanced occasionally at Harrison who was holding court. Cupping their hands over their mouths, they obviously did not want anyone to hear their conversation. They consumed shot after shot of whiskey. They were essentially ghosts amongst the crowd.

Half a dozen tables were grouped together, seating Harrison's family and his closest friends. Throughout dinner, many of the locals who had already purchased the book approached Harrison asking for his autograph. He happily obliged. Those who knew Harrison kept ordering him White Russians, his favorite and only drink, to the point where there had to be at least three gallons of the sweet nectar in front of him. Efforts to get a "to-go" container were met with much finger wagging by the waitresses.

Shortly after eight o'clock, Harrison and his closest friends departed Diamonds and headed over to Earnie's house for the after party. Earnie's brother Jake was due to arrive soon, always excited to talk with Harrison about trout fishing. Patrick Armstrong, Earnie's Army buddy, was traveling in from Fayetteville with his lovely wife Irene. Earlier in the day, Earnie's wife Tammy had decorated the garage, with Ms. Kelly's help, with an assortment of photographs showing Harrison's life from the time he was a baby until his last fishing trip.

When Harrison got up to leave Diamonds, the two men caught a quick glimpse of him, and their blood began to boil.

Reaching the door, Harrison turned back to wave goodbye. Instantly the hair on his neck stood straight up when he locked eyes with the two men sitting in the dark. Their menacing stares sent a shiver down his spine.

"Why are they staring at me that way? Who are they? What do they want?"

Troubled, Harrison tripped on his way out and skinned his knee. Driving to Earnie's house was a blur. He had a bad foreboding.

Luke and Jaxson were distant cousins. They were raised in a remote coastal town just north of Charleston, South Carolina where they spent their youth oystering and clamming. When Jaxson's dad passed and left him an old flat bottom Jon boat, they decided to drop out of school. With just ninth-grade educations, they were still able to eke a meager living selling their catch to local fish houses.

Sadly, just after he left school, Luke's parents were killed in a car accident leaving him homeless. Jaxson's mother took him in. They lived in an old, two-bedroom ranch-style house built in the fifties. The boys were both seventeen at the time when Jaxson's Mom passed away succumbing to emphysema. With no money available for a funeral, the boys buried her in the backyard and marked her grave with an old beat-up push lawn mower.

Each stood at six-feet-four-inches tall. Jaxson weighed two hundred and thirty pounds, ten more than Luke. They did not have an ounce of fat on their muscular builds. Both men had seen their fair share of time in the local jail. Jaxson was locked up mainly for fighting in public. But Luke served time for sadistic crimes. Many a neighbor filed charges against Luke for shooting or mutilating their pets in such unspeakable manners that many considered him clinically insane.

As Luke entered his late teens, even Jaxson at times was afraid of his cousin whenever he witnessed some of the sadistic acts he committed in plain sight. If a fight broke out in one of the local juke joints, Jaxson would normally subdue his opponent with one solid punch and simply walk away before the police arrived. Luke would do the same, but he would lean over the fallen combatant and bite off chunks of the man's cheek or his ear. Once Jaxson saw Luke bite off a man's nose. Luke would chew on whatever he bit off and swallow it.

The cousins had saved enough money to give their uncle Chester six hundred dollars for an old 1974 Dodge pickup truck that he had stored in his backyard shed. They never bothered to get new tags since they traveled only a few miles each day to the local boat ramps. They knew the local sheriff wouldn't care. The truck body was in bad shape but got them to the local boat ramps. They nicknamed the old truck "BOB", claiming it was nothing but a Bucket of Bolts.

The runoff from all the new housing construction wreaked havoc on the local waters. Century old fishing grounds were polluted and sadly wiped out. As a result, the two cousins were going broke. When the old house they lived in went into foreclosure due to unpaid taxes, they decided it was time to move. Having lived in South Carolina for thirty-one years, the pending move would be hard to cope with, but they didn't have a choice.

They had a distant aunt, Lilly Maynard, who lived in Middle Sound where she operated a small landscaping and gardening company named Lilly's Garden. Although it had been decades since their last contact with her, they figured since they were family, she couldn't say no to their request for help. After they got in touch with her explaining their dilemma, Lilly agreed to help them out by giving them some part-time work. She strongly suggested they spend most of their time fishing. Lilly told them to hold off traveling for a week until she could find them a place to rent. She would call them back once she found something.

Three days later Lilly called and informed them that she had found a trailer near the water with a boat ramp at the end of the street. The next day, the cousins left South Carolina and arrived in Hampstead during the spring of 2019. The rental Lilly had found them was a 1969 dilapidated mobile home. It sat deep in the woods, off Factory Road in Hampstead, about a quarter of a mile from the neighborhood marina.

As in South Carolina, the cousin's primary source of income came from oystering and clamming in the creeks adjacent to the Intracoastal Waterway. The most productive areas were in the Topsail Sound area. Occasionally, they would venture south and scour the crystal-clear creeks bordering Figure 8 Island. On those outings, they would launch their Jon boat using the small neighborhood ramp at Mason's Marina. From there it was a short trip to the creeks meandering all around Figure 8 Island.

The cousins felt at home in Hampstead, since it reminded them of their old stomping grounds in South Carolina. Just a ten-minute ride outside the city limits of Wilmington, Hampstead was a rural area inhabited by small farmers and fishermen. Back in the sixties, Hampstead was just a blip on the map, with one flashing yellow caution traffic light marking the center of town. When Jaxson and Luke arrived, the area had witnessed tremendous growth both residential and commercial. Despite the growth, much of the area was rural, especially along Factory Road leading down to the waterway.

When COVID-19 hit the area in 2020, their source of income dwindled down to near nothing. The boat ramps were shut down just like everything else, preventing the cousins from making money from oystering and fishing. Lilly had to pay their rent several times to keep them afloat.

Before the virus hit, the area was booming with new construction, especially new apartment complexes built by key construction companies such as Harold K Jordan and Clancy & Theys. For reasons the cousins couldn't understand, construction was deemed as "essential" and was allowed to continue, but they couldn't. They made several attempts to secure jobs at these construction sites, to no avail.

Luke and Jaxson began to sneak onto construction sites at night and steal whatever they could. Mostly tools found lying around, to sell at the pawn shops in Wilmington. They were eventually caught, but not a charged with any crimes. They were detained for only two hours and released due to the virus scare.

When the restrictions finally lifted in the fall of 2022, the cousins resumed their oystering and clamming. Due to the highway and new bridge construction at Topsail Beach, many of their favorite fishing areas were closed by the local Fish and Game Commission. They concentrated their efforts solely around Figure 8 Island since those creeks were still open. Oysters were harvested between the prime months of October and March. This was also the season for the much sought after speckled trout.

This was Harrison's favorite time to be out on the water, to catch those speckled trout. He had mastered the jerk-jerk-pull technique to such perfection, he could catch his limit of four trout, within twenty minutes of reaching one of his many trout holes scattered throughout the creeks in the Middle Sound area.

He had a yearly ramp pass at Mason's Marina, just a quarter of a mile from his house. During trout season, he used the ramp four or five times a week. The cousins also used Mason's Marina since it was directly across from Figure 8 Island, allowing them to get to prime oystering areas within minutes. The old timers used to say you could harvest oysters in any month that contained the letter "R", but April could be off limits if the weather got too warm. This year, the cousins were fortunate that the weather during the first week in April remained cold enough for them to make one last haul.

After a long night of fishing, the cousins eased into the narrow channel leading to the boat ramp at Mason's Marina. They beached their boat directly onto the concrete ramp. Luke remained in the boat while Jaxson walked toward the parking lot to retrieve their truck and boat trailer. Waiting in line to launch, Jaxson noticed that Harrison was pulling a brand-new Jones Brothers boat fully decked out with a brand-new Ford F-150 king-sized pickup truck. Walking within a few yards of Harrison's truck, Jaxson overheard Harrison speaking to the passenger how he was sick and tired of those smelly mud rats always blocking the ramp.

Irritated, Harrison stepped out of his truck and walked down to the ramp to confront the other fisherman.

"Hey bud, you're blocking the whole ramp. How about pulling your boat over to the dock so I can launch?" Harrison asked in a sarcastic manner.

The man paid no attention to Harrison and never looked up, as he continued shifting the baskets of oysters inside the boat.

Fifteen minutes later, Luke and Jaxson pulled their boat out and parked on the side of the parking lot, stopping to tie down their oyster baskets. They stood there watching Harrison launch his boat, then watched him park his truck about twenty yards away. Harrison jogged down to the small finger dock holding his boat, jumped on board. Harrison eased down the channel toward Pages Creek, which led out to the Intracoastal Waterway.

"Would you look at that arrogant son of a bitch?" Jaxson said, spitting out a chunk of chewing tobacco.

"Who is that guy?"

"I don't know, Luke, but I'd like to beat the shit out of him. When I passed by his truck, he called us smelly mud rats."

Luke and Jaxson were angered to no end by the incident, especially Jaxson. They wanted to find out who this conceited jerk was. They figured that their aunt Lily might know, since she also used the ramp.

Lilly lived just a short distance from the marina. They drove over to her house hoping she might know. Lilly was packing for a long weekend trip to the west coast of Mexico to check on her house she rented out on a regular basis in Puerto Escondido. Apparently, the last tenant caused some damage and Lilly needed to meet with a local contractor to review his repair estimates.

"Hey Aunt Lilly," questioned Jaxson. "Who is that arrogant clown with that preppy new boat and fancy-ass truck we see all the time down at the ramp? You know the guy that wears those $100 dollar fancy fishing shirts and those high tech $200 sunglasses."

"Oh, that must be Harrison. He's the one that wrote that novel that became a huge hit. I hear that they may even make a movie about it. He lives right around the corner over on Marlin Court. Everyone says he is the best trout fisherman in the area. I've heard he has made a lot of money, but at least he gave some of it to UNCW, I'm told. I've also heard that he bought his son and grandkids all brand new cars, too."

"Screw him, he's an arrogant son of a bitch," Luke chimed in. "He thinks he owns the ramp, and who goes out fishing dressed up like that? Well, Mr. Hollywood and all his fancy crap, can go to hell. He needs his ass kicked."

"Nah, Harrison is a good guy. He's a perfect gentleman. I've done a ton of work for him in his yard, and he's always been very gracious to me," countered Lilly. "Here, I'll give you my copy of the book so you can read it."

"You know we don't read so well," Jaxson interjected. "Just tell us the story."

For the next hour or so, Lilly told the story, occasionally reading key passages out loud for emphasis. Most of the time, the cousins sat there snorting and shaking their heads in disbelief.

"What kind of bullshit story is that?" Luke questioned. "Who the hell would believe such shit?"

"Look, you idiots, if you had stayed in school and read a little history, you would know that long ago, this area was a haven for tons of pirates raiding ships all over the place.

"Have you ever heard of Money Island? Well, legend has it, that an old black man, living in a small fishing shack, saw a ship anchor out in the water just south of Bradley Creek. He saw some people get off the ship into a rowboat with lanterns, and they rowed over to a small island not too far from his shack. After they left, apparently the old man went to investigate. Weeks later, when nobody saw the old man, some locals went out to find him. Not finding him in the shack, they noticed a mound of dirt piled up on the tiny island maybe one hundred yards away. The six-foot hole they encountered was empty, and the old man was never seen again. So maybe, just maybe, he found treasure and hauled ass. So, my point is, the story in the book is believable."

Since the cousins had a little time to spare before making their scheduled drop offs at local restaurants, they decided to drive past Harrison's house. Harrison came home early due to a sudden thunderstorm. Just as he was backing his boat into the driveway, the cousins drove by unnoticed.

After completing their deliveries, the cousins went to Diamonds. They took their seats at the far end of the bar. A huge crowd had gathered around several rectangular tables on the opposite side of the bar.

Curious, Jaxson asked the waitress what all the commotion was about. She didn't have time to chat and slapped a flier on the bar advertising the book signing. The flier had a picture of Harrison sitting in his boat, sunglasses dangling from this neck, wearing a pink Columbia fishing shirt. The picture infuriated them. Luke grabbed the flier and tore it in half, throwing the pieces on the floor.

"That son of a bitch is lying his ass off," said Jaxson. "Did you see all the shit in his driveway today?"

"Yeah, that fancy-assed boat he got must have cost him sixty to a hundred thou," Luke added, tossing his head back, throwing down another shot of whiskey.

"There is no way he got all that stuff from just selling a damn book," Jaxson argued. "Remember that story Aunt Lilly told us about the old black man, well maybe the same thing happened to this guy. I think the story he wrote is true. He found a huge stash or treasure somewhere; yeah, that's where all the money is coming from. I figure he's spent at least a quarter mill on all that shit, maybe more. There's no way he got that from one book. He's taking the treasure little by little, selling it somewhere, and living like a king. Lilly said he gave money to that college, right? He's hiding the cash to keep the IRS off his ass. We need to get it before the IRS does."

Luke asked, "Reckon he has it at his house or maybe buried in the backyard? Hiding it from the feds, I bet."

"Well, we know where he lives, right? So, let's go get that shit."

After a few more shots of whiskey, Luke and Jaxson hatched a devious plan, one they felt had to take place right away. The timing was perfect in their minds. They figured that Harrison would be at home, maybe with his wife, before leaving for the book signing tomorrow. All the neighbors would probably already be at Mayfaire. No witnesses. They figured there would only be two people in the house.

Subduing the wife would be easy. The cousins were big men so a woman would in no way hinder their efforts. They would take her down within seconds. To gain access inside the house, their plan was to walk up, knock on the front door and act like they wanted an autograph. The posters on the wall at Diamonds said the book signing was at 2:30 p.m. They would scope out the house first, making sure there were no nosy neighbors lurking on the street. They would start their assault at Harrison's house at 2:00 p.m.

There was a vacant lot just around the bend from Harrison's house that was overgrown with tall weeds where they could have a good view of people coming and going. It was well hidden. There were no houses on either side. They would sit there and wait for 2:00 p.m.

"Look, we have to get him or his wife to open the door," instructed Jaxson. "Once the door is open, you get the wife and I'll dance with Mr. Hollywood. Knock her out and tie her up. Understand?"

What the cousins didn't know was that the law firm of Baker and Baker had re-written the contract totally in favor of Harrison's position. Sir Jeremy Middleton was enraged, as his crafty plan fell completely apart. The film studio also gave Harrison a large check, after the Baker brothers paid them a visit. All the new vehicles, even the boat, were all leased by the film studio to be used by Harrison's family during filming, all for publicity.

One stipulation of the new contract stated that all items leased had to be returned once the movie was released. It was the future movie royalties Harrison would receive that really angered Sir Jeremy. The contract was written to keep all book and movie rights in the hands of Harrison. Going against the advice of the Baker brothers, Harrison insisted on a provision to pay Sir Jeremy a portion of the royalties at his discretion. He figured his services might be needed in the future.

The contract further stipulated that Baker and Baker would be Harrison's agent. That entitled them to receive a portion of the movie royalties. That was Rex's "cut them in on the deal" idea. They set up an LLC for Harrison where all checks would be deposited into the law firm's account. Much to the delight of Harrison, he would have to come to the office to get his check. Harrison was hoping a check would arrive every day.

"Oh, Vanessa, you certainly are a sight for sore eyes."

CHAPTER 6

An hour before the book signing, Harrison told his wife Kelly to go on ahead. He would be there shortly. He was still fighting off an awful hangover incurred from the party the night before. It was one of those hangovers where your hair itches, your teeth hurt, and your tongue is asleep. No doubt in his mind, his poor performance on the golf course earlier was a direct result of this nasty hangover.

He was also in a panic because he forgot to take his Metamucil the night before. If he did not complete his normal morning ritual before he left, he would be in a lot of pain due to his diverticulosis. He thought maybe a little hair of the dog might get things moving, but he decided not to. He did not need to have booze on his breath at the event, since underage children might be present. And since he was in the so-called Bible Belt, he sure didn't need to offend anyone.

To look the part, Harrison donned his favorite oversized bright orange fishing shirt and khaki fishing shorts. The shirt and shorts combined had at least fourteen individual pockets where one would have to pat themselves down just to find their keys. Adding to his outfit, Harrison slipped on his favorite tan boat shoes.

Over the years, Harrison had collected nearly eighty hats which were all displayed side by side, hanging on nails, all around his office walls. If he was wearing a green shirt, he could find a matching hat that had a green emblem or some sort of green insignia on it. Today's choice was a white hat with bright orange embroidering, identifying the LFishman Flooring Solutions company that matched his shirt perfectly.

Harrison stood in front of the full-length mirror in the master bedroom, admiring his attire. Satisfied, Harrison leaned in closer and smiled to check the condition of his teeth. It was a constant battle removing the coffee and tobacco stains. Today they didn't need any further cleaning.

Harrison did notice a few dozen ugly looking hairs protruding from his eyebrows. Those grey mini-tree trunks seemed to sprout overnight. Even more attention was needed to weed out the hairs protruding from his ears. He could not fathom how and why so much hair grew in these spots, and not on his nearly bald head. If only he could transplant those ear hairs on his duck fuzz scalp, he could regain his much sought out youthful appearance.

He still had plenty of time, so he removed his shirt and headed into the bathroom to tidy himself up. Retrieving his mustache scissors and a set of tweezers from the medicine cabinet, he leaned in close to the mirror and within five minutes removed all the unsightly hairs from his eyebrows and ears. Putting his shirt back on, he packed his armpits with new rolled up wads of tissue paper. He took one last look in the mirror. With a slight adjustment to his ball cap, he headed back to the kitchen.

Harrison prepared some coffee in his favorite cup. Against his better judgment, he added in a double shot of Kahlua.

Heading for his favorite recliner in the living room, he wanted to relax and enjoy his coffee and hopefully the urge to use the toilet would hit him soon. He had positioned his recliner in just the right spot where he could look directly out the back window and have an unobstructed view of the bluebird house he mounted on the neighbor's fence post just ten feet away.

At this time of year, the bluebirds were actively building their nests. Harrison sat in his recliner enjoying the constant activity of his bluebirds flying in and out of their box, dragging in twigs and strands of pine straw through the inch-and-five-eighths opening. Just as he was thinking about heading to the bathroom from the caffeine overload, Harrison thought he heard the doorbell ring, so he turned down the volume on the TV to listen again. Seconds later, he could clearly hear the doorbell ring. Irritated, Harrison slowly got up from his recliner, removed the soggy paper towels from his armpits, and approached the front door.

The main front door was already open and through the full-length glass storm door, Harrison could see two shabby looking men standing on the brick porch. One man, with his back towards the door, was facing the street smoking a cigarette. The other one cupping his hands around his face looking inside the glass door. Both men were huge, with shoulders almost as wide as the door frame. They wore leather gloves.

At first, Harrison did not recognize the two unshaven, burly looking men, and it made him a little uneasy. To the best of his recollection, he had never seen these men before in the neighborhood or anywhere else. But that look, that sinister look coming from the man's eyes made the hair rise on the back of his neck.

Since the book had been published, it wasn't unusual for folks to come by for a variety of reasons to see Harrison, but he knew most of them. Usually, they would have a copy of his book with them requesting an autograph. He would step outside to graciously thank them and sign their books. He always added a personal note that started with their first name.

Harrison stepped closer to the storm door to get a better look. Dressed in blue overalls with white marsh boots covered in mud, he was alarmed by their unkempt appearance. He briefly glanced outside to his right and noticed a faded red pickup truck, parked directly behind his truck. It was leaking oil onto his recently power washed driveway. The old truck was riddled with rust matching the tattered look of the two men standing before him.

He also noticed they didn't have a copy of his book, so why were they here? Something wasn't right. There were multiple signs throughout the neighborhood prohibiting solicitation. The only folks that occasionally ignored those signs were neatly dressed Jehovah Witnesses. These fellows were not church members.

Without unlocking the storm door, Harrison asked the men what they wanted.

"We just wanted to get your autograph," the visitor said, motioning his hands together as if signing something.

"I'll be at a book signing in about fifteen minutes. I can give you an autograph there."

Neither one of the men answered.

"It's at the Barnes and Noble bookstore up the street in the Mayfaire shopping center," Harrison said, raising his right hand and pointing to the left with his index finger.

The other man, who had been facing the street, turned around and stood next to the man requesting his autograph. He turned his head and spat out a stream of tobacco juice into the nearby bushes.

"We have a landscaping job to do down the street for Lilly's Garden, our Aunt Lilly, so we can't go. We're late. It won't take a minute, huh?"

"You know Lilly, don't you? She told us to come by on our way over to cut the grass at the church around the corner," the first man spoke up.

Harrison had known Lilly for many years. Every spring he hired her to clean out his azalea beds in front of the house and along the side yard. Harrison and Lilly had become close over the years. Since they were both originally from up north, they had a lot in common. Harrison let his guard down, thinking it would be okay to let them in since they worked for Lilly. He unlocked the storm door and pushed it open, allowing the two men to enter the small foyer.

"Let me get a piece of paper and a pen."

Harrison barely took two steps when he felt the entire weight of one of the men crashing down upon him. Falling forward and smashing his face onto the hardwood floor, Harrison felt his front teeth rip through his bottom lip. A puddle of blood spewed onto the flooring.

The attacker shifted quickly upwards and hammered his knees into the center of Harrison's back. The heavy blow knocked the wind out of him. The left side of his rib cage cracked. The excruciating pain left Harrison gasping for air. Every breath felt like a hot searing cattle prong pushing against his ribs. He struggled to breathe. Pinned to the floor, he couldn't move.

The other man came around and grabbed his arms, wrestling them onto his back. His wrists were then zip-tied together. His fingers went numb.

In a split second, the first man lifted Harrison up and slammed him through the office door. Harrison violently careened off the office door and hit his head on the corner of the nearby bookcase. He spun and crumpled to the floor. Lying face down on the Berber carpet, he was amazed at the sheer speed and strength of this individual. He could taste blood.

"Get up, you piece of shit," screamed Jaxson, standing directly over Harrison. Luke was standing in the doorway to the office, blocking any escape.

"Where is that bitch wife of yours?"

Harrison was dazed from the blow to his head, as blood poured down his cheek and from his mouth onto the floor. The attack was all a blur as he laid there face down on his office floor. The wind had been knocked out of him and he was still struggling to breathe, let alone speak. It took a few seconds before he was able to roll over and face the person that attacked him.

He was terrified by the anger on the man's face. Harrison tried to recoil, but the pain from his cracked ribs would not let him. At that very moment, he recognized the two men as the ones he had encountered the other day at the Marina. Were they there just because he asked them to move their boat? He didn't insult the men or say anything derogatory. He just simply asked them to move their boat out of the way so he could launch his and go fishing.

"Answer me, you son of a bitch," ordered Jaxson as he drove his boot into Harrison's chest. Harrison felt the pain of another rib being broken and he curled up into a ball.

Gasping for air and choking on his own blood, he couldn't speak. He laid there like a rag doll, motionless.

Just as Jaxson was about to deliver another vicious blow, Harrison spoke.

"She is at the event, she is not here," mumbled Harrison through all the pain.

"Go look for it. I'll handle this punk," Jaxson said.

"Now, tell me where the money and other stuff is at. I know you have it somewhere."

Barely conscious, all Harrison could say was, "What the hell are you talking about?"

Harrison laid there in enormous pain, completely confused. He was dumbfounded when the man asked about money and stuff. The attack obviously wasn't about the issue at the marina. It was something totally different that Harrison couldn't comprehend. Nothing was making any sense at all. The pain made him vomit blood.

Suddenly, Jaxson grabbed Harrison by the throat, picked him up off the floor and drove his monstrous fist into Harrison's face. The blow split his nose, sending blood all over the office desk. Jaxson's fist was so massive it split Harrison's left eyebrow wide open and shattered his orbital eye socket. Blood splattered everywhere and Harrison's knees buckled under him, sending him to the floor again. Jaxson landed another kick to the ribs, then picked Harrison up and slammed him into his desk chair. Harrison tilted forward and leaned over onto his desk, spewing blood all over the keyboard.

Harrison could faintly hear in the background the sounds of the other man going from room to room, ransacking everything in the house. The pain made him dizzy with vertigo and the uncontrollable shivering from the beating he took did the work that Metamucil would have done, and he defecated all over himself.

Luke came into the office and told Jaxson he didn't find anything, and that nobody else was in the house.

"Just beat it out of him," Luke encouraged.

"What do you want?" Harrison asked, dazed and confused. He no longer could focus on the man in front of him.

"Listen to me carefully. We've driven by this house several times, and we've seen all the fancy new cars in the driveway and that new boat you've got. We've heard your family has all the new cars. We figure you've bought four or five new ones. Aunt Lilly even has told us that you took the entire family on a couple of cruises, and she also said you bought a brand-new house for your son. We know there is no way some stupid book you wrote could pay for all this stuff, no way.

"The money is coming from somewhere else. That story in the book is about you going out metal detecting and finding buried treasure on some beach, right? Well, we think you found some shit out there and loads of it. You're selling bits and pieces of it to somebody, and it is bringing in a ton of money. So, cough it up."

"I don't own any of . . ." Harrison wasn't able to finish his statement. Jaxson grabbed a handful of hair, pulled Harrison's head back and hit Harrison so hard that he knocked out three of his front teeth. Harrison slumped in his chair.

Harrison had no idea how long he was unconscious. As he slowly opened his eyes, he could hear the men talking, no doubt, from the kitchen. The three-bedroom house was a typical ranch style built back in the early seventies. A small hallway connecting all three bedrooms led into the adjoining kitchen and living room. It was easy to know the two guys were in the kitchen, with the relatively small layout of the house, and he could also hear the kitchen cabinet doors being opened and slammed shut.

Beaten half to death, Harrison knew he needed to think fast. Trying to reason with these two men was totally out of the question. Any more battering at his age could leave him crippled or dead from internal bleeding. He had to come up with a story, a ruse, to get out of the house where maybe someone would see him and come to his rescue.

It was a Saturday and there had to be neighbors out working on their lawns, he thought. The slightly curved street Harrison lived on had thirteen houses with well-manicured lawns that his neighbors were constantly tending to during the spring and summer months. He just needed to do something to get outside and scream for help. If these idiots really think he has treasure or money hidden somewhere, just go along with it and get out of the house before you are beaten to death. Being stuck in the house was no doubt a death trap but getting outside meant freedom.

Surely, Harrison thought, Mr. Fitzgerald, the retired Coast Guard veteran who lived next door, would be on his usual neighborhood watch. Confined to a wheelchair, the seventy-five-year-old Mr. Fitzgerald spent his days peering out of his living room window, carefully watching everything like a hawk. He was even known to call his neighbors to let them know it was raining outside, and that they needed to roll up their car windows. If any of the neighbors were going to go out of town for a few days, they would call old man Fitz and ask him to watch over their house while they were gone. He was back on duty, armed with his daytime binoculars and his infrared night vision binoculars, with his cell phone on speed dial to the police. He would send at least four text messages while you were gone, telling you everything was fine.

Harrison was counting on his neighbor to be at his normal post, with binoculars in hand, and would see that something was out of place and call the police, giving them a detailed description of the vehicle and the men, he saw.

The two men came back into the office finding Harrison awake slumped in his office chair, staring at the ceiling in a daze. Luke got behind the high-backed chair and spun him around to face Jaxson, who was leaning on the armrests, with his face inches from Harrison. With his nose smashed in and bent off to the side, Harrison's labored nasal breathing had a faint whistle to it. As Jaxson leaned in closer, he had to recoil away from the man's horrible breath. Harrison could see that the man had maybe six or seven teeth and they were riddled with brown stains and gapping cavities. His breath was wretched. Harrison had to hold his breath as the man got closer and closer.

"I'm going to ask you one more time and if you don't tell us the truth, we're gonna torch this damn place, ya, hear me?"

The thought of having his house set on fire and burned to the ground terrified him even more than the man standing in front of him. He could not let that happen. Ms. Kelly and Harrison had just finished a thirty-five-thousand-dollar renovation of their home the year before, and to see all that work go up in flames was unfathomable.

"Where's the fucking money at?" Jaxson asked, grabbing Harrison's throat with his massive left hand, and drawing back his right hand that was balled into a fist, ready to strike again.

"I've hidden it," Harrison babbled. The strangle hold crushed his carotid artery. He passed out.

Fueled with elation, the two men began to tear the house apart again room by room but were coming up empty-handed. Within ten minutes, they knew they were wasting their time. It became clear to the two men that Harrison had not hidden anything of value in the house, but somewhere else.

"Shit, go get some water so we can wake this asshole up," Jaxson ordered, while grabbing Harrison's hair and yanking his head back.

Luke retrieved a pot sitting on the kitchen stove, filled it with cold water from the sink, and returned to the office. He emptied the contents onto Harrison's face and waited. Harrison began to stir and moan, slowly raising his head.

"Where the hell is it?" Jaxson demanded. "You said you hid it, where asshole?"

Harrison groaned, then sputtered, "On the island."

CHAPTER 7

Harrison was never late, never. It was a trait ingrained in him by his father at an early age. His father was the most regimented person he ever knew. In his dad's eyes, being tardy for anything was totally out of the question, and if you were, it was usually met with a few good licks across the back of the legs with a leather belt.

It was almost three o'clock in the afternoon, and Harrison had not arrived at the book signing or called anyone saying he would be late. After placing multiple calls to Harrison's cell phone that went unanswered, Ms. Kelly asked her son Dalton to drive back over to the house and let her know where Harrison was. On a rare occasion, he was going to be late, he would always, call to let her know exactly how many minutes he was running behind.

Many of the patrons were leaving, and Mr. Calder tried his best to convince the remaining crowd to stay a little longer. It was one thing waiting for a well-known celebrity or a high-profile politician, but an unknown local author was another. By three fifteen, most of the crowd had dispersed. Just a handful of dedicated fans remained, still eager to get their books signed.

The Barnes and Noble staff had begun to remove the dozen or so books which were on a display rack, packing them in boxes to be stored in the back room. They dismantled the two tables covered with white linen cloth and took them to storage.

Thoroughly disappointed, Rex Calder packed up the small public address system he had set up earlier.

Dalton left the store and did a quick search of the parking lot, hoping to see his dad's truck. Not seeing it, he jumped into his new Toyota Tacoma and sped toward Middle Sound. It took a little less than eight minutes to arrive at Treasure Cove, the small subdivision where Harrison and Ms. Kelly lived.

Pulling into the driveway, Dalton noticed that his dad's old 2006 Ford pickup truck was still there along with his new 2022 Ford F-150 truck. The front door was open, only the glass storm door was shut, but that was nothing unusual. When Dalton approached the front door, he noticed a red smudge on the glass door. As he got closer, he could tell the smudge was blood and there was more blood on the foyer floor. Calls to his dad were unanswered and a terrible feeling came over him as he noticed more blood splatter trailing down the hallway toward the office. He followed the blood trail and eased down the hallway, cautiously entering the office. He was shocked at the sight of the ransacked office. When he noticed a large pool of blood on the desk, he got sick to his stomach. He could taste bile rising up into his throat.

Dalton bolted from the office. His hands were shaking so badly, he could barely dial 911. After contacting the police, he called his mother and told her to come home right away and that something terrible must have happened.

"What do you mean, did he fall down in the shower or something?"

"There's blood all over the office and he's not here. I've called 911 and they're on their way."

Two sheriff cars and one fire emergency truck converged upon Harrison's house minutes before Ms. Kelly and the grandkids arrived. Complete chaos erupted amongst the family members when they saw the blood on the glass door. Because Ms. Kelly had her cell phone on speaker, those fans that had remained at the book signing heard everything Dalton said. As a result, they lit up social media spreading the word that something terrible happened to Harrison.

Soon a hoard of people descended upon Treasure Cove. Even the local TV stations arrived and began to set up their satellites, with reporters standing at attention with microphones in hand. The police struggled to secure the area.

With its single and only entrance heading west off Market Street, Middle Sound Loop Road was a two-lane road winding through the community. A short distance from Market Street, across the street from the Ogden Elementary School, a circular round-a-about directs traffic either north to the left or south to the right. Within minutes after Dalton's 911 call, all traffic was stopped on Middle Sound Loop Road by well-armed North Carolina State Troopers. They were searching each vehicle coming and going.

Officer Robert Wilson of the New Hanover County Sheriff's Office was the first law enforcement official to arrive at the house, with Dalton standing on the steps of the front porch. Officer Wilson's partner, Corporal Geoff Nixon, was on his cell phone contacting the detective division, while he stood guard at the front door. After identifying himself to Officer Wilson, Dalton tried to open the front door to go inside, but the officer stopped him. He was told to wait until the detective squad arrived first.

While Officer Wilson was escorting Dalton off the front porch, Ms. Kelly approached trying to enter the house. She was stopped by the officer with the same directive. Ms. Kelly would have no part of that, and ignoring the officer, she shoved him to the side and bolted into the house. Officer Wilson raced after her. Ms. Kelly stood in the hallway trembling, gasping for air. She was frozen in place. Holding her face with her hands she sobbed with a deep wail.

With a comforting tug, he escorted her back down the hallway into the kitchen. Officer Wilson noticed that Dalton had slipped inside so he motioned for him to come over and comfort his mother.

"Please, please don't touch anything until our detective and forensic people get here. We don't want to contaminate the area."

The policeman suggested they take a seat in the living room and wait for the detectives to arrive. Dalton and Ms. Kelly reluctantly sat down on the large couch in front of the bay window. Wilson took out his small notebook and pen and began asking the usual standard questions. Did they know of anybody who wanted to hurt Harrison? Did he have any known enemies? Dalton and Ms. Kelly were too upset to answer his questions and just shrugged him off.

A four-member forensic team from the New Hanover County Sheriff's Office soon arrived and immediately began their investigation of the crime scene. Another Sheriff's patrol car, with two more officers, pulled up into Harrison's front yard. Departing from their vehicles, they began to drape multiple layers of yellow crime tape across the premises to restrain the growing crowd. Once completed, they joined Officer Nixon on the front porch for added security. The crowd of nearly fifty people was growing and anxious to get as close as they could.

The forensic team observed the results of a struggle which had resulted in injuries. The first team member took multiple samples of blood from the office area, hallway, and the front door. The two others dusted for fingerprints. The fourth member, a blood splatter specialist, took a series of photographs, at different angles, of the blood evidence from locations throughout the house. The house was obviously ransacked. With the beds overturned, the dresser drawers pulled out and every bookcase emptied, it looked like a burglary gone bad. But where was Harrison? A quick search of his work shed out back revealed nothing.

The youngest member of the forensic team, Jennifer Watkins, approached Ms. Kelly holding a large clear bag about the size of a five-gallon trash bag.

"Ma'am, I need to pick up several articles of clothing that Mr. Thomas might have been wearing in the last twelve hours or so. I'll be handing that over to our K9 unit so the dogs will get a good scent if we need them later.

"Okay, follow me into the bedroom. I've got just what you need," Ms. Kelly said, heading down the hallway to the master bedroom.

Lying on the floor between the bed and a chest of drawers were Harrison's favorite black sweatpants and a white T-shirt with a single pocket. Ms. Kelly stopped at the end of the bed and pointed out the two items to the technician.

"There ya go, I'm not touching those nasty assed sweatpants, so have at it," Ms. Kelly said holding her nose.

The technician bagged the sweatpants first and was about to place the T-shirt into the bag when she noticed a reddish stain next to the front pocket.

"Mike, come quick, I think I have found more blood," shouted out the young technician.

"It's not blood, honey, it's spaghetti sauce. Go ahead, and smell it, if you don't believe me. We had spaghetti dinner the other night and, as usual, my husband spilled half his food on his shirt. The man won't sit down at the table and eat like the rest of us. He will sit his fat ass in the recliner and dribble his food all over his shirt. He does it all the time."

The young technician couldn't help but giggle, but she wasn't about to put her nose anywhere close to that T-shirt. With the sweatpants and T-shirt bagged, Ms. Jennifer was satisfied that she had plenty to hand over to the K9 unit.

Several more sheriff patrol units arrived. Officers canvassed the residents, going door to door, interviewing all the adjacent neighbors. Unfortunately, no one saw or heard anything. Not a single neighbor had seen Harrison in the last few hours. All the neighbors reported they had been at the book signing event earlier that day. Marlin Court was empty during the time of the attack. Several days prior to the event, Ms. Kelly hand delivered flyers advertising the book signing to all the neighbors asking them to please attend and apparently, they all did, including old man Fitz and his wife Hilda.

An hour later, things began to settle down some, and most of the people and press gathered outside had departed. The fire emergency truck left along with all the sheriff's deputies except for Officer Nixon, who remained on site, waiting for the detective unit to take over. The forensic team completed their work by four o'clock that afternoon. As they were packing the retrieved evidence in the back of their van, the lead detective, Anthony Decker, arrived, parking his black sedan across the street. After chatting with the head forensic technician for a few minutes, he headed inside the house.

With the detective in charge of the investigation, Decker told the two sheriffs they could leave. Seeing that Dalton and Ms. Kelly were visibly upset, he suggested they remain in the living room while he did a quick search of the house. Detective Decker returned to the living room and took a seat on the raised brick fireplace hearth with Ms. Kelly and Dalton seated just a few feet away to his right. He reached the same conclusion as the forensic team leader had, that it looked like there were several people involved, just not one, but he would keep that to himself for now.

"Let's start from the beginning," Decker said, pulling out his notepad and pen.

For the next ten minutes, Dalton and Ms. Kelly gave the detective a brief description of their events that day. Dalton explained that he had spent the night with his parents and left with his mom to help set up the event around one thirty or so. That was the last time they both had seen Harrison.

"Did you see anybody, or did you see anything out of order? Were there any vehicles on the street you didn't recognize?" Decker asked.

"I really don't think so. Dalton and I were so excited that we didn't pay attention to anything other than the event we were headed to."

"Okay, I want both of you to take your time and carefully walk around the house to see if anything is missing. Don't touch anything. Start in the office. As it appeared, the initial attack took place there. Look for anything to be out of place," Decker instructed, upset with himself for using the word attack, as it clearly upset Ms. Kelly and Dalton.

Although Harrison normally kept an immaculate office where everything had a place, right now it was destroyed. With the sight of Harrison's office all torn apart, coupled with the pool of blood, neither Ms. Kelly nor Dalton could face what they were seeing. They quickly returned to the living room. After a few more questions from the detective, he informed them a technician from his department would be coming by shortly to provide them with a means to tape any conversation and track any calls to their cell phones.

"If Harrison's been kidnapped, somebody might call you asking for some sort of ransom."

"You think he's been kidnapped and not murdered?" Ms. Kelly asked.

"Sit tight. Everything is going to be fine. We'll get to the bottom of this. Let me get back to the office and check in with our forensic people, and I'll be in touch."

Before leaving, the detective assured Ms. Kelly that he would bring Harrison home. Walking out into the front yard, he motioned to Harrison's grandchildren that they could now go inside. They almost knocked him over as they rushed by screaming for their Grandmama.

Several tearful hours passed before anyone attempted to clean up the carnage throughout the household. The task of cleaning the front door and hallway was completed rather quickly. Dalton volunteered to undertake the office cleanup by himself. Since he had spent hours in the office as a kid, he knew exactly where everything should go. He wanted to make it perfect. His dad kept his office so neat, that if someone took a pencil out of his glass jelly jar holder, he would know it immediately. He recalled how many times his dad would call him or his mom, just livid about a missing pencil.

"Hey, where the hell is my yellow pencil?" Harrison would scream into the phone.

"How many times have I told you if you use something, put it back in the same spot where you found it?"

Mom would totally ignore him, even if she took the pencil. She thought his neatness was a sickness, and she wanted no part of it. How can a man get so upset about one stupid pencil when he had fifteen others within reach? She never admitted she took it, not once. Dalton, on the other hand, was always honest and would confess where he left the pencil.

The office was one thing, but God forbid if you misplaced a tool from the workshop. That would set off a verbal tirade that even a drunken sailor couldn't match. Harrison would come flying out of his workshop, unleashing cuss words in multiple languages, just totally out of his mind. And if he had a few cocktails in him, he was like an F-15 coming in hot getting ready to strangle someone in the house.

"Shut your mouth and take off your shoes," Mom would fire off the first shot.

"Go back and look where you used the damn tool the last time and quit blaming us, you fool," Mom would fire the next shot, leaving Dalton safe for the time being.

Many times, Dalton actually had taken the tool and did not want to face the oncoming onslaught, so he would run out the front door and place the tool on his dad's truck bumper. No way was he going to get caught with any tool he did use and forgot to replace.

It took Dalton nearly three painstaking hours to get the office in pristine order. He was proud of his work and knew his dad would be pleased. Everything was in its place, except Dad. Unsettled with that thought, Dalton eased into the office chair and wept. After a few minutes, he rose from the chair and looked around one more time. He could sense something wasn't right. He could feel it, but just couldn't put his finger on it. Whoever did this didn't steal anything but his dad. They didn't even bother to take the rifles which were mounted on the office wall. They were worth a lot of money.

Over the next few hours, several neighbors stopped by offering various plates of food. Ms. Kelly had no desire to cook. Most of the plates were just picked at by the family members and it was a shame most of it had to go to waste. No doubt it was going to be a long night.

CHAPTER 8

A few minutes later Harrison regained consciousness, and for the time being, he avoided another beating. He was struggling to breathe, as the blood from his missing teeth continuously dripped down his throat, causing him to gag. When he glanced up, he thought he saw the two men high-fiving each other several times.

"What is that all about," he wondered, with his head swirling in pain.

"We knew you were lying; you piece of shit!" Luke yelled.

"So, where is this island?" Jaxson asked.

Harrison, still dazed, vaguely remembered he told them about hiding the stuff on an island somewhere. At the time, it was the only thought that came to mind, so he could get out of the house. Maybe he could tell them this island was way down on the Cape Fear River down near Southport, just to keep them off base. Or maybe he could tell them that the island was way up north in the Outer Banks to throw them off. However, the thought of another beating made Harrison think otherwise. He would keep the story of the island close to home to make it more believable.

"It's off the Intracoastal Waterway across from Porters Neck. We all call it Earnie's Island."

"What the hell are you talking about? We ain't never heard of any island in these parts called Earnie's Island," Jaxson said, glaring down at Harrison.

"It's just a nickname we use. My buddy Earnie, a couple of summers ago, found it when he was out scouting around, looking for a new place for him and his family to go camping. When a group of us went out there for the first time, we just named it Earnie's Island after him. The only way to get there is by boat, and it must be high tide to travel up a small creek that leads to the island," Harrison explained.

Harrison had a momentary flashback, vividly remembering the first camping trip to the island after Earnie told everyone he found the perfect camping site. A group of eight people, on a Saturday evening, headed off to the island on Earnie's twenty-two-foot Bayliner just before sunset, loaded down with all their camping gear. When Earnie turned off the Waterway into the small creek leading up to the island, the boat ran aground and came to a complete stop. Frustrated, Earnie rammed the throttle forward and created a huge rooster tail of sand and mud, spraying on everyone in the boat. The motor's overheating alarm sounded off and shortly after that, the motor choked out and died. The tide was rapidly falling out of the creek, and everyone realized they were stuck, especially when the boat leaned a few degrees on its side, high and dry.

Earnie radioed Sea Tow for assistance, explaining his situation, but was told it might be an hour or two before their small rescue boat could get there. Fortunately, for those on board, it was early October, with the temperatures in the mid-fifties keeping the gnats and flies away. Sunlight was fading fast when the Sea Tow boat arrived with its three-member crew. After assessing the situation, they felt that trying to pull the boat off the sandbar some forty yards might tear out Earnie's transom, so they told Earnie they would be back at high tide around eleven or eleven-thirty that night.

"Just sit tight. I've punched your coordinates into our GPS, so we'll find you," the captain spoke over the radio.

Earnie's 82nd Airborne buddy Patrick, the ever-present joker, couldn't resist and grabbed the radio microphone from Earnie.

"Hey captain, can you label those coordinates with a name or title?"

"Sure can, go ahead,"

"Label it Earnie's Island. I'm sure y'all will be here many more times, the way this idiot drives."

Harrison's short flashback came to an end when Jaxson slapped him across the top of his head. "Let's go dip shit, get up and get in the truck,"

"I need my metal detector to find the spot. It's right there in the corner next to the printer. The Fisher one."

Jaxson grabbed the detector, then yanked Harrison from his office chair. Luke tore off a piece of duct tape and covered Harrison's mouth. The three men headed down the hallway stopping just short of the front door. Jaxson glanced out the glass storm door looking for any nosy neighbors. Seeing that the coast was clear, Jaxson went out first. He opened the passenger door, leaned the front seat forward, and then went around and opened the driver's side door. Looking around, he saw no one and motioned to Luke to come on while Jaxson slipped into the driver's seat and started the truck.

Since they had duck taped Harrison's mouth, the option to yell out to someone was gone. Coming out of the house, Harrison glanced to his left, then to his right and noticed nobody was outside. Not a soul was out in their yards or walking down the street. He felt totally deflated and contemplated his next move.

Faking a fall, he tripped himself, hoping he would stumble and fall on the ground, bringing attention to himself. He stumbled barely a foot when Luke strengthened his grip on Harrison's armpit and picked him straight up, planting him firmly back on his two feet. The grip on his armpit cut off the blood supply to his arm and his left arm went numb. He couldn't believe the strength of this guy and wasn't about to struggle any more.

Luke shoved Harrison into floor of the back seat and ordered him to lie down and not move a muscle. Just then, Harrison's cell phone rang, startling everyone. Luke reached in and grabbed the phone from Harrison's back pocket and smashed it with his heavy boot on the floorboard of the truck. The Life 360 app he had on his phone was of no use now, another option gone.

The red pickup pulled out of the driveway, turned right, and entered Middle Sound Loop Road. Halfway to Market Street, the truck was nearly sideswiped on a blind curve by a speeding driver in a gray pick up that had to be traveling at least sixty miles an hour. After stopping at the Middle Sound Loop Road and Market Street light, they turned right and headed north on Highway 17, passing through Porter's Neck on the way to Hampstead.

At Factory Road, the truck turned right and was now headed east towards the Waterway. About a quarter of a mile before the Waterway, the truck turned left off the paved road and crunched its way down a gravel road for approximately one hundred yards before stopping.

The ride lasted maybe fifteen minutes. Harrison figured he was twenty to thirty miles from his house. That's better than being hours away he thought. The option of seeing someone outside failed miserably. The 360 app was of no use.

Where was he? Does anybody know what has happened to him? What do I do now? Between the raging pain, and his mind swirling in circles, he found himself completely defeated without any solutions to his predicament. Was his big fat lie going to seal his fate? "Damn, how in the name of God am I going to get out of this shitty mess," he thought out loud. Thankfully the two men sitting up front didn't hear him.

While meandering down the gravel driveway and before Harrison was pulled out of the truck, Luke had blindfolded him with a nasty brown rag that smelled like burnt motor oil. Luke grabbed Harrison by his feet and pulled him halfway out of the truck, then grabbed the back of Harrison's shirt and lifted him out of the truck.

Standing upright next to the truck, he could smell the salt air and the odor of rotting seafood. Luke, still gripping Harrison's shirt, pushed him forward for about ten yards until they reached the wooden front porch of the trailer. Luke yanked on his shirt and made him come to a complete stop. Harrison was then told to step up just a few inches and he could hear Jaxson fumbling with his keys.

Once Jaxson got the front door open, Luke pushed Harrison along the wooden porch into the living room. Before he could take a step forward, Luke reared back, and with his arm and fist like a steam-driven piston, he delivered a crushing blow to Harrison's right kidney. The muscles in his back tightened so violently it contorted his body sideways into a C shaped position. Harrison couldn't move, moaning in agonizing pain. Breathing was labored and he began to have the dry heaves. Jaxson stepped forward, guiding him into the recliner which reeked of cat urine.

Luke removed the blindfold, and Harrison's eyes watered, either from the nasty rag or from the cat urine. Luke zip-tied

Harrison's ankles together, then turned towards the front door. Before Luke could close the front door, Harrison was able to view a small section of the front yard. It was littered with old crab traps, oyster baskets, and a couple of gill nets strung between two trees. These guys were fishermen, and now he knew where their strength came from.

When Harrison arrived in Greenville, North Carolina to attend East Carolina University as a skinny freshman in the fall of 1969, he met one of his suitemates in the dorm who was from Salter Path, North Carolina. To this day, he still doesn't know his name, for as many times as he asked him, he couldn't understand his Hoi Toider accent. An unusual brogue that sounds a bit Australian. Regardless, what Harrison remembered the most was the incredible strength his suitemate had with his forearms and biceps the size of tree trunks.

On the first night on campus, a group of guys from the dorm walked down East 14th Street towards Charles Blvd. to get something to eat. On the way there, this popeye-looking freshman walked up to a yellow caution sign, grabbed the outer edges, and pulled the edges together with ease. That was the most incredible sight of strength he had ever seen.

Looking around, Harrison found himself in total filth and wondered how anyone could live like this. He had seen messy apartments and houses before when he worked for the Sherwin-Williams floor covering division. This was the worst he had ever seen. The odor was horrendous. "My God, where the hell am I?" Harrison wondered.

"What is the tide doing?" asked Jaxson, while opening the refrigerator door. "Check the tide chart on your phone."

"Aw shit, it's falling...gonna have to wait probably six or eight hours," Luke hollered as he walked to the bathroom.

Harrison sat in the nasty recliner and for the first time was able to observe the two fishermen as they moved throughout the trailer. They were huge men standing at least six-feet-four-inches tall, with barrel chests, stocky legs, and hands like catcher mitts. Their faces were weathered and deeply wrinkled from decades of being exposed to the sun. It was hard to tell how old they really were. Their enormous weight caused the floor in the living room to sag under each step.

Listening to their muted conversations, it sounded somewhat like a Gullah accent heard along the coastal areas near Charleston. Their overalls were blood stained and stiff from salt residue. Both wore T-shirts that were probably white at one time, but now soiled to a dingy light brown, splattered with tobacco juice and his blood. Their ball caps were ragged and torn, with sweat stains covering most of the outer bills. Between the two of them, they maybe had nine teeth, and those were stained a nasty yellow brown.

While sitting in the recliner directly across from the front door, Harrison glanced around and felt like he vaulted back some fifty years in time. He quickly realized the layout of the mobile home was identical to the one he moved into when he first arrived in Wilmington in 1973, just after graduating from college. He knew it was a two-bedroom layout where the bedrooms were situated on each end. In the center was a living room about twelve feet by thirteen feet that joined the combined kitchen and dining room areas. On the front side of the mobile home, directly behind the kitchen wall, was a small bathroom and utility area. Opposite of the bathroom was a short hallway that led directly into the master bedroom. The recliner was set in the back left-hand corner of the living room, resting against the wall of the guest bedroom. From there Harrison could see the master bedroom door at the end of the hallway.

"Go get the boat ready and make sure to put some shovels on board. Bring the brown tarp, too," ordered Jaxson.

Jaxson gulped down the beer he retrieved from the refrigerator and headed down the back hallway. He turned right into the utility area, where Harrison could hear him shuffling things around. Jaxson came back holding two shotguns and laid them on the kitchen table.

Luke entered through the back door and headed for the bathroom.

"Yo asshole, hand me a box of shells out of the closet while you're back there," Jaxson ordered.

"How many do you want?"

"Get me the Winchester 1200, one hundred round boxes."

The sight of the guns caused Harrison to quake with fear. With shovels, a brown tarp, and the guns he felt that his situation was going downhill fast. He lied to these guys, but they believed him. When they would finally realize there was no treasure, the guns, shovels, and tarp would seal his fate. He knew he was going to get killed, and he needed a plan to avoid that. The fear was overwhelming, and Harrison thought of his family and began to sob uncontrollably.

"You pussy," Jaxson growled as he walked over and backhanded Harrison across the face. The sting from Jaxson's knuckles brought Harrison back to his senses. He had to outwit these jerks to survive, so think, Harrison, think. You only have six hours to plan your escape and survive. In the meantime, you need to buy time. Lots of it to survive, Harrison thought.

"We might not be able to get on the island," Harrison spoke up.

"Why the hell not?" Jaxson asked, glaring down at Harrison.

"I was there last week, and a group of marine biology students were doing something with bird nests, and I couldn't get on the island."

"What, why would they be out there now?"

"It's nesting season I guess for those seahawks, and they'll be out there for weeks."

"Oh, screw that. You're full of it. I don't give a gnat's ass about them birds or those kids. All we need to do is string our gill net across that creek and that will stop them from coming in. And if they don't like that, a little buckshot screaming over their heads will send them pussies running for the hills."

Maybe, he thought, the Corps of Engineers would be out there stringing pipes across the creek doing some dredging. On several trips to the island in the recent past, there were remnants of broken and unbroken iron pipe laying all over the island. On his last fishing trip some three weeks ago, he did notice a dredge getting set up just south of Nixon Channel, and maybe they've moved south with the operation blocking the creek into Earnie's Island. Was the pipe there for a reason or just abandoned? The more Harrison contemplated this scenario, the more he realized it was simply a pipe dream, a total fantasy.

Jaxson and Luke each grabbed a twelve pack of beer out of the refrigerator and went out the back door dragging an extension cord with them and a small radio. Harrison soon heard firewood crackling and both men singing, totally out of tune, to some country western song. Harrison strained to hear their conversation, but between their incomprehensible accent, the blaring radio, and the fire crackling, he couldn't understand anything.

Looking around the trailer again, Harrison chuckled to himself when he saw the beach towels nailed above the front windows being used as curtains. He could remember how he decorated his trailer the same way. Other than the nasty recliner he was sitting in, the living room had one old brown three cushioned couch with duct tape holding together apparent slits in the upholstery, and a television mounted on a one by six pine board held up by two cinder blocks on each end. The back wall of the trailer was completely bare, except for an extra-large Confederate flag beach towel stretched to cover the back window.

The carpet in the living room was vintage sixties orange shag. It was so matted down it looked like the infield of a baseball field. The kitchen had a small stove, and maybe six cabinets, with an oval metal table with three red vinyl metal chairs that must have been popular during the fifties. Harrison, being in the floor covering business since 1979, recognized the old brown slate vinyl floor in the kitchen, as the long ago discontinued Congoleum sheet vinyl style called Spring. The edges of the vinyl floor had curled up all along the brown stained cabinets. The separation of the vinyl flooring from the kitchen to the shag carpet in the living room was covered with two or three strips of duct tape.

The dome light fixture mounted on the kitchen ceiling and the same fixture in the center of the living room were both filled with dead bugs. Both probably hadn't been cleaned out for decades. The once-clear glass covering the light bulbs, was now stained with a yellowish-brown color. No doubt the result of years of cigarette smoking in the living room. The stippled ceiling was covered in water stains. The original white paint now resembled the light fixtures. An assortment of dead water bugs, flies, and crickets lined the windowsill next to his chair.

The paneling on the walls in the living room was probably white when the trailer had been new, but now they were stained yellow from years of cigarette smoke. The wallpaper in the kitchen was an awful orange yellow floral design, covered with daisies. A favorite pattern from the sixties. Most of the paper was peeling away from the walls. Harrison could see an army of German cockroaches crawling in and out of the kitchen cabinets with scouts perched on the dingy handles of the refrigerator. The top handle of the refrigerator must have broken off years ago and had been replaced by a pair of old rusty vice grips holding onto two round holes apparently drilled into the outer face of the refrigerator.

Harrison was still reeling from his injuries, and his head was pounding so hard he just couldn't think straight or clearly anymore. He had no idea how much time had passed. Right now, he needed rest before he could plan another option to buy time. Buy time, you need to buy time; he thought as he drifted off to sleep.

CHAPTER 9

After concluding his interviews with Harrison's family, the lead detective, Anthony Decker, headed back to his office located on the second floor of the newly constructed New Hanover County Law Enforcement Center. With no solid leads, or any witnesses, Decker found himself confronted with a frustrating task. All he knew was the fact that a man was missing. His investigation needed to start with the basics. Class 101, conduct a thorough background check first. Then develop an in-depth profile of Harrison to see if anything in Harrison's past would raise any red flags.

After spending several boring hours in front of the computer screen, he could not find any clues from his efforts. Harrison was as clean as a whistle. Not even a traffic ticket. Decker was hoping to find some sort of domestic disturbance in Harrison's past that would lead him to an individual wishing to harm Harrison, but he found nothing.

Irritated with his results, Decker galloped up the stairs to the third floor, wanting to converse with the department head of forensics, Ms. Nicole Cafaro. Although it was close to five-thirty in the evening, he knew Nicole would still be in her office. Nicole was new to the department with just under eighteen months' experience. She was known for her methodical approach in reviewing forensic evidence. Heading up a team of seven highly trained technicians, each one with a specific area of forensic expertise, Nicole could take their evidence and, like putting together the pieces of a puzzle, could deduce what occurred at a crime scene with uncanny precision.

"Come on in," Nicole instructed after hearing a knock on her office door.

"So, what have ya got for me? By the way, here is a copy of Harrison's background check which is completely clean. There's nothing there that will help us."

"I'm still waiting, but it doesn't look good."

"What do you mean, it doesn't look good?"

"Not a single fingerprint was lifted from the scene, so I really want to examine the area myself to see if my team missed something. I'm going to head over to Harrison's house in a few minutes. Do you want to join me?"

"Absolutely. Let me get my jacket and radio, and I'll meet you out front."

When Nicole had learned that the crime scene investigated by her team was the home of Harrison Thomas, she was deeply upset because she knew Harrison personally. Her Dad, Earnie Cafaro, and Harrison had been close friends for over twelve years. During that time, Harrison treated Nicole as if she was his own daughter. Whether it was her birthday, or graduation from high school or college, Harrison was always present. When the Cafaro household was destroyed during Hurricane Floyd in 1999 from rising flood waters, Harrison and Ms. Kelly housed them at their home for two weeks.

Having full access to the entire house, Nicole was amazed at the number of books Harrison had accumulated over the years, both fiction and non-fiction. When Nicole came across his old school yearbooks that were tucked away in a tall bookcase at the end of the hallway, her curiosity led to a series of question-and-answer sessions lasting hours. With each page of every yearbook,

Harrison had a story to tell, and by the end of her two weeks stay, Nicole developed a deep admiration and respect for her father's friend.

The only aspect of Harrison's personality that she didn't like was all the foul language he used to emphasize events that occurred in all the stories he told. His potty mouth, as Nicole labeled it, was distracting and annoying at times to the point she had to ask him several times to refrain from using such dreadful language. On several occasions, she would let Harrison know that contrary to popular belief, God's last name wasn't dammit.

Harrison explained to Nicole that he got that from his mother, who was raised by her Irish grandparents. They owned and operated a bar and pool hall in Queens, New York, back in the raucous years of the 1920s and 1930s. The bar and pool hall were on the first floor, with an active brothel on the second floor. Harrison's mother lived on the third floor with her grandparents.

After she finished school each day at the local all-girls Catholic school, she would spend her afternoons and evenings helping her grandfather clean up after all the rowdy and foul-mouthed patrons had left for the day. At a young age, Harrison's mother could cuss with the best of them, and unfortunately, she passed the habit of using foul language onto Harrison and his younger brother, Rich.

This was Decker's first major case since being promoted to detective just four months earlier, and he, too, was personally involved. Both he and Harrison had been project estimators in the construction industry, and had spent many hours together, sharing information over drinks while lounging at Earnie's pool. Decker's expertise was in kitchen design for new construction projects as well as home remodels, while Harrison's forte was estimating the floor covering needs for large apartment complexes. Many times, they would feed off each other while estimating the same projects. Whenever they had an audience around them, their whacky sense of humor along with a multitude of racy jokes, would keep people in stitches for hours on end.

It was six years ago, when Earnie and Harrison encouraged Decker to pursue his lifelong goal of being a law enforcement officer. They convinced him to attend the police academy right after he lost his estimating position. Decker, facing unemployment, explained he did not have the finances available to live on and to attend the six-month long course being offered in Fayetteville, North Carolina. He could still remember the evening he stopped by Earnie's house with Harrison sitting at the bar, that changed his life.

"We have decided, and we will not take no for an answer," Earnie said, handing Decker an extra-large manilla envelope that was bulging at the seams.

"Go get your training and don't worry about anything. We've got you covered, buddy."

It wasn't until months after he graduated from the police academy that he learned that it was Harrison's idea to loan him the money. Upon hearing of his buddy's financial woes, Harrison had gone to Earnie with a proposal for Decker, and Earnie welcomed the idea. Earnie gladly contributed fifty percent. Together, they handed him twelve thousand dollars as a gift, an unbelievable gesture that changed his life forever. Now, on his first major case, his buddy was out there somewhere, and he needed to find him.

"Have you called your Mom and Dad?" Decker asked as they approached their vehicles.

"Oh, of course I did," Nicole responded. "They're over at Harrison's house right now and they said it was a mess. That's telling me we are dealing with several people, don't you think?"

"Yeah, I agree, but it's the amount of blood I saw all over the place that really has me concerned."

"We think at this point, the type O blood found is from one person, most likely Harrison's since his medical records showed his blood type to be O. My team found some tissue samples in both the hallway and the office that were covered in type O as well. But type O blood is the most common blood type out there, so we really won't know until the DNA results come in. They also found a couple of teeth and we are waiting for Harrison's dental records to see if they are his."

"So, off hand, what do you think? I know you haven't seen the house yourself, but what is your gut telling you?"

"Right now, I think Harrison, for whatever reason, was severely beaten and got kidnapped. If we can determine why, that might lead us to the perps."

When Decker and Nicole arrived at Harrison's house around six-thirty that evening, the family members were still cleaning up the mess created by the intruders. Each item they touched brought back family memories with Harrison and they could not hold back the tears. At one point, the sight of blood deeply upset Harrison's grandson Bryson, and he had to leave the house. His older sister Andrea followed and found him in Paw Paw's shed in the backyard. This was where Harrison had stored a huge collection of bluebird houses that he had built in his spare time.

A few years back, when Andrea was eighteen, she cut out a picture of a bluebird house she found in a magazine and asked her Paw Paw to build one for her. She wanted it to look just like the one in the picture. Harrison gladly accepted the task and built his first birdhouse that resembled the picture to a tee.

Harrison enjoyed building that first birdhouse so much, he went out and bought a compound miter saw, a brad gun, and a whole assortment of other tools along with twenty or so different colors of spray paint and found himself immersed in a brand-new hobby. Four or five months later, he had built eighty-three and each time he finished one, he sent a picture of it to his grandkids, seeking their approval. That original picture from Andrea was still hanging on the shed wall, and when Andrea saw it, she held her brother close, and both began to shed uncontrollable tears.

Andrea and Bryson adored their Paw Paw even though he wasn't directly related to them. Their real mother was Ms. Kelly's daughter from her first marriage. Their mom sadly passed when they were just babies. When they were able to talk, they called Harrison Paw Paw. He relished his role as a step-granddad and loved them as if they were his own grandkids.

Upon their arrival, Decker and Nicole were greeted with hugs and kisses from the family and they found it hard to concentrate, so they politely asked the family to step outside and let them search the house. They started in Harrison's office and upon entering they found Dalton sitting in his Dad's chair staring at the wall above the two computer monitors. Harrison had pinned two of his favorite phrases on the wall, just above the monitors, that Dalton had read for many years.

"What are you looking at, Dalton?" Nicole asked.

"Look, read that," as Dalton pointed to the piece of paper pinned to the wall. *Learn Through Failure, Don't Let It Define You.*

"Dad said it was something President Bush once said. Read this other one," he said and pointed at the wall. *Aim So High You'll Never Be Bored.*

"When I was younger and would mess up, after Dad would scold me, he would always read these to me." Dalton broke down and had to leave the office.

Decker and Nicole meticulously scanned the areas where blood samples had been taken, starting in the office, the master bedroom, the guest bedroom, then moved on into the hallway and finished at the front door. Their search once again revealed nothing new. Not a single clue was left behind, not even a fingerprint other than those of Harrison and his immediate family members. Perplexed, they asked the family to come back inside, and they all were interviewed again, this time by Nicole. Same questions, same answers.

Decker motioned for Nicole to join him outside, not wanting the family to hear what he was about to say. He stood on the back porch scratching his head.

"I really think it's time to call in the Feds. I'm clueless on this one. We need outside help."

Nicole agreed. They knew that their personal feelings would probably cloud their thinking. Reaching out for help was their best option.

Decker made the call to the local FBI office and was told an agent would come by the house around nine o'clock that night to meet with him. In the meantime, Decker was hungry and suggested to Nicole that they go to Diamonds for something to eat. There was plenty of time before the FBI agent would arrive. Nicole had not eaten all day, so she welcomed the idea. She was looking forward to having her favorite appetizer, a basket full of fried pickles.

Just as Decker and Nicole sat down, Willow, the ever-present waitress at Diamonds, came over and asked if Harrison had been found. She, too, was visibly upset. Harrison over the years, had been a perfect gentleman towards her and always left her a generous tip after each visit. It amazed Decker and Nicole how fast word had spread about Harrison's disappearance.

"Have y'all heard anything strange from anybody lately?" Decker asked.

Willow thought for a moment and replied, "No, haven't heard a thing."

"If you see or hear anything, you call me right away. You've got my card, right?"

"I sure do, honey. I'll call ya if I hear anything," Willow said, winking at Decker.

Nicole rolled her eyes at Decker, then gave Willow her order. Fried pickles with a glass of sweet tea. Decker ordered his usual cheeseburger and fries with a glass of water with a lemon.

Decker and Nicole ate in silence. As they headed up to the bar to pay the bill, the other waitress, Lisa, approached them.

"Hey look, I'm not sure if this will help y'all, but I remember seeing two guys sitting over there at the corner of the bar. I had never seen them before. They weren't regulars, and they weren't friendly at all. It was odd, but they kept looking over at the table where Harrison and that group of friends were sitting the other night."

"Can you describe them to us?" Nicole asked.

"They were big fellows, I mean huge. Their hands were filthy. If I remember correctly, they wore overalls and they both wore ball caps. They seemed to be whispering amongst themselves. They stayed huddled together the whole time and didn't speak to anyone."

"Did you hear any of their conversations?"

"No, not really. They sure were cussing a lot though."

"Can you remember anything else that could help us?" Nicole asked.

"Well, I do remember they smelled bad. Like when the tide is low. You know what I mean, like when the tide gets so low it has that rotten fishy smell to it."

"Do you remember anything else about what they were wearing?" Decker asked, pulling out his notebook and pen.

"Nah, not really. I was busy that night and didn't notice."

Decker asked Lisa to show him exactly where the two men were sitting, and she pointed to the last two bar stools next to the jukebox. The officers walked around the bar and stood behind the two bar stools that Lisa pointed out. They could see where the two men had an unobstructed view of the table where Harrison was sitting with his friends the night before.

"Reckon we should get your team to dust for fingerprints here at the bar?" Decker asked Nicole.

"Honey," Lisa interrupted, "We've cleaned that area many times since then. You won't find any fingerprints there at all."

"Well, here's my card. If you happen to think of anything else that might help us, give me a call," Decker tried to hand Lisa his card, but her hands were full of drinks, so Decker leaned over and slipped it into her blouse pocket with a big smile on his face.

Nicole, disgusted with Decker's apparent advance towards the waitress, made the call to her team anyway, with instructions to dust everywhere, including the bar stools.

Decker jotted down some notes in his notebook, thinking maybe he had his first clue. He was anxious to meet with the FBI agent. Just before they left, he asked Lisa if Diamonds had any inside cameras, and she just laughed. Decker and Nicole thanked Lisa for her help and headed out the front door.

While heading over to Decker's car, Nicole glanced to her right and spotted a 24-hour ATM housed in a small building in the adjacent parking lot. She noticed a camera mounted on the nearby power pole that pointed directly toward the machine. It also pointed in the direction of the Diamond's parking lot. Nicole walked over and found a small label on the back outside wall which identified the name of the attending company. She took a photo of the label then sent it to her team with instructions to contact the ATM people. She also instructed them to get the videos from that camera for the last twenty-four hours and call her as soon as they had something.

"Oh Lord, I hope that camera was working and recording everything," Nicole said, looking at Decker.

"Me too, it could be our first solid lead."

"You, my Dad, and Harrison have been going to Diamonds for years and years, so you'll be able to identify most of the people that were there the other night. We'll ignore those that you know and concentrate on those you don't know and start from there."

"I know we can run vehicle tag numbers, but does your lab have facial recognition abilities?"

"We have limited capability, but that's where the Feds can help us."

During the short ride back to Harrison's house, Nicole recalled how Harrison, Decker, and Robert got together every Thursday night in her Dad's garage for cocktails where they would shoot pool, play cards, tell jokes, or discuss recent sporting events.

"Hey Decker, the last time all you guys got together at Dad's, did Harrison act strange in any way? Was he upset about anything?"

"Nah, he was his usual jovial self. In fact, he was really excited about the book signing and was looking forward to it."

"Did he mention if anybody strange called him or spoke to him in the last few days?"

"Not at all. What about you? You gave him a ride home in the golf cart last week because he drank too much, right?"

"I guess you're right. I didn't notice anything out of order either."

"I think you are grasping at straws, Nicole."

"Really, you were grasping at something else earlier, you dirty old man."

"Do you know that he tried to give me a tip when I dropped him off last Thursday night?" Nicole smiled getting out of the patrol car.

"That's Harrison, always the gracious one."

CHAPTER 10

The chafing and burning on Harrison's buttocks were becoming unbearable and he could not find, as much as he tried, a comfortable position to sit in. Both cousins were still outside, and it suddenly dawned on Harrison that he didn't even know their names. When they talked to each other, it was either dumbass or asshole, back and forth constantly. Is it possible, Harrison pondered, that their mother felt compelled to name them at birth this way? Harrison heard someone opening the back door. Jaxson entered and walked over to check on Harrison's bindings.

"Good God man, it smells like shit in here."

"Hey man, look, I messed myself. Do you have an extra pair of pants I could wear?" Harrison asked, with a painful look on his face.

Hearing that, Jaxson grabbed Harrison by the back of the neck and dragged him across the living room. Opening the back door, he flung Harrison out into the backyard. Harrison landed hard on the dirt ground, narrowly missing the red-hot burn barrel.

Harrison, with his hands tied behind him, couldn't turn his body enough to the side, so he landed on his chest, briefly knocking the wind out of him. After finally catching his breath a few seconds later, he slowly turned his head to the left. All he could see was woods. There was a small patch of dirt around the burn barrel. It was littered with dozens of beer cans. There were no other structures or homes in sight, just thick woods. Harrison thought he heard a dog barking. As hard as he strained to listen, there weren't any other sounds he could hear other than the whining of a pesky mosquito twirling around his ear. He rolled over on his back, and seeing Jaxson angrily standing over him, he almost messed his pants again.

The sun was setting, casting long shadows through the trees onto the property. One single ray of sunshine peaked through and hit directly upon the eight-inch Bowie knife that Jaxson was holding in his right hand. He grabbed the bottom of Harrison's orange fishing shirt, placed the blade against the bottom button, and with one swift upward movement, cut open Harrison's shirt with the same dexterity as if he was fileting a fish. He unbuckled Harrison's belt, pulled it out from the belt loops, and tossed the belt off to the side. Jaxson reached down and grabbed the bottom edges of Harrison's fishing shorts and with one quick pull, he yanked the shorts completely off and threw them in the burn barrel.

"Jesus, you really did shit yourself didn't ya?" Jaxson said, looking down at Harrison's soiled underwear.

He carefully slid the edge of his knife just under the outside edge of Harrison's underwear and cut through the fabric, causing the elastic lining to spring open, leaving him lying there fully exposed. Luke came around from the side of the mobile home and after seeing his naked captive, muttered something under his breath about the movie *Deliverance*.

"Oh Lord," Harrison thought, "this is not good."

"Hey dipshit, grab that garden hose over there and wash this asshole down while I go and see if I can find him some pants," Jaxson ordered, heading back into the trailer.

Harrison turned his attention to Luke, who was standing about three feet away with both hands on the hose pressed against his crotch, swinging the hose round and round. The look on Luke's face was the same look he'd seen in the movie *The Shinning* with Jack Nicholson. His eyes were bulging wide, his eyebrows raised up into a V shape, with his lips just barely open, showing the tip of his bright red tongue. His eyes were devoid of any color, just glazed over and pure black. The hair on his forehead was quivering, beginning to stand straight up. It was an utterly crazed sight; an inhuman look Harrison had never seen before. Even though he had been kidnapped and beaten, for the first time he was truly frightened looking into the eyes of the devil himself.

Luke turned on the water and readjusted the nozzle, creating a strong thin stream of water. He directed the powerful stream directly into Harrison's groin area and pelted his testicles for several seconds. Writhing in pain, he rolled over and curled into a ball, exposing his chaffed butt. In his sick twisted mind, Luke now directed the forceful stream of water straight at his rectum. Harrison screamed in agony, hoping someone would hear him. Unfortunately for Harrison that only infuriated Luke more. Bending over and placing his left hand on Harrison's hip, Luke started bringing the nozzle closer and closer to his rectum.

"I'm gonna clean you out real good boy, so hold still," he laughed.

Jaxson came back outside holding a pair of jeans, and seeing what his cousin was about to do, he rushed over and grabbed the hose anyway from him.

"What the hell are you doing you moron. You'll kill him like you did that dog. We need him alive you idiot."

"Aw man, I was just having some fun."

"Get yo ass in the house and start gettin' things ready," Jaxson ordered.

The damage was already done as a small dribble of blood oozed out of Harrison's swollen anus. Jaxson knew if he had waited any longer, Luke would have continued with his sadistic ways and quite possibly killed their only hope of retrieving their bounty.

"Well, I'll be. Look at that, the little pussy is having his period," Luke belted out. Both men chuckled, but Harrison didn't find any humor in what Luke had just done.

Lying face down in the cigarette butt ladened mud, whatever strength he had before was now gone. He was physically and emotionally drained. The relentless abuse by the two men was taking its toll. He was broken and didn't know how much longer he could hang on.

"Stand up you piece of shit," ordered Jaxson. He twisted the nozzle to create a wider spray and ordered Harrison to turn around in circles so he could rinse him down. After two turns, he was too weak to stand and collapsed to his knee's inches from the burn barrel. The warmth emanating from the burn barrel and the water drizzling over him, was somewhat comforting. He had the sudden urge to urinate. It felt like he was peeing razor blades. Looking down, Harrison was horrified to see nothing but a steady stream of blood. He passed out falling to the ground barely missing the edge of the barrel.

When Harrison regained consciousness, he found himself in new clothes at least, but the mildew smell of the clothes made him gag. His hands were still zip-tied, but now his thighs and feet were zip tied as well. For whatever reason, the cousins had decided to zip-tie his hands in front of him this time. When the two noticed he was awake, they both came into the living room and picked him up and dragged him over to sit at the kitchen table. They had an old AAA North Carolina Road map spread out on the table. The last time Harrison saw a map like this one was when his family traveled each year from Delaware to Florida for Easter break. Back then, I-95 had not existed, and the only highway south was US Hwy 17 and even that highway wasn't one hundred percent complete.

While he was in Boy Scouts, one of the merit badges he was trying to obtain was the Cartography badge and with his dad driving, he would help navigate the entire trip using a map from AAA, just like the one he was looking at now. Because of those trips, he excelled at map reading and even went on years later to receive a minor degree in cartography at East Carolina University.

"Where is this island at?" Jaxson asked, pushing the map in front of Harrison.

"I can't see without my readers," Harrison blurted out, which was met with another back hand from Jaxson. The blow opened his lip again.

Jaxson ordered Luke to go get his glasses that he left in the truck. When he came back, Jaxson placed the glasses over Harrison's eyes and ordered him to point out the location. Harrison was used to wearing readers that were 2.00 magnification, and these were obviously less, so he struggled to focus moving his head back and forth. Jaxson slapped Harrison on the back of his head again.

"Quit jerking us around and tell us the location."

"Okay, Okay, show me where we are on this map."

Jaxson landed a crushing blow with his fist that sent Harrison to the floor. His eye swelled. His lower lip was split, and blood dripped on the floor.

"You need to know nothing. Just show us *your* spot," Jaxson growled, picking Harrison off the floor with one arm. Jaxson slammed Harrison into the kitchen chair with a thud. Jaxson slid the map over and pushed Harrison's nose into it.

Harrison figured he was in Hampstead. He had driven from his house up to the Hampstead Marina a hundred times in the past and knew every turn and bump in the road along the way. Although he couldn't see earlier, lying on the floorboard of the truck, he was certain it was Hampstead. They were just twenty minutes from his house. He could also smell low tide, so he knew he was close to the water, maybe less than a quarter of a mile away. He was hoping to get his location pinned down more, but quickly realized these two were not about to reveal their location.

Seated once again at the kitchen table, Harrison decided to obey them to avoid any more beatings. His best option right now was to point out to them the location he had in mind. The map was so old, many of the North Carolina modern landmarks and highways were missing, and the terrain details along the waterway were also missing.

"See this area here? There is a golf course there today, and across from it is the island, about right here. That's the island. That is where we need to go."

"If you're lying to us, and there's nothing there, that island will be your grave," Jaxson exclaimed. "Do you want to take another look, to make sure?"

"No, that's the island, that's the truth."

Jaxson stood up, went over to the kitchen counter and retrieved a pen from a small ceramic bowl, then handed the pen to Harrison.

"Circle that island," Jaxson ordered. Harrison did as he was told and circled the island three or four times.

91

"So, it must be high tide, huh? We can't get there now at low tide?" questioned Luke.

"There's only a few inches of water in that creek at low tide, so, yes it has to be high tide."

"So, what are we going to find once we get there?" Jaxson asked. "What's the metal detector for?"

"There are a lot of people that go out on these islands looking for stuff, and someone with a good detector could find the stuff easily. So, I took a bunch of the scrapped iron pipe that the dredge guys left there and scattered it all over the place. In that way, after an hour of digging up junk, most hunters will leave. Even if someone was directly over the spot, I've placed a large piece of aluminum over it so if they started to dig, they would hit that junk within a few feet and move on, never thinking to look a few feet under it," Harrison explained. "The aluminum makes a very distinct sound with the detector, different than plain old iron, so I'll know the exact spot."

"What do ya mean by stuff? What stuff are you talking about?" Jaxson asked, sliding his chair closer to the table.

"Look, just like in the pirate movies, you would think treasure would be found in a large iron box or chest if you want to call it that, filled with gold coins, chunks of silver and various jewels, right? Not in this case. It seems that someone had a bag of some sort, maybe a leather satchel or something else they stashed the coins in. There must have been a large tree on the island at one time, and this person or persons dug deep under that tree and shoved the bag way up into the root ball. Over the years, that root ball completely engulfed the bag. Follow me here. It seems the only time the root ball loosens its grip on the bag is after a heavy rainstorm. I only go back out there after a big storm, and sometimes I find nothing, but sometimes I might find a bunch of coins."

Harrison wandered along with his tale. He held their attention.

"I dug out another big hole down about four or five feet, poured in probably four or five hundred pounds of concrete and set a large safe deposit box into the concrete. Even if someone found that, they would never be able to pull up my safe without heavy equipment. Also, they would also need the set of two keys to open the safe deposit box, which I have hidden out on the island as well."

Harrison anxiously awaited their response, hoping they would fall for it. He was really going out on a limb with this ridiculous story, but he was formulating a key part of his plan. It was imperative these guys believed what he was saying.

"Yo, Jaxson," Luke popped up. "Remember that old creek bed near our house where we would find all those sharks' teeth after it rained for a few days? Instead of sharks' teeth showing up, it's gonna be gold, baby!"

It worked. They bit, hook, line, and sinker. Harrison couldn't believe he was getting away with all the hogwash he was feeding them. Apparently, their greed and lust for treasure completely overtook any rational thinking. Harrison now knew the name of one of the men, the man who beat him so badly.

"Wait a minute, what kind of bullshit is this?" Jaxson asked while grabbing Harrison by the neck and glaring at him. "Why would you bury a safe in concrete and leave it out there?"

Harrison realized that Jaxson was the smarter of the two and if he didn't come up with a brilliant explanation, his plan would fail and fall apart, and he'd no doubt receive another beating.

"Look, I started finding those coins maybe seven or eight years ago and I would take them to the bank and put them in my safe deposit box. The boxes were all in one room and there was another room next to it where you could close the door and be in private, with nobody watching what you were doing. There's always an attendant with a master key and you give them your key so they can open the drawer to get to your box.

"During one of my trips, maybe six years ago, I was in a hurry and didn't close the door completely to the private room. When I reached into my pocket to pull out the coin I had, I dropped it on the floor, and it rolled out into the other room. When I went to get it, the attendant who was still there had picked up the coin and was standing there with it in his hand. He looked at me real strange like and asked me where the hell I had found it. I told him that my grandfather left it to me in his will."

"Come on dude, what the hell are you telling us?" Luke inquired.

"That banker, I tell ya, had a real funny look on his face, and he scared me. I thought maybe he was going to report me to the Feds or something. Maybe he thought it was stolen property, but whatever, I figured I needed to get the coins out of the bank. I did about two or three days later.

"I didn't want to keep them at my house or anywhere on my property if anybody showed up looking for them. I was freaking out big time trying to find a place to hide my coins. I had been on the island many, many times, so I figured it would be the safest place I could hide them. It is such a remote spot. It is extremely hard to get to, but still close to my house. For a little added security, I encased the safe in concrete. I'm glad I did it, because about a month after I cleaned out my box at the bank, our house got broken into and somebody stole our small fire safe boxes.

One was my wife's that had her collection of wheat pennies and the other one was mine that was filled with old silver dollar certificates. We got hit again three months later. Anyway, I always thought that banker had something to do with it, so to throw him off, I wrote a book about finding treasure and. . . ."

"Then why in the hell did you write a book about finding treasure? No wonder they broke into your house. You ain't too bright are ya?"

"Did you read my book by any chance?"

"Nah, don't have time for that shit," Jaxson belted out.

"I wanted this banker, or whoever robbed my house, to leave me alone and get off my ass, so I wrote a book about an old man finding treasure on a beach one summer while out metal detecting. That treasure, as I clearly described in the book, was one single gold coin. Just one, not a bunch of them. I did that on purpose because I wanted that thief to think there was only one coin."

"Did it work?" Luke asked.

"Well, to make sure it did, just after the book was released, to help publicize it, I contacted the *Wrightsville Beach Magazine* people to have them come interview me. Luckily, I had a gold coin that my great grandfather left me, so I had them take a picture of me standing with my Fisher metal detector and the gold coin in my hand. I lied and said I found it on the beach metal detecting stating it was the only gold coin I ever found."

"Does anybody else know what you really did?" asked Luke.

"Oh, hell no," Harrison answered. "Nobody knows but me."

"Did anybody hit your house again after you did that interview?" Luke asked.

"Nope. Whoever it was, left us alone after that."

"Freaking bankers, they're pieces of shit," Jaxson said releasing his grip on Harrison's neck.

As Jaxson sat back down on his kitchen chair, Harrison breathed a huge sigh of relief, knowing then that they believed his story for now. Recalling what he had just said, Harrison realized his story was full of holes, and he had to be prepared to counter any questions these two guys might ask him later. Harrison waited patiently, ready to respond, but surprisingly, Jaxson and Luke turned their attention to the old map without asking any further questions.

CHAPTER 11

Detective Decker and Forensics Director Nicole Cafaro returned to Harrison's house around eight-forty-five and anxiously awaited the arrival of the local FBI agent. When no one showed at nine o'clock, Detective Decker called asking why. He was told they determined the incident was not a federal matter, and the case would be turned over to the State Bureau of Investigation in Raleigh. The desk clerk at the FBI office gave Decker the number to the SBI office in Raleigh. After placing the call, he learned that agent Sebastian Vickors was assigned the case, but he would not be there until the next morning.

"What time is he going to arrive?" Detective Decker asked the female SBI duty officer.

"Agent Vickors said he would be there at six-thirty sharp."

The detective, always the charmer, spent the next ten minutes inquiring about agent Vickors but also chit-chatted with the young lady on the other end. The conversation ended when he found out she was married.

Director Nicole had to leave when she received a call from her team. They had retrieved the video tapes from the company that operated the camera mounted near Diamond's parking lot.

"Looks like my team retrieved the video, so I'm heading back to the office."

"Great, I'll follow you in."

Leaving Middle Sound, both cars headed west on Market Street. About four miles in, they encountered a terrible four car accident at Station Road which blocked traffic in all directions. Nicole radioed Decker, telling him she was going to pull into the parking lot on her right and wait for the wreckage to be cleared away. He radioed back with a simple 10/4, and followed Nicole into the small parking lot, pulling up in the space next to hers.

"Look, you stay here. I'm going to see if I can lend some assistance. It really looks bad," Decker said, turning and jogging over to the accident scene.

Nicole turned off the engine, pulled up on the seat lever and eased back two notches. She opened both windows and closed her eyes, allowing the cool evening breeze to pass through her vehicle. Reflecting on her past, she felt truly blessed to be in the position she was now in. She was totally elated she would be working alongside Detective Decker, who she had known since she was eleven-years-old.

Being an Army brat, Nicole had spent time in South Korea and Germany before landing in Youngstown, Ohio when she was ten. One year later, her dad Earnie retired, and the family moved to Wilmington, North Carolina. They bought a home in the Treasure Cove subdivision adjacent to Middle Sound Loop Road.

She breezed through her early years in school, graduating from high school in just two years. She graduated from UNCW in two years as well. Because of her outstanding grades, she received a Forensic Pathology Fellowship at East Carolina University. She completed that program with honors and became the youngest member of the American Academy of Forensic Sciences. Many municipalities and county law enforcement agencies from all along the eastern seaboard recruited the phenom, but her heart was in Wilmington. Although her forensic abilities were never fully tested in the field, it was her superior academic abilities they all wanted.

An hour later, the vehicles involved in the accident had been cleared away and traffic once again was flowing. Nicole and Decker arrived at the Sheriff's Office fifteen minutes later, parked in the underground parking lot, and took the elevator to the second floor. Standing in the elevator, Decker couldn't help but notice that Nicole was wearing the exact same attire she had worn the first day she started her job. She wore the same outfit every day since then. Her hair was pulled back in a bun. The pleated gray slacks, the thin collared light gray blouse, and her gray block heel shoes, gave Nicole her own dull look. Her attire was far different from all the other ladies in the department who wore colorful skirts or long flowing dresses.

The forensic team, along with Detective Decker, gathered around the flickering computer monitor, anxiously waiting for the video to start. The video was extremely grainy. After watching just a few minutes, he excused himself returning to his office. He picked up his guitar and headed back upstairs to the breakroom, just a few doors down from Nicole's office.

A few minutes later, the team heard Decker strumming his guitar and belting out one of his honky-tonk ballads. The girls in the department just loved him. With his quick humor, he always kept things jovial within the department, and with a constant smile on his face, always had kind words for his fellow officers.

Dark complexioned, with bushy eyebrows and a thick black mustache to match his jet-black hair, Decker was a dead ringer for Juan Valdez, the fictional Colombian coffee farmer whose face was on coffee cans during the late fifties and sixties. On several occasions, the good-natured detective would go along with requests from the girls to pose with them wearing a white cowboy hat, emailing their friends, saying they had a visit from Juan that day.

"Anything yet?" Decker asked, popping his head into Nicole's office.

"Nope, it's slow going and nothing important has shown up yet."

"Okay ladies, I'm done for today."

Heading out, Decker sang a *John Denver* song... *"Hold me like you'll never let me go, 'Cause I'm leaving on a jet plane, don't know when I'll be back again, oh babe, I hate to go....*

As he reached the rear stairwell, he could hear cackling in the background.

Agent Sebastian Vickors left Raleigh and arrived at Harrison's house at six-thirty on the dot. Agent Vickors parked his unmarked four-door black sedan in the driveway. Decker greeted the agent from the front porch. He watched the strikingly handsome light-skinned black man step out of his car. Agent Vickors wore a tasteful black two button Gangster suit with white pinstripes. A heavily starched white shirt with no collar rode up high on his neck. Decker noticed his black, wingtips were militarily polished.

"Good morning, sir, I'm Detective Anthony Decker of the New Hanover County Sheriff's Office. Thanks for coming."

"Wopnin, chingas tus ya," Agent Vickors replied in what Decker thought was a British accent and had no idea what he said.

"What, what did you say?" he asked with a puzzled look on his face.

"Oh-ye, sorry mate, old habit. Right, I was born and raised in Bermuda, and that's how we greet one another on the street. Sorry for that bro. Let me walk about for a bit. I'll meet ya back inside where you can fill me in."

From his short conversation with the SBI clerk, Decker had learned that Agent Vickors was a well-seasoned investigator whose best talents were solving kidnapping cases.

"Agent Vickors is blunt and straight to the point and if he asks you a question, you best have an answer. You should pay attention and take notes." Decker remembered what the young lady had told him.

Decker watched as the agent pulled out his cell phone, set it to video. He meticulously videoed the entire front yard in a panoramic sweep, then continued along the side yard, eventually circling around the property. At an even slower pace, the agent reversed his earlier movements.

"I don't see anything of value here. Did your forensic team scan the property? Did they bag any evidence?"

"Yeah, they found nothing. All the evidence is inside the house, so let me take you inside to meet the family members and you can do your thing. How does that sound? Maybe a little *chingas* is in order?" said Decker using his best impression of a British accent.

"Yo, bro, watch what you say. When we have some time later, I'll tell you about the neighborhood I grew up in, north of Dundonald Street, where what you just said could get your throat slit ear to ear."

Eyeing Vickors with bewilderment, Decker opened the front storm door and guided him into the residence. Vickors approached Ms. Kelly. She was standing in the kitchen just ten feet away with her jaw dropped ever so slightly. She couldn't help but notice the eloquently dressed, extraordinarily handsome young man in his early thirties was the spitting image of her favorite actor Denzel Washington. It momentarily took her breath away.

"I'm Agent Sebastian Vickors of the North Carolina SBI. And you are?"

"I'm Kelly Thomas, Harrison's wife. Nice to meet you," Ms. Kelly responded, coming back to earth, but still enthralled with his good looks and charming accent.

Detective Decker introduced Agent Vickors to all the family members present and ushered him down the hall to Harrison's office. Decker reviewed his notes with the agent in private, away from prying ears. Agent Vickors pulled out his cell phone once again and proceeded to video the entire residence, starting in the office, and ending his video in the living room where he took still photos of each family member. Same questions with the same answers were all he got after interviewing each one. There was no reason for Harrison to be kidnapped. It had to be a burglary gone bad. Very bad was Agent Vickors' conclusion, but he did not reveal his thoughts to the family.

Agent Vickors turned his attention to Decker, motioning to him to come back outside.

"Come with me and let's sit in my car for a few minutes while I upload the videos from my phone to my computer. I'll send everything to my team in Raleigh. In less than thirty minutes, we'll know everything about everybody in that living room."

Decker watched the agent attach his phone to a fourteen-inch ThinkPad laptop mounted on a Jeto-Desk stand. Within seconds, all the information was sent to Raleigh.

"Did you do a preliminary background check on Mr. Thomas?"

"Yes, I did, and..." before Decker could finish his statement, Vickors interrupted him.

"Did you copy that info on your phone?"

"Yeah, why?"

"What's your cell number?"

Decker gave the agent his number and then watched as Vickors' fingers flew across the keyboard and with a final click on the Enter key, Decker's background check information popped up on the laptop screen.

"Holy shit, how the hell did you do that?"

"You don't need to know; just know I can find you or anybody else pretty quick if need be."

As soon as he got back to the law enforcement center Decker was going to contact his IT people and learn how to do this hack.

"You're telling me that not one single neighbor witnessed anything?"

"No, nothing. We assume that they were all up at the event."

"Did any of the neighbors have video cameras, or any other home surveillance?"

"Nope."

Both men returned to the house.

"Does anyone here have a recent photograph of Mr. Thomas? I need one that I can keep. It would help if you had one where Mr. Thomas is standing with friends or a group photo at some gathering."

Agent Vickors scanned the living room looking for pictures of Harrison when a large brass picture frame caught his attention. Inside the brass frame, accented with a green mat, were three yellow legal-size sheets of paper covered with numbers. The top sheet was dated Wednesday, Sept. 18, 1991.

"What's this?"

"It's a record of all the contractions Grandmama had twenty-four hours before giving birth to Dalton," said Andrea.

"Jesus, look at this, would ya?" Agent Vickors turned to face Detective Decker. "This guy is one anal character. Who the hell would do this?"

His cell rang before he could answer. Nicole was calling him explaining while reviewing the tapes, she believed she may have found something that he needed to see.

"We have a video of two guys leaving Diamonds shortly after Harrison's group left."

With that news, Decker and Vickors excused themselves. They sped off heading for Nicole's office. On the way in, Decker radioed Agent Vickors and told him he was going to stop by Diamonds first and see if any of the waitresses were on duty so he could bring them in to view the tapes. Decker luckily found two waitresses at Diamonds prepping for the day and using his charm, was able to persuade them to come with him to the police station.

Within twenty minutes, everyone had gathered in Director Nicole's office with their eyes fixed to the large screen monitor mounted on the side wall. Nicole inserted the flash drive into her laptop, hit a few keys on her keyboard, and the video came into view. She fast-forwarded the video, stopping at six forty-five that evening. One by one, they could see Harrison and his group leaving Diamonds, getting into their separate vehicles. Nicole and Decker identified each one they knew, pausing the video in ten-second intervals, to allow Agent Vickors to take notes. Eight minutes later, they saw two rather large men leaving Diamonds and getting into a dark colored pickup truck. The pickup was parked within ten yards of the front door under a huge live oak tree. The two men were visible walking for approximately six seconds before their images were blocked by the tree. Nicole rewound the video and paused it, showing the best image of the two men.

Detective Decker took a copy of the photos and ushered Lisa into his office. At the same time, Director Nicole took Willow to her office. Pre-planned, each one asked the same questions. "Do you recognize these guys? Did you see them at any time in the bar?" When they regrouped, Decker and Nicole shared their findings.

"Willow said she couldn't recall. Frankly, I think she's lying."

"Well, Lisa confirmed that she saw the two in question. She was pretty sure about it," said Detective Decker. "She said that she remembered that blue ball cap one of them was wearing and that they were sitting at the end of the bar last Friday night."

"Is there a shot of the truck license plate?" asked Decker to the others..

"Unfortunately, not. The truck was parked facing the camera, so when they left, the camera never picked up the plate numbers."

"Well, at least we may have two suspects," said Vickors.

Agent Vickors gave instructions to Nicole to send the videos to his forensic people in Raleigh. He wanted to see if they could zero in closer, especially inside the truck. Maybe they could get something on facial recognition files to be investigated. The video was a bit grainy, but it was worth a shot.

"Nicole, did your team find anything on Harrison's computer?"

"Nothing, absolutely nothing to work with," she replied with her head down. She was beginning to even doubt herself and wondered if she should hand over the duties to a more experienced team member. That might even help with morale. Several more experienced team members had been passed over when the department announced that she would be the director. That decision did not sit well with many of the team members. Maybe her own judgment was clouded since she knew Harrison so well.

"Were there any pictures saved on his computer?"

"Oh, there are hundreds of shots, mostly shots of Harrison holding up fish he caught."

"Have someone go back through all those pictures and print out any that have Mr. Thomas in the company of anybody, and I mean anybody. Get those pictures to me right away."

Nicole needed help, and she knew it. Agent Vickors' request should have already been done. She missed a simple, but crucial step, and everyone present knew it, too. She had to swallow her pride and seek advice from the one person that hated her the most. She had to turn to a senior officer, namely Gretchen Banks.

Gretchen, with eighteen years of service, had the most tenure of all the current forensic team members. When she was passed over as Director of Forensics, she immediately handed in her resignation. After a heated discussion, her boss convinced her to stay on a little longer. She was bitter and she let it be known amongst her peers.

Gretchen joined the New Hanover County Sheriff's Office shortly after she turned twenty-one, having served a two-year stint in the Marine Corps as a field nurse. Even as a Patrol Deputy, it was obvious to her superiors that she had a knack for forensics. The department transferred her to that division starting out as a Crime Scene Investigator. By the time Gretchen turned twenty-eight-years-old, she had obtained her associate degree in criminal justice from Cape Fear Community College and a four-year forensic science degree from UNCW. In the field,

Gretchen soon became a ballistic expert as well as a blood splatter expert, and even excelled at forensic photography.

"Come in," Gretchen said, after hearing a knock on her office door.

"Ms. Banks, I need your help. I am at a dead end, and I have no one else to turn to," Nicole said, being as humble as she could.

"You're the director, figure it out or go ask someone else," Gretchen replied, not even looking up.

"But you are the best, and I really need your help."

"Get out of my office and don't let the door hit you in the ass," Gretchen belted out, pointing her finger in the direction of her office door.

Dejected, Nicole started for the door, but hesitated when she heard Gretchen's chair slide back.

"What was the first thing I told you about a crime scene, when you started working here?" asked Gretchen who was standing erect, leaning over her desk with her arms outstretched.

Totally surprised, Nicole turned and approached Gretchen's desk. "You said there is always a clue or a set of clues at every crime scene no matter what."

"That's right. So, you and everybody else have overlooked something. There is something there you're not seeing. Go get me everybody's notes, the videotapes and all transcripts of the interviews and be back in my office in one hour."

Nicole turned to leave just as Agent Vickors was entering Gretchen's office. Closing the door behind her, Nicole glanced back to see Gretchen and Agent Vickors hugging, in what she thought was more than just a friendly hug, but something much more intimate. That's strange, she thought, and she knew she was in for a tongue-lashing once the agent told Gretchen about her rookie mistakes.

107

When Nicole left Gretchen's office, she ran into Detective Decker in the hallway and put up her left hand with her fingers spread wide open, indicating to him to stop while placing her index finger of her right hand perpendicular to her lips. Decker was startled, and quickly ushered Nicole downstairs into his office and closed the door behind him.

"What's going on? Why are you being so secretive? What the hell happened?"

"Ah, how do I explain this without sounding silly. When I was leaving Gretchen's office, Vickors passed by me and before I could close the door, I glanced back and saw him hugging her in a, well I guess, a rather passionate way. I clearly saw him grab her butt for God's sake."

Decker got to his desk and leaned over, signaling for Nicole to come closer.

"Look, not too many people know this, but Ms. Banks and Agent Vickors were lovers a decade ago and their short-term affair damn near got them fired, I've been told."

"Oh my God, really? What the heck happened?"

"Well, they were at the same training academy in Salemburg back in 2007 or maybe 2008, and while all the guys in the class were constantly hitting on her, she had eyes for only one person. Geez, guess who, huh? Anyway, being half black and half Chinese, even you should admit she is drop dead gorgeous."

"Yeah, I'll admit I'm a little jealous. She doesn't even wear any makeup and her natural complexion has a golden glow that makes her look tanned all the time. She really is naturally pretty."

"She's drop dead gorgeous, but her raspy voice that almost sounds like a growl negates all that, doesn't it?"

"Yeah, it's a shame. That growl of hers, has really turned people off. Reckon it is some sort of speech impediment?"

"It could be. You're right, it is a shame. Looking at her, I would say she is a solid ten, but when she opens her mouth, she drops down to a five."

"Oh, have you ever seen her with her hair not tied up in a bun?" Decker asked.

"Well, no, I haven't."

"Well, I have. Several months ago, I heard through the office grapevine that she would work out in the gym every day around five o'clock in the morning and exercise for a solid hour before work. When I heard about this, I decided to visit the gym one early morning. Man, when she strolled in wearing a skintight jumpsuit with her hair down, I was shocked. Half of her perfectly straight silky black hair fell over her shoulders reaching within about one inch above her hips and the other half nestled between her rather large breasts reaching to her exposed belly button. You wouldn't know it when she wears her normal uniform, but my lord, she has a voluptuous body with bodacious tatas."

"You're nothing but a dirty old man. Keep that nonsense to yourself please."

"Just telling you what I saw sweetheart."

"So, anyway, tell me how they got into trouble?"

"Okay, so as the rumor goes, during their training, one of the supervisors saw Vickors leaving Gretchen's hotel room during a weeknight at two in the morning. To keep his job, he had to report it to his boss. I heard they got into a lot of trouble with HR, but I really don't know more than that, and I've never asked. Just keep your mouth shut about this. We never had this conversation, right?"

"Okay, you can trust me. I won't say a word. I really don't care about that but tell me about this Agent Vickors guy. What do you know about him?"

"Well, from what I gather, they knew each other while they were in high school somewhere in upstate New York. Vickors' parents divorced, and his mother moved to upstate New York when he was about fifteen. Both graduated at the same time and Gretchen went into the military after high school while Vickors returned to Bermuda to help his dad run some sort of gift shop. Apparently, they kept in touch and a few years later they ended up at the academy together in Salemburg. From there as you know, Gretchen settled here in Wilmington, and Vickors went on to attend the Special Agent Academy in Raleigh where he took an interest in solving kidnapping and rape cases. From what I hear, he is the best, so I'm glad he is here to help us."

"Interesting stuff. Do you think we need to tell them that we are personal friends with Harrison, or keep our mouths shut?"

"No, we need to tell them right away. Look, Harrison and I attended all your graduation ceremonies, and I am sure there are tons of pictures taken by your Dad and Ms. Kelly that has all of us standing together, so we can't hide from that."

"Yeah, you're right, I'll go tell them,"

"Knock first."

CHAPTER 12

It was close to nine o'clock when Jaxson and Luke finished loading up their boat with its antiquated 40 hp Evinrude engine. Over Harrison's objection that they wouldn't find anything since it had not rained in two weeks, the cousins loaded the boat with a set of shovels, their shotguns, the brown tarp, and a 150-foot-long fishing gill net. To thwart Harrison's objection, they added one other key tool: a sixteen-inch chainsaw. Luke got the rusted-out boat trailer hitched to the truck with everything secured. It was time to kick back. The tides weren't right yet to venture off to the island. Jaxson returned to the trailer while Luke siphoned gas from the truck's gas tank to fill up the boat's gas tank.

When Jaxson had pulled Harrison's soiled pants off earlier in the day, he found Harrison's wallet with $315.00 cash in it. He also found a Visa card and put that in his own wallet. Luke came back into the trailer through the back door and found Jaxson sitting at the table with the cash spread out in front of him, counting the bills. He shoved the bills back into the wallet.

"Hey, take this here wallet with the cash and go buy us some damn good whiskey," Jaxson said, tossing the wallet to Luke.

"Oh, make sure you dump that damn wallet where nobody will find it."

"Ah Jesus, Jaxson, I just hooked the boat up to the truck, now I've got to unhook it, dammit," Luke said, cussing on his way outside.

"Hey Luke, don't forget to get some water and ice, too," Jaxson hollered out.

Harrison now knew the other man's name, and it wasn't dumbass. It was Luke. Since they said Lilly was their aunt, Harrison assumed they were related to each other somehow. He also knew they weren't from this area or anywhere else in North Carolina. The only other time he ever heard a Gullah dialect was whenever he would visit his friend Jay Moore and chat with his mother Zora, who had a thick Gullah accent. Zora traveled from Charleston, South Carolina to Wilmington each year to spend the summers at Jay's riverfront home on the NE Cape Fear River. He and Zora would spend hours fishing for catfish off Jay's dock. Listening to her accent was something Harrison never forgot.

Zora explained to him that her descendants were slaves, originally from the from western or central parts of Africa. They were brought to Charleston in the late 1500's where they were forced to work on large plantations in the cotton and rice fields. Those that settled in Charleston are referred to as Gullah, while the ones that settled in Georgia are Geechee. To most people the dialect sounds the same.

Since Jaxson and Luke had the same accent, Harrison assumed they were originally from Charleston as well.

After unhooking the boat trailer, Luke eagerly set off for the local ABC store located up on Highway 17 about nine miles away. With very little traffic on Factory Road and US Highway 17, he reached the ABC store within ten minutes. Pulling into the parking lot, he parked in the last parking space next to a green dumpster on the edge of the blacktop. He removed the cash from Harrison's wallet and was about to exit the truck when a customer drove in and parked two spaces away from where he was parked. He waited until the elderly man entered the store, then stepped out of his truck and walked just a few feet away, reaching the dumpster. He lifted the plastic lid to the dumpster just a few inches and, with a flick of his wrist, threw the empty wallet into the dumpster.

A minute later, Luke reached the front door and entered the small ABC store just minutes before closing time. With only two aisles, it wasn't hard to find the bourbon section where he picked up three half gallons of Jim Beam Black, something that was normally way too expensive for them. The female assistant manager locked the front door just as he was paying for his bourbon. He was their last customer for the day and after paying for the bourbon, the assistant manager ushered Luke to the door, twirled her biker chain key ring around a few clicks and let him out. He was in and out of the store within five minutes, and while heading back to his truck, he noticed his truck was the only vehicle on site, so he felt confident no one saw him throw the wallet into the dumpster.

Luke placed the bourbon on the front seat of the truck, then walked over to the gas station adjacent to the ABC store and picked up two bags of ice and four packs of cigarettes. Leaving the ABC parking lot, he drove across Highway 17, directly into the small community shopping plaza parking lot, and parked in front of the Food Lion grocery store. With plenty of cash still on hand, he bought a loaf of bread, a package of beef baloney, two cases of spring water, a twenty-four pack of Pabst Blue Ribbon beer, two Stouffer chicken TV dinners and a small container of Duke's mayonnaise.

While standing at the checkout counter, he added a few small bags of Lays potato chips, a small box of aspirin, and three more packs of Marlboros. Pleased with his purchases, he placed the groceries in the front seat of the truck and headed back to the trailer.

When Luke returned to the trailer, he found Jaxson intently watching the small flat screen television in the living room. Jaxson seemed agitated, leaning out from his kitchen chair with his hands on his knees.

"Geez, look at this. The cops are everywhere," Jaxson said, pointing at the TV.

"They think bonehead over there was kidnapped, and since no one has called in for a ransom, they said he may be dead."

"We need to get the shit and haul ass, bro," Luke chimed in, placing the groceries on the kitchen table.

"Calm down. They said on the TV that the cops don't have any leads and no suspects."

Jaxson stood up and approached the kitchen counter to see what was in the plastic grocery bags. "Hey, did you dump the wallet?"

"Yeah, I threw it in the dumpster behind the liquor store. Ain't nobody gonna find it."

"Well, these cops are smart, and sooner or later they'll come crawling up our ass for sure," Jaxson said, stuffing a pack of cigarettes into his shirt pocket.

"We'll be long gone before they even get near us," said Luke while putting the beer in the refrigerator.

"We might have a good jump on them, so I think we'll be alright."

Jaxson went out the back door and a few minutes later returned with a ten-gallon red cooler with a broken lid. The two cousins began packing it with ice and a dozen or so water bottles, along with the lunch meat and mayonnaise. Watching how they angrily crammed the cooler full, Harrison could tell their demeanor had changed. Harrison guessed the news on the TV had upset them. It gave him a little sense of relief to know at least the police were involved. Was his dear friend Decker working on the case? Harrison prayed he was.

When Luke put the two TV dinners in the oven, a hoard of German cockroaches escaped from its greasy insides. Harrison almost gagged, watching hundreds of roaches scurrying over the kitchen countertop, then disappearing behind the sink. There was an old saying that if you saw just one German cockroach, there would be thousands behind the walls. Seeing hundreds just then, Harrison knew the whole trailer was infested with them and it made his skin crawl.

"Can I have some water, please?" Harrison pleaded, hoping he would get a bottle of water from the cooler Jaxson had just brought in.

Jaxson went over to the sink and filled up a mason jar with tap water and brought it over to Harrison. The water must have come from a swallow well, as it tasted like sulfur, which was typical of the water taste along the coastal area. Harrison gagged and spat a mouthful out with the bulk of it landing on Jaxson boots. Jaxson reared back to land another thundering punch to Harrison's face.

"For Christ's sake, I'm seventy-years-old, my ass is bleeding, my ribs are cracked and if you continue this, you're gonna kill me. You'll end up with nothing."

Jaxson retreated into the kitchen, cursing under his breath. Picking up a bottle of Jim Beam, he untwisted the cap, tossed it to the side, and took a long swig. Harrison took the opportunity to add some fuel to the fire. If he could interject some confusion, to get these guys to alter their plans, it could buy him more time. Obviously, the police were on the case, but Harrison knew it would take time for them to find him. He needed to delay these guys as much as possible without getting another beating.

"Hey, with the cops on your ass, how are you going to get out of this? Where ya gonna go?" Harrison asked, trying not to sound condescending.

"You don't need to know shit," Jaxson shouted in anger, taking another swig from the bottle.

"Even if you get some of the gold, how and where are you guys gonna sell it? You can't take old gold coins to the bank and cash them in."

"Shut your damn mouth," Jaxson screamed and then ordered his cousin to follow him outside. They stayed out in the backyard for at least twenty minutes before returning. Harrison could barely hear them, but they were for sure arguing about something. Were they changing their plans or not? Harrison was hoping for his comments to interrupt their plans, and maybe buy more time. Or did he mess up and inadvertently speed things up?

Back inside Jaxson asked, "So, where do you take the stuff and get cash for it?"

Luke appeared out of nowhere and put a pistol to the side of Harrison's head.

"And don't you friggin' lie to us, ya hear?" he said, pushing the barrel of the gun deeper into Harrison's temple.

"Give me a bottle of water first, please, and I'll tell you."

Jaxson reached into the cooler and retrieved a bottle of water while taking another long swig of his Jim Beam. He tossed the bottle to Luke who caught the bottle in his left hand while still holding the gun against Harrison's temple. He handed the bottle to Harrison and pushed the barrel even harder into Harrison's temple.

Harrison's wrists were bound together so tightly that he couldn't open the bottle, and in his attempt to do so, he lost his grip and the bottle fell to the floor. Jaxson picked up his kitchen chair and sat it down in front of Harrison. Bending down, he picked up the bottle, twisted off the top and handed it to the prisoner. Harrison emptied the bottle in three gulps, fighting through the pain from the cool water which hit the openings in his gums.

Jaxson walked back to the kitchen to retrieve his bottle of bourbon, then returned to his chair facing Harrison. Taking a long pull from the bottle, he handed it to Luke who leaned towards Harrison with pure anger in his eyes. Was he going to question the story Harrison had told earlier? Did he finally figure out it was all bullshit? Harrison feared this worst, as beads of sweat rolled off his forehead.

"Now tell us how you do it, asshole," Jaxson demanded.

That was sweet music to Harrison's ears. They stupidly believed him for now. Keep going Harrison, add to the story and buy more time, he thought.

"I take it to my brother, up on his farm in Burgaw."

"Okay, we get the shit, pay him a little visit and get the hell out of this hell hole," Luke spat out, pushing the barrel of the pistol even harder into Harrison's temple.

"Jesus, you guys just don't get it, do you?"

"It takes my brother sometimes weeks to move just one coin. It's not like he is sitting there with wads of cash. He contacts some guy that I don't know and brings me the cash later. He doesn't really trust his contact, so we only sell a few coins at a time. We sure as hell don't want to bring attention to ourselves. I don't want to keep all those coins at my house or at my brother's either. That's why I built that concrete safe."

117

Harrison waited. He knew he was pushing it with his out and out lies. Just how much longer will these guys continue to believe him? They had to, he needed time.

"How much do you get for a coin?" Jaxson asked.

"Anywhere from $1,500 to $2,000," Harrison answered with a huge sigh of relief.

"So how many coins ya reckon are in this safe of yours?" Luke asked.

"Hundreds, probably two or three million dollars' worth."

The two men returned to the kitchen and sat at the kitchen table drinking shots, and neither one said a word. Harrison really had them thinking things over. No doubt he interjected a wrinkle in their plans, enough of a wrinkle to buy time. Seconds turned into minutes and the minutes turned into hours.

Shot after shot, the two men boiled between excitement and anger. Harrison was hoping they would just pass out, giving him the opportunity to escape. However, they continued drinking their bourbon as if it was water. Each one had consumed half their bottles, and there were no signs of any change in their demeanor. These guys, Harrison thought, could really hold their liquor better than anyone he had ever seen.

Harrison couldn't believe the predicament he was in and feared the consequences. "Is this what you get from a little fame"? he thought. For the first time in his life, he made a good chunk of change, and the future looked bright for him and his family. He had always wanted to write a book, and now that he did, he found himself half beaten to death, tied up and sitting in cat piss. What karma caused this, and why? Harrison pondered over and over the horrible situation he was in. What was he facing when they found out he was lying to them all along?

Jaxson suddenly stood straight up, walked over to Harrison, grabbed him by his neck and hauled him towards the kitchen. He was whispering something in Harrison's ear that was nothing but babble, then slammed him into the chair facing the sink. Jaxson's breath reeked of alcohol, and his body odor was like rotting cabbage. "These guys are animals," Harrison thought and shuddered to think what was going to happen next.

"You know what, Slick? We really don't need you or your brother," Jaxson shouted, taking another long swig from his bottle.

"We've got some people we know back home that will move whatever we bring them, so screw you and your brother. Plans have changed."

With that said, Jaxson unfolded the old AAA map and spread it out on the kitchen table.

"You tell us right now where that shit is buried. Point to it on the map right now," Jaxson said, pushing Harrison's face into the map. Luke pushed the pistol to the side of Harrison's head and cocked the hammer with a loud click.

How in the world, Harrison thought, could the consumption of so much booze allow a man to think clearly? They obviously changed their minds and had come up with a new plan. All they wanted, much to Harrison's surprise, was the exact location on the island. Once they got that, they would dispose of him, get the stuff, and move on. This was their new plan and Harrison had to counter their newfound intelligence, and quickly.

"Listen to me and listen carefully. I am the only one, the only person that knows exactly where the coins are hidden. If anything happens to me, that information goes with me to my grave. Do you understand that?"

Luke released the hammer on the pistol and sat back down across from Harrison, still pointing the barrel towards Harrison's head.

"You're not getting anything unless I take you there and I need to be alive to do so," Harrison further explained, staring down the barrel of the pistol.

With Jaxson holding onto the map, the two men went outside. Again, Harrison could barely hear them, but he could tell they were in another deep discussion. In less than five minutes they returned. Jaxson dragged Harrison across the kitchen back into the living room and sat him down in the old smelly recliner. He went back into the kitchen and sat down in his chair with a thud, and the two men started taking shots again. Jaxson kept pounding on the map with his index finger while Luke waved the pistol around, sometimes pointing it directly at Harrison with evil in his eyes. Luke was so erratic with the pistol, Jaxson finally reached over and took it away from him, placing it down the front of his jeans. Harrison knew his bluff had worked.

Harrison must have drifted off to sleep, as he was suddenly awakened by a crashing sound coming from the kitchen. Luke finally had succumbed to his drinking and fell out of his chair onto the kitchen floor, slamming into the cabinets. He didn't move.

The only light illuminating the trailer was coming from the ceiling fixture in the middle of the kitchen. Jaxson was nowhere in sight, but Harrison thought he heard snoring coming from the room in the back. Maybe Luke has a concussion, maybe Jaxson is totally passed out.

"It's time to escape, now or never. This could be your only shot."

Harrison sat up in the recliner as best he could and contemplated his options. He needed to figure out how to cut himself loose and run to safety without being heard. He needed to free himself from the zip ties first. He deduced that the most likely location of a knife, a pair of scissors and some other cutting utensil had to be in one of the kitchen drawers. He had to figure out a way to maneuver across the living room in some fashion and reach the kitchen counter. With his thighs and feet wrapped so tightly together, just walking into the kitchen was not a viable option. The only option he could think of was crawling across the floor.

Harrison thought he heard the clap of thunder off in the distance.

CHAPTER 13

With her arms full, Director Nicole entered Gretchen's office with all the pertinent information she had requested. In her meticulous manner, Nicole spread out all the information in chronological order on top of Gretchen's desk. Reaching into her pants pocket, Nicole also handed Gretchen the flash drive that contained the ATM video footage from the Diamonds parking lot. Gretchen pulled her laptop from underneath a stack of papers lying behind her chair. She placed it on her desk, spinning it around to face Nicole. Taking the hint, Nicole powered up the computer, and inserted the flash drive.

"Have you heard anything back from our SBI boys in Raleigh about the video?" Gretchen asked.

"No, not yet."

"Well, get on the phone and push 'em. We need whatever they've got, and we need it now."

"And get Decker in here," Gretchen barked. "He conducted the interviews with the family members, right?"

Nicole didn't answer. She went into the hallway and called Decker on his cell phone. He could hear the desperation in Nicole's voice and said he would be there in two minutes. Nicole nervously waited, then finally spotted Decker coming down the hallway.

"Where the hell have you been? The sour pus wants to see you, and she's not in a good mood."

"Jesus, you can't even take a crap in this place without getting *nicoled* and dimed, Nicole."

Decker chuckled and smiled, trying to get Nicole to calm down a little. She was not amused with his little pun.

Decker opened the door to Gretchen's office, let Nicole enter, and he followed in behind her, trying to avoid the first verbal salvo that surely was coming their way.

"Sit down, don't move and don't say a thing unless I ask you something, ya hear me?" Gretchen spoke sternly and looked up, daring them to say anything.

The message was received loud and clear. She could really be a total pain in the ass at times, Decker thought, and since Mr. Charmin didn't do his job, he was faced with a double calamity.

For the next forty-five minutes, Gretchen, in total silence, poured over all the information and made notes of her own on her yellow legal pad and on an assortment of different colored sticky notes. She didn't seem pleased at all. Several times she got up, walked over to the window that overlooked the adjacent courthouse, and seemed to talk to herself, shaking her head.

Gretchen got out of her chair and came around to the front of her desk taking a seat on the edge with her arms folded in front of her. Facing her two colleagues in the chairs directly in front of her desk, Gretchen leaned over with blood shot eyes, and eyed them back and forth for about ten seconds. It felt like an eternity. Releasing her intentional mental grip on them, Gretchen unfolded her arms.

"You both have done a pretty good job. Your notes are in order and all procedures were followed to the letter, and as you have indicated, there are no clues to be found. This is highly unusual. There must be clues. There is always at least one clue for God sakes. So, we start over again. We are going to conduct new interviews, search for leads, but this time we'll do them here in my office. Go call the family members and get them in here as soon as possible."

"A man just doesn't vanish without leaving a clue!" Gretchen screamed, turning her back to Decker and Nicole as they raced out of the office.

Nicole headed towards her office while Decker needed to make a second visit to the men's room.

Before they could even close the door, they heard Gretchen yell out, "Tell that fingerprint guy to get into my office right away."

Eric Johnston, the fingerprint specialist, with his office right next to Gretchen's, heard the entire conversation and he just about knocked over Decker rushing into Gretchen's office. Eric was a sheepish young man in his early thirties who usually kept to himself. He was intimidated by Gretchen, so he did his best to avoid any contact with her. Eric stumbled into the office.

"Yes ma'am, what can I help you with?" Eric asked with his head down, trying to avoid any eye contact.

"Don't you ma'am me, you're the same age as I am. Did you dust everything at that Diamonds bar near where these two guys were sitting?"

"We did, but nothing came up. The waitresses had cleaned the bar top multiple times after those guys had left."

"Well, did you bother to dust under the bar lip? Did you bother to dusk up underneath the bar stools? Did you think that maybe one of these clowns picked his nose and stuck it under the bar stool? Get your ass back out there and do your job right."

"Yes ma'am, right away ma'am."

Gretchen sat down, leaned way back in her chair, and plopped her feet up on her desk. She was satisfied that she was somewhat in control. It was time for her to shine and prove to the dim-witted department heads that they had made the wrong decision. She should be the Director of Forensics, not some straight A rookie just out of school. Although she told Decker and Nicole that they had done a decent job, her notes indicated otherwise. She wasn't about to tell them. She wanted to embarrass them during the next set of interviews to prove she was superior.

"Mr. Juan Valdez and his sidekick are gonna see who really runs this place."

Before the family members would arrive at Gretchen's office, she copied several shots taken from the videotape of the red truck leaving Diamonds and sent out a statewide APB, something else Nicole and Decker had failed to do. Gretchen also set in motion requests for court orders to obtain Harrison's bank account statements along with his cell phone records.

She called the front desk and requested that a patrol car pick up Rex Calder, the book publisher, and bring him to her office within the hour. Both Decker and Nicole had failed to interview Mr. Calder, another mistake, Gretchen had keenly noted.

"How the hell did those two not think of doing these steps in the first place?"

Forty minutes later, bewildered and confused, Rex Calder found himself being escorted into Gretchen's office. Learning that his client was apparently kidnapped was hard to fathom. He was visibly shaken. Gretchen instructed Calder to take a seat while she stood a few feet away, leaning back on her desk. At first, in a calm voice and not wanting to reveal key details of the case, she presented Calder with just enough basic information about the kidnapping to keep his attention. Returning to her chair behind her desk, Gretchen pulled out her legal pad and began interrogating Calder. Within five minutes, Calder felt he was being held responsible for the kidnapping. It sent shivers down his spine. How ludicrous he thought to himself.

"Do you think I had something to do with this?" he blurted out. "Are you kidding me here? What would I gain from such a ridiculous notion? You're way off track, sweetie. You can kiss my ass, ma'am."

Gretchen was furious at the lack of respect and flung her legal pad clear across the room, knocking over a potted plant on the windowsill, spilling its contents all over the floor.

"I don't give a damn what you think. I need a list of names of everyone you and Mr. Thomas have been in contact with for the past several months. After I talk with them, maybe I'll think differently about your involvement. In the meantime, don't you dare leave town, or I'll have you arrested. If I call you, you better answer right away. And don't call me ma'am, now get out of my office."

"Yes, Ma'am," Calder said, flicking a huge ash onto the floor from his smoldering cigar. Calder could hear the enraged woman demanding that he clean up his mess. He ignored her. He couldn't help himself giving the finger to the patrol officer who had brought him to the station.

Shortly after Calder left, Ms. Kelly arrived with her grandkids Andrea and Bryson and her son Dalton. Irritated, they all waited outside Ms. Bank's office. Gretchen had them wait while she buzzed Nicole and Decker on the intercom summoning them to her office on the double.

"Nicole, fire up my laptop with the parking lot video and project it on the big screen behind me."

Gretchen had Nicole pause the video when it showed the best view of the red truck, then told Nicole to let everyone in. Ms.

Kelly was offered the only chair in the office while the others had to stand in front of the big screen.

Gretchen then instructed Nicole to play the video of the red truck leaving Diamonds parking lot but pause it every five seconds. At each pause, Gretchen asked if they recognized anyone or noticed anything out of place. None of the family members provided any clues.

She then placed the photos Agent Vickors had gathered across her desk and asked the family members to identify each person seen with Harrison. She wanted to know everything about these other people, everything, and the process was exhausting. Since only a handful of names were given to Gretchen, she felt that something wasn't right and maybe one of the family members was hiding something from her.

Gretchen asked the family to step outside her office and wait for further instructions, knowing they were getting frustrated hoping one of them would slip up. She brought in each member separately and slowly interrogated each one. Everyone was a suspect. She didn't care, and she needed to find a clue.

Four hours later, the family members were excused, with instructions not to leave town. Gathering outside in the parking lot of the police station, all the family members were horrified to realize they were being considered possible suspects. Detective Decker came out to console the family because he knew what they had just gone through.

"Look, she is just doing her job. She will investigate everything and everybody."

"My God, does that crazy woman think any of us would leave town right now while Dad is missing?" Dalton interjected, throwing his cigarette on the pavement, and grinding it into shreds with the heel of his shoe.

"I know you're upset, but it is all part of the investigation. She's desperately searching for clues, and we just don't have any right now. Let her do her job and the best thing y'all can do right now is just go home and sit tight."

At that point, Earnie Cafaro and his wife Tammy pulled into the parking lot, driving his new Ford Raptor pickup truck. When the family members were reviewing the photographs, there were a lot of Harrison and Earnie standing together in different settings. Gretchen wanted to know who this Earnie fellow was. Harrison's grandson Bryson let her know that the book, *Earnie's Island*, was named after Earnie. That sparked Gretchen's interest, and she had her assistant call the Cafaros, asking them to come to Gretchen's office immediately.

"What the hell is going on?" asked Earnie.

Detective Decker said his goodbyes to the Thomas family members, then escorted Earnie to the side.

"Look man, you and Tammy are going to get interrogated by Ms. Bitch. Everybody is considered a suspect."

"Oh really, screw her! She can kiss my ass."

"Just answer her questions. Let the crank do her job. Maybe she'll pick up on something we've all missed. Calm down and call me later."

Over the next two hours, Gretchen grilled Earnie and Tammy, but in the end, she did not learn anything new. She released them with the same instructions not to leave town. At the end of the day, Gretchen felt confident that the family members and the Cafaro's had nothing to do with the kidnapping. Her gut told her that the perps were likely unknown to the family. She would not disclose her thoughts to them or anyone else at this point.

"Dammit," Gretchen hollered out after everyone had left. "What am I missing here?"

Gretchen was brilliant with her forensic methods and techniques. Over the years, due to her significant findings, she helped prosecutors win many complicated cases in a relatively short period. She was well-respected by her peers. Many were shocked when she was passed over for the directorship.

Her office was a mess with papers and files scattered all over the place as if a tornado had come through. Her case files were filled with handwritten notes and plastered with multiple sticky notes. It was her system, and it worked for her. The year before Nicole was named the department head, a highly successful prosecutor basically forfeited an important case when Gretchen lost some valuable notes due to her sloppiness, resulting in an acquittal of a known criminal. That mistake, she thought, was her downfall that led to the hiring of Nicole instead of her.

She had to admit that Nicole's office was neat and organized. All her case notes and findings were safely tucked away in a computer, and each case file backed up on a flash drive. The young kids today were so proficient with computers. Gretchen was old school, and she wasn't about to change. She was going to solve this her way and prove to all she was the best and should have been selected as the director.

Gretchen could hear Decker playing his guitar down the hall. Needing a mental break, she strolled into his office taking a seat in the corner next to the window not saying a word. Peering out the window, Gretchen could see Thalian Hall, and it reminded her of the high school days when she was active in the drama club. It brought back fond memories as Decker continued with his gentle serenade.

"You are good friends with Harrison, aren't you?" Gretchen asked.

"Oh yeah, we've known each other for probably twelve or thirteen years."

"So, what do you think? Why would anyone kidnap him?" she asked, turning her attention away from the window and staring at Decker.

"It just doesn't make any sense at all. Everybody liked Harrison. I've never heard anyone say a negative thing about him."

Decker strummed his guitar and sang out *where seldom is heard a discouraging word* from the song "Home on The Range." They both chuckled.

"Seriously, what is your gut reaction to all of this?" Gretchen asked, staring intently at Decker.

"Like I said, Harrison was a generous guy who was always willing to help his friends and neighbors. He was always joking around and made people feel comfortable around him. Hell, he would walk up to perfect strangers in Walmart or Publix and start talking to them, leaving them with a smile on their faces. He was a natural born salesman with the gift of the gab. I can't think of anybody wanting to harm him, let alone kidnap him.

"He wasn't by any means a wealthy person at all, so that can't be the motive. I did a background check on him and found absolutely nothing. There was nothing in his bank records that caught my attention other than the fact he gave most of the monies he received from the book sales to his son, grandkids, and UNCW. Do you realize out of the first one hundred thousand dollars he received; he gave away nearly eighty-five percent of it? So, there's nothing there for someone to gain. It just doesn't make any sense at all."

"Yeah, I agree. It's killing me that we can't find any direct clues to go on."

"Something's gonna come up."

Decker strummed his guitar and started singing the Beach Boys hit...*Don't Worry Baby*...

Gretchen chuckled at first, then completely cracked up. She no doubt was beginning to warm up to Decker. She liked his sense of humor.

"Ya know what, you play pretty good. Your voice is kind of, how would I say, salty. I like it. Have you written any songs yourself?"

"Yeah, I'm working on the lyrics right now matter of fact."

"Oh, really, what's the title?"

"*You caught my eye when your boyfriend knocked it out.*"

For just a split-second Gretchen had a complete blank look on her face, then completely lost it in a fit a laughter. At this point she sincerely appreciated Decker's humor.

Slowly shaking her head, Gretchen got up and headed back to her office while Decker continued playing his guitar, singing the first few lines of *Devil with A Blue Dress On.*

Gretchen smiled. A crime had been committed and Gretchen realized she needed to push aside her pride for the time being and be a team player.

"Come on in," Nicole said, hearing a knock on her door.

"How are you doing?" Gretchen asked, slowly entering Nicole's office.

"Yeah, fine, ah, have a seat," Nicole stumbled over her words, shocked to see Gretchen in her office for the first time. It was totally out of character for Gretchen to visit another team member in their own office. They were always summoned to Gretchen's office.

"I understand that you and Decker are really good friends with Mr. Thomas?" Gretchen asked in a soft tone Nicole had never heard.

"Well, he's good friends with Decker, not really me. He's like an uncle to me if you know what I mean? My Dad, Decker, and Harrison are like the three musketeers. They are an absolute hoot when they get together."

"Tell me about your so-called uncle. What's he like?"

For the next half hour or so, Nicole basically reiterated what Gretchen just heard from Decker. Nicole added in a few personal stories outside of the three musketeer adventures, but Gretchen didn't pick up on anything that she would consider a clue to explain the kidnapping. Not wanting to get too chummy with her adversary, Gretchen abruptly got up and headed for the door without saying thank you or goodbye.

"You're welcome, ma'am."

CHAPTER 14

As much as Harrison tried, he could not loosen the grip of the zip ties which were wrapped tightly around his torso. Frantically twisting and turning in every possible direction, he could not get the bindings to budge. Sweat was pouring down from his forehead and he was convinced that his anus, from straining so much, was bleeding again. His pants felt wet.

With Luke passed out on the kitchen floor and Jaxson nowhere in sight, Harrison realized this was his best opportunity to try to escape, but he knew he needed to act fast, but do so quietly. He had earlier deduced that just standing up and walking into the kitchen was out of the question. His only option left was to get on the floor somehow and crawl his way over into the kitchen.

Harrison twisted his body around and scooted up just enough to get his hips on the edge of the recliner. Shifting his weight forward, he attempted to slide out of the recliner, but he momentarily lost his balance. As if in slow motion, he landed on the floor with a loud thud. He laid there motionless for a moment, then with a quick glance, he eyed Luke still lying on the kitchen floor. Harrison did not move a muscle, and neither did Luke. He was safe so far. The snoring Harrison heard coming from the back room told him that Jaxson was passed out cold, just like Luke. With both men passed out from their enormous consumption of bourbon, he figured he might have an hour at best to escape and reach freedom before they awoke.

Harrison needed to keep going, so he began to inch along the living room floor like a worm coming out of the ground after a spring rainstorm. As he rose up on his elbows, he put one elbow in front of the other while pushing with his toes, and inch by inch he got closer and closer to the kitchen. He had to rest after each attempt to crawl on his elbows, as the pain from his cracked ribs would not allow him to move in one continuous motion. He traveled about five feet when the pain in his rib cage brought him to a full stop. He rested to let the pain ease off some. He was losing valuable time, but the pain was excruciating.

The odor of the shag carpet was a mixture of urine and rotten fish. Using his chin occasionally to help inch along was almost unbearable. Matted down and caked with sand, the old shag carpet was like crawling on sandpaper, leaving Harrison's elbows raw and bleeding. He had to keep pushing on. He hoped to reach the cabinets near the kitchen sink to retrieve any type of cutting utensil he could find in one of the drawers before Luke awoke. There must be a knife in one of those kitchen drawers, there had to be. He could cut himself free and get out of this hellhole.

Harrison crawled halfway across the living room when he heard movement from the back bedroom where he assumed Jaxson was. At first, Harrison heard bed springs squeaking. Was Jaxson just rolling over in bed? He was petrified when he could hear him shuffling down the hallway heading towards the living room. Harrison held his breath and froze in fear. He struggled to hear as the pounding of blood in his ears was deafening. If he was caught in this position, he knew another beating would soon rain down upon him with sheer vengeance. Jaxson, half asleep, turned to his left before reaching the living room and staggered into the bathroom and never noticed Harrison lying on the living room floor.

Fearing that Jaxson may wander into the kitchen wanting a glass of cold water, Harrison closed his eyes in defeat and waited. There was no way he could turn around at this point and return to the recliner to safety. All he could do was glance towards the hallway and wait. After expelling what he figured was at least a gallon of urine, Jaxson attempted to return to the bedroom, but stumbled over something in the hallway causing him to crash into a chest of drawers. He landed and bounced on the bed making so much noise, Harrison thought for sure Luke would wake up. He glanced into the kitchen, watching him raise his head up about two inches, lift his leg, then ripped one and rolled over, motionless. Harrison found new energy, realizing he just dodged a bullet.

Harrison was close, only two feet away before he would reach the vinyl flooring, where he could slide a lot easier than inching along the filthy shag carpet. The odor of the carpet was bad enough, but what Luke expelled out of his body was even more disgusting and Harrison almost vomited. He waited half a minute until the air cleared, then moved on. He was only inches away from the vinyl flooring now, and he anticipated his movements should be much easier once he reached the smooth surface.

Reaching the vinyl floor, and still using his elbows to crawl, his right elbow slipped and collapsed violently to the side when he placed it on some, what he assumed, spilled bacon grease. Unable to react soon enough, his chin slammed into the floor with such force it opened a two-inch gash on his chin. Blood poured out freely, creating a small pool of blood on the floor. It wasn't the cut he was worried about; it was the noise and reverberation that surely would wake Luke up out of his drunken stupor. Harrison laid there dead still with his right cheek against the floor, staring at the drunken mess in front of him. Holding his breath, he looked for any movement from him, but all he heard was heavy breathing and noticed no movement, not even an eye twitch. Only one more foot and he would be within reach of the cabinets.

Just as he was about to lift himself up on his elbows, the biggest rat he had ever seen in his life came out from underneath the refrigerator, vigorously sniffing his way towards him. The twelve-inch rat had the same dark beady eyes just like Luke. As the rat came closer and closer, he tried to backpedal, but without the help of his feet, he couldn't move. When the rat got within inches of Harrison's exposed face, it stood up on all four legs and looked down at him.

Was this rat getting ready to pounce on him? Harrison tried to create the sound of a cat hissing, but with his front teeth missing, all he could produce was a *thuuu* sound that sounded nothing like a cat. For some reason, the rat turned away and headed towards Luke. Harrison breathed a heavy sigh of relief, but that soon turned into complete terror as he watched the rat approach the drunken brute watching it climb up his outstretched leg. If there ever was a time for him to break wind again, now was the time for surely the rat would run away, disgusted with the smell. The rat continued up his leg, stopping at his knee. Luke's knee twitched and the rat abruptly fled to the open AC vent at the bottom of the kitchen cabinet.

Harrison was only inches away from Luke. He knew that one false move and all his efforts would be wasted. Any movements had to be done in complete silence. In a prone position, Harrison slowly drew his knees up and rolled upwards toward his left side while pushing down with his bound hands. He had to get on his knees. His body was racked with pain, but he finally rolled up on his knees and now sat still with his legs underneath him.

To raise up from his sitting position would be difficult. His first attempt failed. His thighs had been bound so tightly, it cut off the blood supply. They lacked the strength to propel his body upwards. Not even moving an inch, Harrison realized in a moment of panic that he was stuck. He knew if he was found in this position, the two men would probably beat him senseless. He cussed himself for not keeping in better shape these past couple of years. He vowed to himself, should he succeed in escaping this horrible mess he was in, he would join a local fitness gym and get back in shape.

"You can't give up now, keep going dammit, get up."

The cousins had tied his wrists in a manner where the right wrist was on top, crossing over his left wrist, leaving all his fingers free to move around. He pulled his hands up close to his mouth, and he licked all the fingers on his right hand, then ran his thumb against each finger several times to get them somewhat sticky. He had one last chance and hoped he had more strength in his hands than his thighs had.

Harrison could barely reach the outer edge of the cabinet, but he was able to place four fingertips of his right hand on the edge of the counter. They stuck. He paused and closed his eyes. He wanted to visualize his next move. He recalled an interview he watched featuring Jason Day, his favorite pro golfer, just after he won the PGA Championship. Jason explained how his visualization technique of closing his eyes before every shot would in most cases result in that perfect golf shot. A simple mind over matter mental technique many professional athletes used to excel in their sport. A few seconds later, Harrison opened his eyes and with all the strength he could muster, slowly pulled himself up to a standing position. Sweat gathered on his forehead. Blood rushed to his head.

His knees started knocking violently. He feared he would topple over and fall on Luke. Physically exhausted, he had to rest against the counter for a few minutes. Mentally, he was energized knowing that freedom from his captors was only a few moments away. His heart was pounding so hard he could hear the blood rushing through the veins in his neck and sweat ran profusely into his eyes, blurring his sight. He shook his head from side to side and finally the sweat left his eyes. He glanced toward the living room where the television was still on the Weather Channel. With both eyes swollen, it was difficult to see. In the left-hand corner of the screen he could see it was three fifteen in the morning.

Using his thumb and index finger of his right hand, Harrison grabbed the handle of the drawer in front of the sink and slowly, without a sound, pulled it out about six inches. Looking down into the kitchen drawer, he found exactly what he was looking for. A ten-inch filet knife, with its steel blade glistening from the overhead kitchen light. Harrison couldn't believe his eyes. Lying at the bottom of the drawer was a knife identical to the one his son Dalton had given him for his sixtieth birthday.

"I'm coming, buddy, I'm coming home," Harrison whispered to himself.

Harrison retrieved the knife from the open drawer and placed the butt of the knife in the right side of his mouth, clapping down hard with his canine tooth. He turned the blade up, brought his hands up and over the blade, and began sawing at the twist ties. The knife was dull as hell, but he found one tiny spot that was sharp enough to do the job. After several minutes, his hands were free. He grabbed the knife from his mouth, and seriously thought about slicing Luke's neck wide open. Clearing that thought from his mind, he reached down and cut away the ties around his thighs.

Able to spread his knees apart, Harrison concentrated on cutting the ties off his ankles. Just the thought of being free filled him with elation. That elation was short lived. Instead, panic took over when he tried to bend over and reach his ankles. His attempt was six inches short.

Because he had let himself go over the last few years, his extended belly would not let him bend forward far enough to reach his ankles. He made yet another vow to himself that he would quit drinking those fattening white Russians and quit eating Breyers vanilla ice cream and get back in shape. But that thought could wait. He was so close now, he had to get free.

Harrison reached over and grabbed the edge of the counter with his left hand with the knife in his right hand. He figured if he could just do a deep squat, he could reach down and cut himself free. He spread his knees apart and let gravity take over but the effort to do a deep squat shot enormous pain up his anus and, wrenching in pain, he accidentally dropped the knife. The butt of the knife hit first, bounced in the air away from him, and landed within four inches of Luke's lifeless face. Harrison froze and he once again found himself staring at Luke looking for any movement. He thought again about just slicing the man's throat, cutting himself free, then ending it all by stabbing Jaxson to death in the other room. Just those thoughts made Harrison shiver, and he brought himself back to reality, focusing on his escape.

Harrison inched over to get into position to retrieve the knife and, knowing he would face immeasurable pain, proceeded to squat again. He was so close now; he could not stop. Fighting through the lightning bolts of pain, he squatted down and grabbed the knife with his right hand, and with one powerful slice, he cut through the plastic bindings around his ankles. He stood up and blood rushed into his feet. The resulting pins and needles sensation made him unsteady on his feet. His whole body was cramped from being tied up for hours on end, and it took a few minutes for him to regain his physical composure.

The whole ordeal took at least forty-five minutes, Harrison judged, but he was free. Standing over Luke with the knife still in his hand, it took everything in his psyche not to bend over and slice the man's throat wide open. Erasing that thought from his mind, he carefully placed the knife on the kitchen counter. Taking tiny steps, he tiptoed towards the front door, keeping a watchful eye on Luke the whole time. Thankfully, he wasn't moving. The only things moving were the cockroaches making their way into the cooler. He gingerly opened the front door, leaving it slightly open. One squeak from the rusted door hinges could end in disaster. He pushed open the screen door and slipped out without a sound. He quietly closed the screen door, not allowing it to click fully shut.

"Oh, thank God I am free," whispered Harrison to himself as he looked around standing on the wooden porch.

It was pitch black outside, with not a star in the sky or any moonlight whatsoever. Harrison remembered seeing the porch the one-time Luke had left the front door open for just a few seconds. It should be about six feet wide extending out from the trailer. Harrison slowly slid his right foot forward, followed by his left foot shuffling along inch by inch, trying to feel for the edge of the porch. With caution, he continued. Twenty seconds later, he found the edge with his right foot. He slid his left foot forward and now with both feet together, he was standing on the balls of his feet with half on the porch and half hanging over the porch. He eased his right foot over, expecting to feel a step down, but to his surprise, it rested on the ground. Stepping off the porch with both feet, he closed his eyes and stood dead still, listening for any sounds in the distance that would guide him to safety. His body raged with adrenaline. All he could hear was the constant thumping in his ears that was matching his every heartbeat.

With the trailer located directly behind him, Harrison knew his escape route had to be either straight ahead or a few degrees to the left or right. He then remembered the sound of the cousin's pickup truck tires crunching gravel for maybe one hundred yards or so just before they reached the trailer. It was to his right. He figured that had to be the driveway, and he knew that must lead to a paved road. If he could just find the gravel driveway, he could follow it to the paved road and maybe, just maybe, somebody would come along and find him.

He decided the best route would be slightly to his right. He began blindly walking with his arms stretched out in front of him to avoid hitting anything. The goal was to reach the gravel driveway. Constantly turning his head from side to side, he was keenly listening and looking for any signs of life. The only sounds he could hear were the tree frogs screaming for rain.

Harrison walked just a few yards and stopped dead in his tracks. A tad off to his right, he noticed a faint light with a yellowish tinge flickering way off in the distance. Without hesitation, he decided to head directly toward the yellow light and reach freedom. The light had to be either a streetlamp or maybe even a house. In either case, he figured people had to be nearby.

He snapped his head back towards the trailer as fear jolted through his entire body, when from inside the trailer he heard Luke yell out, "That son of a bitch, I'll kill him!"

Luke opened the front door to the trailer, but before he even opened the outside screen door, Harrison was on the move. Jacked up with fear and adrenaline, he took off as fast as he could run, heading for the distant light. Gaining speed, he was in full stride when his left foot hit the gravel driveway. Then everything went black.

CHAPTER 15

It was now Monday, and even though tragedy had struck the family, everyday life went on as usual. Dalton returned to work at the Distribution Center of the New Hanover County ABC Board. He arrived at six o'clock in the morning. All the employees gathered around and hugged Dalton expressing their concern. Many of the ABC employees knew Harrison. They all stayed at the distribution center during the last two hurricanes which hit directly along the New Hanover County coast. Up to thirty people stayed at the distribution center during those storms because the facility had a generator, running hot and cold water, food, and live cable broadcasting. Between the two storms, the employees spent over six days together, and they all got to know Harrison quite well. They enjoyed his jokes and wild fishing stories. Most of them had attended the book signing as well.

Ms. Kelly arrived at work in a complete daze. She lasted about an hour before her immediate supervisor sent her home. Not wanting to go home, she went straight over to see Tammy Cafaro, her best friend. She didn't want to be alone and needed the comfort of a dear friend.

It was agonizing that there were no new developments about her husband, and she feared the worst. Ms. Kelly was an avid viewer of TV crime shows, and most of them always implied that if a person wasn't found within the first forty-eight hours, they usually were later found dead or never found. She just couldn't get those thoughts out of her head, and she dreaded the possibility of the police coming to her with devastating news.

After Dalton completed his normal duties for the day, his immediate supervisor had received a late request to send five cases of liquor to a neighboring store in the next county. He asked Dalton if he would drive to Hampstead to make the delivery. Although totally worn out from the three deliveries he already completed that day, Dalton agreed to do it. He figured he could make a few more overtime bucks and since he would be halfway to his girlfriend's house, he would make the delivery and continue up Highway 17 a few more miles and pay her a visit in Surf City.

It was a small delivery, so the five cases of assorted liquor were placed in Dalton's back seat. He headed north toward Hampstead and ran into a traffic jam. A tractor trailer pulling out of the Lowes parking lot overturned blocking all northbound traffic. It delayed Dalton for almost two hours. He eventually arrived at the Hampstead ABC store around two forty that afternoon.

A cold front that was approaching from the north collided with the moist humid air mass hanging over the area creating a blanket of cumulus clouds, resembling a derecho formation. It blocked the sun's rays but filled the sky with a glorious deep red glow. Dalton stepped out of his truck, but he paused for a moment to gaze upon the horizon to witness a weather phenomenon that usually developed at dusk, and he began to sob. He could remember his Dad saying to him, "Red Sky at Night, Sailors Delight...the fishing tomorrow son will be great!" He remembered how many times he slept in, to find that his dad had left, but not in the boat.

"Hey mom, where did Dad get off to?"

"Well, you didn't get up at 5:30 a.m. like Dad wanted you to, so he put the boat back in the shed and went off somewhere to do something else."

He had done this too many times to his dad, and now he sincerely regretted it. His heart was filled with so much grief that it was crushing him.

"I'm sorry Dad, I am so sorry."

He broke down and cried. Dalton gathered himself together, wiped away the tears, and brought the first case of liquor into the store. Ten minutes later he had delivered all five cases and was about to leave the store.

"Hey, young man," the female manager said. "Would you mind opening those cases, and placing those bottles in the right spots?"

"No problem, ma'am, I'll be glad to."

Dalton vividly remembered what his Dad told him many times.

"Son, trust me, never ever piss off a female, you'll regret it for the rest of your life."

With that in mind, Dalton finished stacking the bottles and was about to leave.

"Would you please take those empty boxes out to the dumpster for me?"

"Yes ma'am."

Although somewhat irritated, Dalton grabbed all five of the boxes and headed for the small dumpster that was at the end of the parking lot out behind the store. The strange cloud formation he witnessed earlier moved in quickly and darkened the skies so much it seemed as if it was nighttime. The sudden darkness set off an overhead utility lamp mounted on a pole directly over the dumpster that provided him plenty of light to see.

Dalton lifted the plastic lid of the dumpster with his left hand, then tried to toss in the first box with his right hand. His hand slipped off the lid and the box bounced out into the parking lot. Now really irritated, he slammed back the plastic lid so it would remain in place behind the dumpster, giving him plenty of room to throw all the boxes in. To make sure he did have enough space, he leaned over the outside edge of the dumpster to scope it out and search for the best spot to throw the five boxes.

At first, it did not completely register in his mind.

"No, this is not possible, it can't be."

Lying at the bottom of an empty, open Skyy vodka box, Dalton could see a brown leather wallet that looked just like his dad's. He stood there completely mesmerized. He couldn't move. It was the same three-fold style wallet his Dad bought for him at Walmart and later bought one for himself. The thick rubber band always wrapped around the wallet wasn't there, but the indentations of the rubber band were.

"Oh my God, it's Dad's wallet," Dalton yelled out, looking around to see if anyone heard him. He reached down inside the box and grabbed the wallet. His hands were shaking so badly, he could barely open the wallet.

The North Carolina driver's license, tucked inside the first fold of the wallet, was in fact that of Harrison M. Thomas. Dalton kissed his Dad's picture on the license, then reached for his cell phone.

Dalton fumbled with his cell phone and dialed 9-1-1. He gave the lady who answered his call a brief description of what he found. He then called his Mom with the news. He could hear the sirens already approaching from the south. Searching in his own wallet, he pulled out Detective Decker's card and dialed the number. Decker answered on the first ring.

"Mr. Decker, it's Dalton. I've found my dad's wallet."

"Did you find it in his office, or what?"

"No, up here in Hampstead at the ABC store. I found it in the dumpster out back."

"Don't move, stay right there. I'm on my way!"

Decker immediately called Nicole, told her to tell Gretchen the news, and then he called Agent Vickors. All agreed this was a huge break in the case, a lead that could solve the kidnapping.

Minutes later, several police vehicles were en route to Hampstead. The area around the ABC store was completely sealed off by the local sheriff with yellow police tape, and all traffic on Highway 17 was temporarily brought to a standstill. With the darkening skies overhead and all the red and blue lights emanating from the police vehicles reflecting off the low cloud cover, it looked like a Christmas tree lighting ceremony.

Someone who was stuck in the halted traffic called the news desk of WWAY-TV because the news crew van, arrived and parked in the adjacent BP gas station to set up their satellite feed. People across the street that had been shopping at the small shopping center walked over and gathered at the scene. Cell phone screens lit up the faces of those texting out their version of what happened, setting social media on fire.

Agent Vickors, flashing his SBI badge, took control of the crime scene, and barked out instructions to the law enforcement personnel present. It was pure chaos, as the little township of Hampstead had never seen so many police vehicles gathered in one spot before.

"Gretchen, get your team moving. I want fingerprints from this entire place. I want the videos from inside the ABC store. I want names and addresses. We've got a break in this case. Do your jobs and be as thorough as hell. And get all these people the hell out of here right now."

When Vickors approached the BP station, an anxious reporter shoving a microphone in his face.

"Was the ABC store robbed? Did somebody get hurt?"

"No, nothing like that. We have apparently located the wallet of Harrison Thomas, who was, we think, kidnapped recently. That's all we've got right now. If anything further develops, I'll let you know. Our forensic team is gathering information and maybe we'll have some information later."

"Have the kidnappers asked for any ransom money yet?"

"I don't have any further details for you right now. Like I said, if something develops, I'll let you know. Now excuse me, I have work to do."

Agent Vickors absolutely hated reporters. He found them to be nothing but a bunch of piranhas and compared them to a nagging hemorrhoid. Heading back to the ABC store, the first thing he wanted to do was to view the videotapes with Gretchen. His intuition kicked into high gear, and he knew that finding Harrison's wallet was an important clue. Just outside the front door, he was met with a peeved stare from Nicole. She heard it loud and clear what Agent Vickors said earlier.

"Gretchen, get your team going."

Nicole was letting Agent Vickors know she should have been the one he directed his order to, not Gretchen. In her mind, Agent Vickors was not following the proper protocol and she would confront him about that later.

"Come with me, Nicole. We're going to view the tapes."

The agent knew Nicole was upset, and he wanted to smooth out his blunder. He needed to keep the entire team focused. He motioned to Decker to have him join them as well. Decker had been standing with Dalton in the parking lot. Decker told Dalton to sit tight and suggested he might want to pound social media with some real facts about what really happened to thwart the growing crowd.

They all entered the front door and headed for the manager's office in the back left-hand side of the small twelve hundred square foot store. Standing next to each other, Nicole and Agent Vickors could have passed as brother and sister. Both were tall individuals, with Nicole being nearly six feet, but Agent Vickors towered above all the rest at six feet five inches tall. His suit was the same color as Nicole's outfit, except for his shoes that were black. Agent Vickors' military looking crew-cut and his beady eyes let everyone know he was in charge.

Vickors knew that every ABC store had a multitude of video cameras. He asked the manager to rewind the tapes, but she had no clue how to operate them. Fortunately, there was an ALE officer, Mr. Daniel Thornton, on site who did.

"Excuse me, let me sit down and get to work." He turned toward Vickors for instructions.

"Do you have cameras outside showing the dumpster site?"

"Oh yeah, we have both, several outside and more inside. They all run twenty-four seven, all year long."

"Show me the dumpster and take us back twenty-four hours to start."

Mr. Thornton made a few clicks on the computer keyboard. The monitor flickered for a second, then a clear picture appeared on the screen. The entire team gathered around and intently focused on the fourteen-inch monitor screen. They might have to stare at the monitor for hours before it showed a person or persons near the dumpster. A tedious procedure, but one that had to be done.

Agent Vickors asked Thornton if he could speed up the footage and zoom in on the dumpster more. All they needed to see was someone opening the lid to the dumpster. With another few clicks on the keyboard, Thornton had the footage running four times faster. A few minutes later, the image of a truck pulling up alongside the dumpster came into view.

"Hold it right there, zoom in please," Agent Vickors instructed, as he bent over to get a better look.

"That's the truck. Holy shit, that's the same truck we saw from the video at Diamonds!" Nicole screamed out. "Oh my God, we've got the bastard now."

Some of the team members standing close by were rattled and totally shocked at what just came out of Nicole's mouth. They had never heard her cuss, not one time since she was hired. She was known to even scold her team members if they cursed in front of her.

Nicole called into her office and told one of the assistants to text her a screenshot of the pickup truck at Diamonds. Nicole received the text message within ten seconds and held up the picture on her phone next to the truck shown on the monitor and they matched. High fives erupted in the small office.

Agent Vickors asked Thornton to zoom in on the man at the dumpster and on the license plate of the truck. Thornton was able to print out multiple still shots of the truck and the driver coming and going from the property. He handed them to the investigative team. The clarity of the photos was remarkable, enabling Agent Vickors to take pictures of all the photos with his cell phone. He immediately sent them to his office in Raleigh with full instructions to his team members to get him all the information within the hour.

There was one small obstacle Agent Vickors was facing. The tags on the pickup truck were from South Carolina, but he had a good friend in Myrtle Beach he could count on for help.

Agent Vickors said he was returning to the office to wait for the information from his team. Just before exiting the ABC office door, he turned and addressed the team.

"Not a word to the press, ya hear? We don't want to spook this guy."

Nicole asked Mr. Thornton to find videos of the driver when he was in the store, specifically looking for anything or any spot he may have touched while in the store. They viewed the footage and could clearly see Luke entering the store and heading straight for the bourbon section. He brought the bottles to the front counter, pushed them toward the attendant, reached into his pocket with his right hand, and placed the money on the counter. While waiting for his change, Luke placed his left hand on the counter, strumming his fingers.

"Hold it right there, I need that shot. Print that photo out for me please," Nicole said, patting Thornton on his shoulder.

Nicole handed the printed photo to her team so they would know exactly where to retrieve the fingerprints. Once obtained, she instructed them to send them to Agent Vickors right away. The evidence was obtained within minutes, and copies were sent to Agent Vickors' cell phone and laptop.

"We've got the rotten son of a bitch now," Nicole leaned over and whispered to Decker.

"Well, let's just hope he's got a record somewhere and his fingerprints are in the national database, or else we've got nothing to go on."

"Yeah, I hope so too. The store manager said she had no idea who this guy was after my team showed her all the photos."

Detective Decker left the office and went back outside to chat with Dalton, bringing with him the photos of Luke, hoping that he would somehow recognize him.

"You got any idea who this guy might be?" Decker asked, handing the photos to Dalton.

"Nah, I've never seen him. Who is he?"

"Well, he's the guy that threw your dad's wallet in the dumpster, and now we have his fingerprints. We've sent them up to Raleigh, so we should hear something soon and catch this guy. Best thing you can do right now is just go home and sit tight. If I hear anything, I'll call you," Decker said while giving Dalton a hug.

"Hey Decker, do you believe in fate?"

"You're damn right I do."

CHAPTER 16

The pain was excruciating, nothing he had ever experienced in his life. It was all a horrible nightmare drifting in and out of consciousness. Harrison awoke and found himself laying down on the floor, with two men standing over him. Confused, he didn't know who they were or where he was at. As he was slowly regaining consciousness, he noticed one of the men had a thick nylon rope and was tying it around his right ankle.

"Oh, Christ, the pain," Harrison yelled out with his eyes rolling back into his head.

"You stupid asshole, wake up, don't you dare die on us, you dumbass," screamed Jaxson.

Luke knelt beside Harrison and slid his left arm under Harrison's neck and, at the same time, using his right arm, he reached underneath Harrison's right knee. Luke slowly raised Harrison's head, then cradling Harrison's knee, he squeezed his arms toward each other until he was able to clasp his hands firmly together in front of Harrison's chest. With his head now lifted off the floor, Harrison was horrified to see that there was blood everywhere and his right leg, just below his knee, was bent outward at about a ten-degree angle. When Luke had Harrison in the position he wanted, Jaxson raised his right calf and rested it on one of the kitchen chairs.

"What are you doing for Christ's sake?" Harrison asked, grunting through the pain.

"Aw, don't ya worry. We're gonna set your bone home boy," Jaxson answered with a weird smile on his face.

"Just don't move when we say three," Luke added, looking straight down at Harrison. The look of genuine concern on the man's face worried him.

Luke then sat down on the floor and began to wrap the excess rope around his upper torso and then tied off the end around Harrison's right ankle. Luke extended his legs, placing his left heel on Jaxson's hip and his right heel squarely on Harrison's right buttock. Luke then reached over and grabbed Harrison's leg just above and below the break area. Harrison could feel Jaxson tightening his grip and he could feel the rope tightening on his ankle as Luke was easing his upper torso back just a few inches. The two cousins looked at each other and nodded.

"Now, on the count of three, we're gonna pull and straighten out your leg, okay?" Luke explained.

"Ready, one, two, . . ." he never got to three.

Harrison had no idea how long he had been out, but the pain in his leg made him vomit all over himself as soon as he gained consciousness. The cousins must have picked him up, as Harrison found himself in the recliner once again with his right leg propped up on one of the kitchen chairs. He looked down at his leg which was wrapped up in a brown blood-soaked towel, and to his amazement, it appeared to be straight. He couldn't fathom why the cousins still had his wrists zip tied in front of him, given the crippled state he was in.

"I need some water," Harrison begged.

"Oh, so you're awake, are we?" someone said in the background.

"You are one stupid fool," said another voice in the background, Harrison couldn't recall.

154

Harrison shifted his weight in the recliner to get more comfortable, but that effort shot so much pain down his leg, he blacked out again. When he came to about two hours later, Jaxson and Luke were sitting at the kitchen table. It all started to come back to Harrison. The escape plan went well until he tried to run to safety. Then, for some reason, he blacked out and now found himself in the recliner again with his leg propped up on one of the kitchen chairs.

"What happened to my leg, you assholes?"

Jaxson picked up his chair from the kitchen, crossed into the living room and sat it down next to the recliner. It was as if he had some sympathy as he began to tell Harrison what happened to his leg.

"To our surprise, you somehow managed to get loose and when you tried to run away, you ran slap into the tongue of the boat trailer."

"That steel bar ain't gonna move, boy. Completely cracked your bone. When you hit that tongue of the trailer, it sounded like that Dong sound you hear on those Taco Bell commercials on TV. On top of that, you started screaming like a coyote in heat out there," Luke interjected.

"That's what happened," Jaxson explained. "The cut on your leg was very deep, so I had to burn it to stop the bleeding."

"Are you kidding me? You burned my leg?"

"Had to, did you want it to get infected?"

"What the hell did you burn it with?"

Jaxson ignored Harrison as he reached over and began to unwrap the brown towel. With the last turn, a chunk of skin, some four inches wide and an eighth of an inch thick, came off, sending nerve-shattering streaks of pain down Harrison's leg. He shuddered and screamed in pain. Looking down, Harrison was

155

horrified. The outer edges of the wound had turned black, and the center area was bright red, covered with oozing yellow pus.

"Do you see that black flesh? Do you have any idea what that is? That's gangrene!"

"Relax dude, I've seen worse. You're such a sissy boy, aren't you?" Jaxson starred at Harrison with his eyebrows lifted.

"I need to get to a hospital right away. If I don't, I'll be dead in twenty-four hours or less," Harrison said with a vengeful look on his face.

"Oh, shut your face," Luke said as he went over to the refrigerator and grabbed the jar of Duke's mayonnaise and a paper plate from the cabinet along with a box of table salt.

"It's just burn marks, relax."

Luke proceeded to make a paste out of the mayonnaise and a large amount of the table salt, stirring the contents on the paper plate. He scooped up a large clump of his concoction and spread a thick layer of the redneck medicine on Harrison's gaping wound. He then went back into the kitchen and retrieved a roll of duct tape from the middle drawer. Grabbing the small bag of potato chips, he tore it open and poured the contents onto the kitchen table. Harrison couldn't believe what he was seeing as Luke came over and placed the potato chip bag over the paste on his leg. He wrapped the duct tape tight around the homemade bandage several times.

Jaxson had stepped outside and returned with two wooden planks from a freight pallet and placed the two-foot-long planks on either side of Harrison's leg. Luke wrapped the planks tightly with duct tape against Harrison's leg making a makeshift splint. At least his leg was straight now, and not bent outward as he had seen earlier. The paste burned at first, but now was surprisingly easing the pain of the deep gash on his leg

"That should keep him alive just long enough for us to get that treasure. Now let's get going before the tide screws us," Jaxson exclaimed.

Harrison tried to stand, but the pain was unbearable, and he fell back into the recliner, totally defeated and exhausted.

"I can't walk. I need a cane or some crutches," Harrison stated, looking around the room to see if anybody was listening to him.

Jaxson left the living room and Harrison could hear him fumbling around in the utility closet next to the bathroom behind him. He came back into the living room holding a cheap four-foot-long metal mop and a nasty old beach towel. He stood in front of Harrison holding the metal mop in his right hand, then pushing with his right thumb, slowly bent the mop's top six inches over at a ninety-degree angle with ease. He wrapped the beach towel around the bent portion of the mop.

"Luke, give me that duct tape so I can stick this towel around the mop head," Jaxson said, with his hand outstretched wiggling his fingers.

A few minutes later, the two men lifted Harrison out of the recliner. After steadying him with the makeshift crutch, he was able to hobble out of the trailer and make his way to the truck. Nearing the truck, Harrison glanced over at the boat trailer and could see a small piece of his bloody flesh still stuck to the outer edge of the tongue. With great difficulty, he managed to get into the back seat of the pickup truck, while Luke got into the driver's side with Jaxson riding shotgun.

On the way to their destination, the sharp turn to the right, followed by a big dip in the road, confirmed to Harrison they were on their way to Hampstead Marina. He had been a ramp member of the marina several years back and traveled to the ramp multiple times, so he knew the road like the back of his hand. He knew it would be about a twenty-five-minute ride to the island from the marina. Could he still escape? Harrison heard a clap of thunder off in the distance, confirming what he had heard earlier.

Could he fall overboard and swim to safety with his wrists zip tied? It was well over fifty-seven years ago since he took his final lifeguard training test at the Rodney Boy Scout Reservation with his hands tied in front of him. He had to tread water for five minutes to pass. It was easy to do back then, utilizing the dolphin kick to keep one's head above water, but back then he only weighed 145 pounds. Now at 234 pounds with a useless leg, he was nothing but an anchor. He totally nixed the falling overboard escape plan.

They arrived at the Hampstead ramp, just as Harrison had predicted, around seven a.m. To the south, ominous dark black clouds were blustering up and moving north. There were flashes of lightning off in the distance deep within the clouds, followed by rattling booms of thunder. The wind was picking up and there were white caps in the waterway.

"Oh shit, mother of God," Harrison mumbled under his breath.

"What the hell is the matter with you, asshole?" Jaxson asked. "Get your ass up. It's time to get moving."

Harrison didn't budge. He sat there completely frozen. How was he going to explain to these idiots his deathly fear of lightning? It was a crippling fear he had since he was fifteen-years-old. It stemmed from an incident that occurred at the Shellcrest Swim Club in Wilmington, Delaware, while he was a lifeguard at the community pool. His father, who in his youth, was also a lifeguard, told Harrison to always be aware of lightning. If a thunderhead appeared out of nowhere, it would be wise to clear the pool.

On one hot summer afternoon back in 1967, a large thunderhead cloud appeared just over the tree line adjacent to the pool, about a mile away. Harrison blew his whistle to have everyone vacate the pool. Above the objections of the kids swimming and the verbal onslaught from many parents, he prevailed in getting everyone out of the pool just in time. He stepped down from the metal guard stand and walked towards the guardhouse. A huge bolt of lightning erupted from the cloud and hit the top of the guard stand, setting the wooden seat on fire. The bolt bounced off the guard stand, shot directly over his head and crackled into the baby pool in a puff of smoke. Harrison felt the hot tingling of the electricity throughout his entire body. Momentarily blinded by the flash, the following instant clap of thunder sent him to his knees. He wondered if he had been struck by the bolt. To this day, if he heard thunder, he sought safety in the hallway, in the middle of the house, with a pillow over his head. He never could shake that experience.

As if on cue, a bolt of lightning hit nearby, and the cousins stayed in the truck. At least for the moment, Harrison didn't have to explain himself and maybe these guys had the same fear. The storm intensified with the rain blowing almost sideways, rocking the truck. The passenger side window had long broken years ago, and Jaxson was unable to roll it up completely, allowing the rain in, soaking his worn-out T-shirt.

"Oh, shit, let's get back to the house and wait this out."

Another bolt of lightning hit so close, producing such a brilliant flash that Harrison thought for a second, he saw an X-ray image of his hand.

"Oh God almighty," Harrison squealed out like a little girl. He lost control and wet himself.

Hearing the wimpy shriek, Jaxson turned around and saw Harrison curled up on the floorboard moving his hands around outlining the sign of the cross repeatedly.

"You pussy, do you really think the big daddy, junior, and spook are gonna keep you safe?"

Both cousins were laughing as Luke reluctantly turned the truck around and headed back to the trailer. Harrison, for the first time in his life, welcomed the lightning, but that thought soon waned as he dreaded the thought of hunkering down in a tin can for the next few hours. Maybe they would let him stay in the truck where the four rubber tires would shield him from the lightning. At least the storm was buying him much needed time.

The makeshift crutch kept slipping in the mud and both cousins had to assist Harrison into the trailer, and all three got soaked from the torrential downpour. Harrison, completely soaked, was ushered into the wretched recliner once again. The two men took off their T-shirts and seated themselves at the kitchen table. Luke got up and turned on the TV to watch the local news to see what the storm was going to do. The radar was showing a massive line of thick thunderstorms running from Georgia all the way up to DC, heading northeast along the coast. All indications were that the storm would hammer the east coast of North Carolina for the next eight to ten hours before it went out to sea.

"Crap, we are stuck, aren't we?" Luke asked, turning to Jaxson. But Jaxson wasn't answering, his eyes were wide open and glued to the TV, watching a news flash that suddenly appeared on the screen interrupting the weather report.

"You fucking idiot!" Jaxson screamed while grabbing Luke by the throat.

"Look what you've done. How could you be such a stupid idiot and throw a wallet in a dumpster?"

Hey, you told me to dump the wallet, so I put it in a dumpster. That's what you told me to do, so go screw yourself," Luke said pushing Jaxson away from him.

They watched the news in silence, not moving a muscle. The breaking news story had a reporter standing in front of the Hampstead ABC store with a caption at the bottom of the screen titled "Wallet of local author Harrison Thomas found in Dumpster."

A still photo of a man standing near the dumpster appeared on the screen, and then a still photo of the cousin's truck appeared with the reporter saying, "Authorities have a possible suspect in the kidnapping of Mr. Thomas. If anyone recognizes this man or this red truck with South Carolina plates, contact the police immediately."

The photo of Luke plastered all over the news headline did not show his face completely, as his ball cap was pulled down enough to cover most of his face.

Although Harrison could not see the TV screen itself, he heard every word. He was relieved to know that the police were on to these guys, and any minute they would come crashing through the front door. This nightmare, Harrison thought, was going to end soon. It needed to end soon so he could get to a hospital and save his leg. Duct tape and mayonnaise would not save his leg. He needed antibiotics and a highly skilled orthopedic surgeon.

Luke stood up and nervously started to pace around the living room, trying to think of a way to solve the problem facing them since the police were now able to identify their pickup truck. He stopped suddenly and with his right index finger pointed to the backyard.

"Look, we'll switch trucks. We'll put old Bob in the shed out back and use our flatbed instead. Even if they run the tags on the pickup, they're gonna come up empty. That old drunk uncle of ours, hell, he may even be dead for all we know. The police aren't gonna get anything from him. He can't remember what he did two hours ago. We'll be long gone before they find us."

Jaxson thought for a moment, then nodded his head in agreement. Harrison's earlier elation flickered out. He had no idea these guys had another vehicle. The trailer was rocking and rolling as the storm outside raged, with lightning popping almost every twenty seconds. The storm should take at least another six hours before it passed. Surely the police will get here by then, Harrison thought, as he closed his eyes to shield the bright flashes of lightning from his view.

Jaxson's assumption about his old uncle turned out to be spot on. Agent Vickors had sent the tag numbers of the truck down to his SBI buddy in Myrtle Beach, Detective Lewis, asking him to run the plates immediately and let him know what they found out. The tags were registered to Mr. Clyde Jefferson, who lived in a broken-down house just south of the Garris Public Boat Landing, approximately forty miles north of Charleston, South Carolina. Agents were sent out immediately to interview Mr. Jefferson but came up empty-handed as the man was suffering from either dementia, or most likely Alzheimer's and offered no helpful information. A thorough search of his residence yielded no clues or leads, either.

"Sebastian, our boys didn't find anything at all, I'm sorry," Detective Lewis told Vickors.

"What about the tags?"

"Oh, hell, they were stolen well over five years ago. We don't have a clue who owns the truck."

"All right, can you get into the Register of Deeds database and search around for relatives of this guy for me?"

"Sure can. I'll get one of my staff members on it right away. I'll email you the full report as soon as they compile it. But don't get your hopes up. The folks down there, especially those in the fishing community, are like gypsies. They'll have babies in their homes, and they'll never go to school. So, a lot of them are ghosts. If they stay out of trouble with the law, we don't know they exist. We'll give it our best shot."

CHAPTER 17

Aided by Dalton's social media entries, the news that his Dad's wallet had been found spread quickly throughout the coastal community. Dalton's cell phone was pounded with call after call to the point he just silenced the ringer. Dalton nixed his plan to visit his girlfriend in Surf City and decided to drive back to Middle Sound to be by his mother's side. On his way there, he got a text in bold print from his mom's best friend Tammy Cafaro, telling him to call her immediately. The text scared him to death, and he had to pull over on the shoulder of the road to try to calm himself down. He didn't think he could take any more bad news. Fearing the worst, he dialed Tammy's number.

"Dalton, look, Patrick and Irene want to cook a big meal for everyone, and your mom is already here, so come over as soon as you can, okay?"

"Oh, man, is she going to cook that delicious Schnitzel like we had last year?"

"No, I think she is going to cook good old chicken and pastry with biscuits this time. If you would, please call and tell Andrea and Bryson to come also. I'll call Decker and tell him to come over as well. Maybe he has some up-to-date information for us that might calm your Mom down some."

"Your text scared the hell out of me. So, everything is alright?"

"Yeah, sorry about that. I tapped the cap's lock key by accident. Are you coming over?"

"I should be there in maybe fifteen minutes"

Most of the invitees arrived at Tammy's house between five and five thirty that evening and Dalton pulled in around six o'clock. The mood amongst the group, at first, was somber with everyone trying not to say anything that would upset Harrison's family. It was Monday, and a little more than forty-eight hours had passed since Harrison was kidnapped. His whereabouts were still unknown. The group remained inside, due to the blustery thunderstorm. They gathered in the living room and adjoining kitchen participating in general small talk.

As expected, the main topic of conversation was centered around Harrison. Irene was busy in the kitchen cooking, while her husband Patrick was grilling his famous beef ribs in the garage with the garage door about halfway open. Earnie and Tammy had four big screen TVs scattered around the house and all were on, each tuned to a different news channel in the event some breaking news would be broadcast.

Tammy loved company, and she was most comfortable and at ease when she had family and close friends gathered at her home. She would go out of her way and bend over backwards to make everyone feel welcome. Even though she knew that her daughter Nicole was upset with Agent Vickors and Gretchen, she invited them both to come over, and they both accepted the invitation. With all the commotion that had taken place over the last twenty-four hours, Tammy and Irene both decided that a relaxing casual get together coupled with a good meal would surely help pacify the tension everyone was feeling.

Tammy and Irene first met each other in 1995 when their husbands were both stationed at Camp Humphreys Army base in Osan, South Korea, during Desert Storm. Tammy and Earnie and Patrick and Irene lived outside the base in small duplex apartments. When the men returned after deployment, Tammy and Irene would welcome them home with a huge smorgasbord of their favorite cuisine. This always had a tremendous calming effect, helping to erase the recent mental scars they sustained while in battle. Under the current circumstances, it was the perfect time to bring everyone together.

The storm coming in from the west intensified, bringing with it southeasterly winds so strong that several trash cans were toppled over along the street in front of Earnie's house. The leading edge of the thunderstorm was approaching fast, bringing with it menacing black clouds which unleashed sheets of rainfall. When a massive bolt of lightning hit close to Earnie's house followed by an immediate deafening clap of thunder, everyone ducked and covered their heads. The dogs ran around peeing everywhere. The bolt hit so close everyone could smell the faint scent of chlorine in the air and many were convinced the bolt hit the swimming pool out back.

"Damn, if Harrison was here right now, we'd find him scared to death crawling on his belly heading for the hallway!" Earnie said.

Everyone broke out in laughter. They all knew of Harrison's fear of lightning, and they all ribbed him about it all the time.

"Yeah, even if Harrison knew that lightning hit in Myrtle Beach, he'd be in the hallway, all covered up with pillows and shit," Earnie added to more laughter.

If a storm was headed towards Middle Sound, several of Harrison's friends would call Ms. Kelly to see if her husband was in the hallway. Patrick and Irene, who lived on the outskirts of Fayetteville, would sometimes call Harrison telling him to get ready as the storm they just had was coming his way.

More and more stories about Harrison's escapades took center stage as everyone sat around the dining room table. Each person who knew Harrison personally took their turn telling stories about Harrison's daring and hysterical adventures, but it was the hilarious stories that Harrison's younger brother Rich told that had everyone crying with laughter.

Rich told stories about his older brother, during his elementary school days and high school years, that those in attendance had never heard before. They all knew Harrison was a tad goofy, but the stories Rich told convinced them he was totally nuts, in a funny way. As Rich proclaimed, his brother was such a free spirit that he and many of his brother's past friends and relatives found him to be a so-called visionary Shalogan. The atmosphere in the room changed, and even the family members were laughing.

As the dinner plates were being cleared away in the kitchen, Nicole, Gretchen, and Agent Vickors quietly slipped away, unnoticed, headed for the garage. Minutes later, the screaming of cuss words from all parties that erupted from the garage sounded like a bomb igniting. In an instant, Earnie and Patrick bolted to the garage as if in a Pavlovic response. After serving multiple tours of duty in Iraq and Afghanistan, any out of the ordinary sounds would trigger the two veterans into combat ready status. Earnie was not about to have such a commotion take place in His house, no sir, not now, not ever.

"Y'all shut the hell up and sit your asses down," Earnie ordered entering the garage, followed by his wife Tammy. Patrick was right behind him with his hand inside his belt gripping his Glock which he always had with him.

Agent Vickors noticed Patrick's hand position, and reacting to his training, began to reach for his own gun, when Patrick bellowed out, "Don't even think about it, I'll blow your goddamn head off."

In a split second, Tammy, with her arms outstretched, separated the two men. She scolded both, telling them to cool it and sit down. Irene entered the garage and grabbed her husband by the elbow and spun him around, then reached up and placed her hands beside his cheeks, calmly telling him to stand down. Both Tammy and Irene knew their husbands still suffered from PTSD, and things could get out of control quickly. Even though both men had been retired from the Army for some eleven years, their PTSD would still rear its ugly head at any given moment.

"I don't know what the hell is going on here, but it stops right now. If you can't control yourselves, get the hell out of my house right now. I will NOT put up with this, y'all hear me?" Earnie roared, with the veins in his neck protruding.

The rage in Earnie's face was scary, and it defused the situation quickly. Everybody involved took a deep breath, and the garage fell silent. Realizing their disrespectful behavior, each one apologized to one another then and headed off in different directions.

Patrick reached into a nearby cooler and pulled out two nearly frozen Yuengling beers, handing one to Earnie. Both men walked outside and stood in the rain, while their wives looked on. Both Tammy and Irene had witnessed their husbands do this many times. From their observations, Tammy and Irene could see that the rain had a tranquilizing effect on their husbands, and they would just leave them alone. When Tammy and Irene first witnessed this behavior, both Earnie and Patrick explained to them that during their seven tours of active duty in the desert, it maybe would rain twice a year. When it did, all the soldiers would stand out in the rain, tilt their heads back, and let the short rain shower wash away all their worries, along with the sand and grit.

All the fighting would come to a halt, and for a short period of time, all was peaceful and quiet.

With emotions still running high, Tammy politely asked everyone to come back inside and have German chocolate cake and ice cream. Things calmed down, and laughter once again filled the room.

Agent Vickors couldn't resist, still visualizing the picture frame in the Thomas' living room on his first visit to their home, and he had to question Ms. Kelly about it.

"Ma'am?" Agent Vickors questioned, motioning towards Ms. Kelly.

"I couldn't help but notice the picture frame in your living room that listed, I assume, were all your contractions. I've never seen anything like that in my life, and I was wondering if you could explain it to me?"

The room fell silent, as everybody was completely stunned by Agent Vickors' question. His question had nothing to do with the ongoing investigation, and it seemed so inappropriate.

Tammy, however, took advantage of the question feeling it would bring more humor into the room, and pleaded to Ms. Kelly to answer. Tammy was worried about Ms. Kelly's mental state. Having her loosen up a bit, might help relieve the tension.

The majority of the group had never seen the picture and, knowing Harrison, the story about to be told by Ms. Kelly was going to be yet another example of his goofiness.

"Oh, Lord, where do I start?" Ms. Kelly said, rubbing her eyes.

"That man, when he got something in his craw, he would not let it rest. When I was pregnant with our son Dalton, he had been studying childbirth on the internet for months and we even attended those Lamaze classes. For some reason, he thought it would be beneficial to have a record of my contractions to present to the doctor when we arrived at the hospital. I don't remember the Lamaze instructor ever mentioning anything about keeping such records, it was something he came up with on his own.

"He was a pest, driving me crazy walking around with his legal pad and a friggin' stopwatch, mind you. He went out and bought a cheap stethoscope and insisted on listening to every contraction and each time he would write down the time, the length of the contraction and he had some sort of pain scale, from one to ten, that I had to assign a number to. I kept telling him I had been through all of this with the birth of my daughter and just leave me the hell alone. I made the mistake of telling him that the doctor would know when it was time to measure my cervix opening. The dang fool went to his computer to research this new revelation and came back into the living room one day with a dang flashlight and his architect scale ruler thingy and wanted to measure my cervix for God's sake."

The room erupted into fits of laughter and the normally stoic Agent Vickors lost control and slapped the table with tears streaming down his face from laughter. Everybody was laughing, and those who knew Harrison well, said it was just like him to do something like that.

"Wait, you're telling me this man wanted to measure your cervix and take notes?"

"Oh, it gets crazier," Ms. Kelly said, holding up both hands with her fingers spread out. He found a ball jar with a bottom about four inches wide, and he wanted to stick it inside my, you know what, and look inside the jar to see how wide my cervix was."

Tammy lost it and peed in her pants. She had to leave the room. Agent Vickors was laughing so hard his stomach was hurting and the volume from all the laughter had the four dogs in the house running around howling. It took nearly five minutes before everyone regained their composure and caught their breath. Earnie stepped up and motioned that he had something to say.

"Remember how Harrison just wouldn't believe the correct lyrics to Bruno Mars' song *Uptown Funk*? To this day, that man thinks the lyrics are 'put a little nigger in it,' when we all know it says, 'put a little liquor in it.'"

The whole room erupted again. Nicole scanned the Spotify playlist on her cell phone and soon the song was being played in the background and Patrick broke out into the funky chicken dance that broke everybody up.

After eating his dessert, Dalton walked out to the garage for a cigarette. He was joined by Detective Decker.

"Can you think of any reason why your Dad's wallet would be in Hampstead?"

"No, it makes no sense at all. I just don't understand. Where's my Dad at?"

"We don't know yet, but I promise you we'll find him and bring him home safe."

"We got a good lead with your find, and trust me, we've got a whole team of investigators here in Wilmington and Raleigh working on it. It's just a matter of time when all the pieces are put together to solve this. Just be patient and watch over your mom, okay?"

Just as Dalton left the garage to go back inside to get more of Irene's delicious German chocolate cake, Agent Vickors entered and stood next to Decker looking round to make sure nobody was listening to them.

"Hey, look bro, I told you I would explain the word *chingas* to ya, right?"

"Oh yeah you did, I'm all ears, bro."

"Certain words used all around the world have different meanings depending on where you might be, how you say them, what tone you use, or even the way you hold your head. I'll give you an example. As a young man when I first came to the States I had an assignment in Myrtle Beach. I was at a beach nightclub one night standing at the bar listening to the music that somewhat resembled my beloved Reggae music. A drop-dead gorgeous chick came up to me and asked me if I wanted to Shag.

"I was totally flabbergasted and of course I wanted to go along with her request. I told her to follow me to my car that was parked just outside the nightclub. She looked at me as if I was totally crazy and I looked at her in the same way. She blurted out that she wanted to dance the Shag and that the dancefloor was the only place she was headed, not the parking lot.

"After a short conversation, she explained to me the word Shag in the South meant a unique dance style that originated in the southern states. I, on the other hand, explained to her the word Shag to Brits and Bermudians meant having sex. We laughed and after that we had a wonderful time shagging to beach music on the dance floor and later shagging at my hotel room."

"So, you're telling me the word *chingas* has the same meaning?"

"Well, yes, and no. It is basically a vulgar word of deep Spanish origin that has different meanings. Depending on what dialect one uses, it can take on a different meaning altogether. The English translation is simply the F word. It can even mean something totally different depending on how soft or loud you say it, what tone you use or even the way you hold your head. Unless you were raised in the back slums of Bermuda like I was, you would never comprehend all the meanings of this nasty word. But I can tell you this, if you ever go to Bermuda or any of the adjacent islands, don't ever use that word under any circumstances."

"Okay, so I used that word shortly after I first met you, just joking around. How did you take that?"

"Ha, the way you said it, specifically your tone, referred to a homosexual, come on. If you had said that to a guy on the street in my old neighborhood, he would have cut your throat in a skinny minute."

"Holy *chinga*,"

"My God, man, you'll never learn, will you? You just said you wanted to have sex with the virgin Mary. Just shut the *chinga* up," Agent Vickors said, raising his voice a few octaves.

Shortly after nine o'clock that evening, the crowd slowly began to leave. Irene and Patrick decided to stay at Earnie and Tammy's house that night while Bryson and Andrea, along with Dalton, went home with Grandmama. Harrison's brother Rich declined the invitation to stay with the family and headed back to his house down near Monkey Junction.

Decker drove over to Harrison's house as he wanted to reassure all of them that he was going to find Harrison and bring him home. He was also dying to see the picture frame that Vickors spoke of. After spending thirty minutes with the family, Decker headed back to his office, figuring he would spend the night on his office couch. He wanted to see if any more information had been sent to his computer.

When he arrived at his office, he noticed light coming out from underneath Gretchen's office door. Figuring she was working late, he lightly tapped on the door and walked in. He quickly realized he should have waited for her to respond first. Both totally naked, Gretchen and Agent Vickors were making passionate love on her couch. They never saw or heard Decker exit the office.

"Okay," Decker thought to himself, "there is no sense in trying to stay here."

Decker quietly left the building and drove home snickering to himself.

"Some things never change, do they? Growl on baby."

CHAPTER 18

As the sun set on the horizon, the storm calmed and worked its way east out over the ocean. It left behind a picturesque orange and purple sunset. Once the rain stopped a little after six o'clock, Luke and Jaxson switched out the trucks. They hooked the boat and trailer to the 1970 F250 truck which was stored in the shed out behind the trailer. After securing the boat and trailer to the flatbed, Jaxson backed the old red pickup truck into the shed and closed the double doors. Tucked away under a tarp, it was time for BOB to take a nap.

After making some last-minute preparations, Jaxson came back into the trailer and cut the zip ties loose from Harrison's ankles but kept the ones on his wrists intact. Now using three zip ties, Jaxson looped each ankle separately then connected Harrison's ankles together with another zip tie, leaving just enough slack where Harrison could walk but had no chance of running, just as if he was wearing leg shackles.

"Let's go wussy, time to hit that island. The tide is about right, and we should be there in about twenty minutes," Jaxson said, lifting Harrison out of the recliner with one arm only.

Jaxson led Harrison out to the flatbed truck and ordered him to climb into the front seat and sit next to Luke, who was nervously tapping his fingertips on the steering wheel. Once olive green, the flatbed truck looked diseased, in need of a tetanus shot, with flakes and patches of rust covering the body. The front window on the passenger side above the bent windshield wiper had a bullet hole surrounded by shattered glass resembling a huge spider web. There were no windows on the driver or the passenger sides. All the handles were missing. The front seat upholstery was long gone, replaced by red boat cushions placed directly over the old zig-zag springs. The backrest upholstery, if any, was covered with beach towels which matched the décor inside the trailer. What was left of the floorboard was littered with cigarette butts, probably dating back to the seventies. Unfortunately for Harrison, he did not have the luxury of sitting on a boat cushion and had to deal with the rusted springs pinching at his butt.

Luke wiggled the stick shift into neutral, then turned on the ignition, not with a normal key, but with a Torx T-Wrench that had been jammed into the ignition housing. What followed was a constant loud grinding noise of tat tat tat, tat tat tat.

"Aw, Jesus Christ, that damn starter," Jaxson spat out.

Jaxson reached into the glove box and pulled out a wood handled ball peen hammer, slammed his right shoulder into the door, got out, then crawled up underneath the truck. Harrison could see Jaxson through the floorboard as he slithered along on his back toward the middle of the truck. Seconds later Harrison could hear two thunderous whacks when Jaxson slammed the hammer onto the outer casing of the starter.

"All right, try it now."

Luke once again grabbed the T-wrench and engaged the ignition. The truck engine fired, bellowing out a plume of gray black smoke from the exhaust pipe, and the cab shook violently as the old engine roared to life. Exhaust fumes were seeping into the cabin, choking both Harrison and Luke, as Jaxson got back into the passenger seat.

Luke gently shifted into first gear, released the clutch, and the old behemoth slowly headed down the driveway. Harrison immediately recognized where he was and took solace, knowing he wasn't that far from home. With the old truck spewing a continuous cloud of black exhaust, it took about five minutes to reach the Hampstead marina. Arriving at the ramp, they spotted an elderly couple launching their 16-foot Carolina Skiff. Luke stopped short of the boat ramp and jammed his pistol into Harrison's ribs, knowing that would inject enough pain to get Harrison's attention.

"Don't think about yelling out. Just sit your ass still or I'll blow out your kidneys and use them for bait."

After several attempts, the elderly couple finally managed to launch their boat. As the old man was walking back to the ramp Harrison hoped the old man would walk by the truck and notice him. Maybe the old man had seen his face on the news and would alert the police.

Harrison's hopes were squashed when the old man walked right by them, not even bothering to look their way. He was too busy swatting away the gnats that enveloped his head. The old man and his wife fired up their motor and headed out, due east, towards the waterway. About one hundred yards from the boat ramp, they turned north. Luke waited until the old couple was at least a half mile away, and with no one else around, he backed the boat trailer down into the ramp, stopping just short of the water's edge.

Jaxson grabbed Harrison by his elbow and dragged him out of the truck as Luke continued to back down the ramp. Jaxson guided Harrison down the gangplank leading to a fifteen-foot-long floating dock where boats, after being launched, would tie up to load gear or passengers before heading out into the channel. Once the trailer wheels submerged a few inches below the surface the boat slid off the trailer with ease. Jaxson moored the boat to the floating dock. Jaxson stepped into the Jon boat and helped Harrison into the boat while Luke parked the truck.

There was no wind at all and thousands upon thousands of marsh gnats engulfed both Harrison and Jaxson. Called No-See-Ums by the locals, the men felt like they were getting eaten alive. It was like having your own personal air force buzzing around your head, dive bombing into every orifice available and setting up camp in your hair and eyebrows.

"Hurry the hell up," Jaxson screamed at Luke, walking back from parking the truck. "We're getting eaten alive, bro."

Luke jumped on board and fired up the old Evinrude motor. Spitting out oily smelling smoke, the motor turned over once and shut down with a hiss.

"You've got to choke her, dumbass," Jaxson yelled.

Luke set the choke, hit the starter once again, and the motor sputtered a few times, but eventually came to life. Once Luke saw that the water pump was functioning properly with a steady stream of water coming out of the pee hole, he pulled back on the throttle handle and engaged the motor into reverse to clear the dock. Once clear, Luke slammed the throttle forward, yelling out, "The wind is your friend."

The wind indeed was friendly as well as comforting, blowing away all the nasty gnats. Once in the Waterway, Luke eased off the throttle a tad and told Jaxson to get the bug spray out of the side panel and spray everyone down. Harrison was relieved to hear the words "everyone." If for any reason they decided not to spray him down, a slow death from sheer agony and torture would descend upon him. Within a few minutes, everyone was drenched in bug spray.

Luke pushed the throttle forward, bringing the small boat up on plane. With no wind and with the complete absence of any chop in the water, the boat skimmed along the smooth water with ease, running at about twenty-five miles an hour.

The cousins made Harrison sit on the tiny bow of the boat which was a piece of plywood about four feet by three feet covered with a piece of green Astro turf. Jaxson sat dead center on top of the live bait well which was filled with ice and about two dozen water bottles. Luke, at the stern, steered the old Jon boat using a five-foot tiller handle extension which allowed him to stand upright and see over Jaxson and Harrison. With the boat perfectly balanced and the water slick as glass, the old Evinrude motor was being pushed to her limits.

Much to Harrison's dismay, not a soul was on the waterway. They were heading south and the old man and his wife in their skiff were heading north, leaving Harrison no chance of flagging them down for help. He had thought of falling overboard if another boat came close enough to witness such an event. A man overboard scenario would surely stop any boater, whereupon he could cry out for help. The ride to Earnie's Island was about a twenty-minute run wide open, and surely someone would come by. Maybe the Coast Guard was out today, or a boat full of Azalea Festival folks out for a joy ride. Somebody had to be out enjoying the slick water and splendid sunset.

There was a small neighborhood marina, exclusive to the residents of Washington Acres, that would be visible within five minutes, and somebody had to be launching from there, heading out for an evening booze cruise. There was a large house on the water with a gazebo dock just past the marina that everyone locally called "The Red Roof Inn" as the entire roof structure was covered in red terra cotta tile. As many times as Harrison fished in and around The Red Roof Inn, there were always people out on the dock gathered inside the gazebo. Not today as they raced past Long Point Channel heading to Greens Channel, yet another fine fishing area Harrison was well acquainted with.

They would soon be passing by the Scotts Hill Marina, where the Sailfish Restaurant building, with a large screened-in porch, sat near the water's edge. Harrison thought about bailing and just falling overboard directly across from the restaurant. There was always a good crowd there, many strolling along the long dock leading out to the waterway, and no doubt someone would see a man fall overboard and possibly call the Coast Guard. Again, no one was in sight, not a single person out on the dock.

They ran wide open past the restaurant heading towards Butler Creek, passing at least eight or nine docks jutting out into the waterway. Passing Butler Creek, they would soon hit Bald Eagle point at Futch Creek, which contained at least thirty individual docks. Somebody had to be boating coming out of Futch Creek.

One single jet ski shot out of Futch Creek and headed south at a blazing speed, never noticing the three men in the Jon boat. Three minutes later, to the port side, they reached the mouth of a large and wide creek feeding into Rich Inlet, Harrison's favorite speckled trout hole. Although named Nixon's Channel on most maps, locals referred to it as Sebastian Cut. Either way, Harrison and his son Dalton had spent years fishing the waters in that creek, and he wondered if he would ever see his son again. Immense depression set in, and Harrison hung his head and began to sob.

"Jesus Christ, what the hell is wrong with you, man? Quit your damn whimpering and pay attention," Jaxson said, slamming his fist into Harrison's shoulder.

"Okay, okay, we're almost there. Ease off the throttle some. See that small creek on the left? Make sure you go in on the south side. There's an oyster bed on the north side. You might want to tilt your motor up some just in case."

As Luke reduced speed to about three knots and steered into the small creek, the gnat attack began again in full force. Even though they were covered in bug spray, the pesky gnats still found their way in and bit into any unsprayed area with vengeance. Just then Harrison realized why nobody was out boating or standing on any of the docks they passed. Along the waterway and maybe a quarter of a mile inland, after a rainstorm, and if there is no wind available, anyone standing outside is fair game for those No-See-Ums. No doubt everyone had retreated to their screened-in porches with their ceiling fans wide open.

The small boat eased into the creek, through a channel no wider than a normal car driveway, for about twenty yards, which then emptied into a small rectangular bay approximately twenty feet by fifty feet. At near high tide, you could not see the bottom of the small bay. The deep bay was teeming with a large school of Red Drum, numbering in the hundreds, that scattered into the adjacent marsh grass as the boat approached.

Harrison could remember sight fishing once in Bradley Creek in the bay next to Airlie Gardens during a high tide, when he came across a huge school of drum nestled within the marsh grass. The drum were not interested in any of the baits or lures he threw their way, but when he reached into his tackle box and pulled out a pack of Danny Joe's Buzz'n Grubs, the drum bite immediately changed. The six-inch ribbed lime green grub with its long curly tail was a bass fishing lure manufactured in Kinston, North Carolina. Harrison vividly remembered tying the

181

recommended Gamakatsu 5/0 offset hook to his fishing line, properly rigged the grub over the hook, and sent out a twenty-five-yard cast. With just a few turns of his reel, there was an explosion in the water, when a hefty thirty-inch drum nailed the grub and took off like a rocket through the marsh grass.

While battling the drum, Harrison could remember seeing a fishing guide with one customer on board, slowly approaching him using a long shaft trolling motor. Once the drum was caught and released back in the water, Harrison had motioned for the guide to pull his boat up next to his. Since he was just a recreational fisherman, he was always respectful to the local guides since they were trying to make a living and needed to produce fish or else social media would eat them alive with negative comments. Harrison had reached into his tackle box and gave the guide two of Danny Joe's grubs and two Gamakatsu hooks. After giving the guide specific instructions on rigging the grub properly, Harrison could remember leaving the bay and looking back to see both men hooked up with huge smiles on their faces.

"Hey, wake up dipshit, where to now?" Jaxson said, bringing Harrison out of his daydream.

"Pull over there on that small patch of sand next to that big piece of driftwood," Harrison directed, pointing off to his right. "Can you see that winding path going up the hill? That leads up to the camp," Harrison said, swatting at the pesky gnats which were once again in full attack mode.

Luke guided the boat onto the sandy bank just as the sun was setting and the gnats set their sights on their newfound victims. No doubt, Harrison thought, it was going to be a long agonizing night fighting off these vampire gnats.

"Does this campsite of yours have a building on it, so we can get away from these damn No-See-Ums?" Jaxson asked, reaching for more bug spray.

"Nope, but there is an old burn barrel up there, where we can start a fire. Hopefully, a fire will help get rid of them," Harrison commented, scratching at his scalp.

"Luke, go on up there and get a fire started. I'll bring our buddy up in a few minutes, along with some gear."

"There's a makeshift picnic table made out of plywood resting on top of a big stump with its corners held up by cinder blocks, where you can store your gear, and keep it out of the sand."

It took several trips, but in about twenty minutes, Jaxson had all the gear out of the boat and sitting on the plywood picnic table. Harrison was ordered to just sit down and not move, while the two cousins quickly gathered firewood. The two men gathered just enough dried wood and some kindling to get a small fire started and stretched out the brown tarp, tying off the four corners to small live oaks trees nearby. The tarp stretched over the makeshift picnic table that was within five feet of the burn barrel. The fire grew, but soon started to dwindle, allowing the gnats to return.

"Guys, you need smoke and lots of it," Harrison interjected, spitting out half a dozen gnats that somehow got lodged in his mouth.

"Go get some marsh grass reeds and get some of those dead palmetto palm limbs. Throw that on the fire and maybe we'll get some relief from these blood suckers. Throw anything that is half dead and half green on the fire," Harrison instructed.

Luke got so mad at trying to pull off some dead palmetto palm limbs, he took out the chainsaw and cut down an entire palm tree down about five feet high and threw the entire tree on the fire.

The tree erupted in flames at first, then bellowed out huge plumes of smoke that choked all three men, but the gnats were driven away for the time being. Seeing the success of this, Jaxson instructed Luke to go cut down as many palm trees as he could. Luke soon returned with five or six palm trees and placed them adjacent to the smoldering fire.

"Did ya bring any of that whiskey with ya, Luke?"

"Yeah, there's a little left, it's in the sack next to ya. But I also brought along our little friend, too."

"Nice bro, fire that pipe up. We'll get stoned and get these yucky gnats stoned too," Jaxson laughed, reaching into his pants pocket for a lighter.

While the two cousins took a few shots and sucked on their pipe, Harrison sat by the fire wondering how he would survive the next day. There's nothing on this island but a bunch of junk. There's no treasure here, nothing but sand, scrap metal and old beer cans. When these two guys eventually find out, there is nothing here, what will they do with him? At this point, not even the onslaught of the pesky gnats bothered him.

Harrison's emotions were raging with dreadful fear. He regretted lying to these monsters. He should have told them the truth. Nothing good ever happens when you lie. If he had told them the truth, he wouldn't be out on this desolate island facing death. Go ahead and tell them the truth now and get this mess over with. He was angry at himself for coming up with the idea of just getting out of the house. How stupid was that? Why drag them out here? They were going to kill him and bury him on his favorite camping site. There is no way out.

He was overcome with negative thoughts. Apprehension and anxiety gripped his soul. Holding his head low and gritting his teeth, he felt so sorry for himself he began to sob. He was defeated. Curling up into a ball to ward off the falling dew, he decided to tell them the truth and face the consequences.

Just when Harrison was at his lowest moment, Jaxson approached with the whiskey bottle in one hand and the pipe in the other.

"Ya wanna hit to keep warm?"

"Just the whiskey. Thanks."

Harrison took a quick shot of the bourbon. It burned.

"Why am I here?" Harrison whispered.

CHAPTER 19

It was six o'clock in the morning when Dalton, Bryson, and Andrea awoke to the wonderful smell of bacon frying in the kitchen. Ms. Kelly was busy preparing breakfast, something she immensely enjoyed as a mother, a wife and especially, as a grandmama. The menu for the hungry crew was eggs over easy, shredded hash browns with grandmama's special seasoning, fluffy biscuits, crisp bacon, grits, and orange juice. Dalton and his mom sat at the L-shaped bar separating the kitchen from the living room, while the grandkids sat facing the television.

Heaven was about to be served as it had been since Andrea and Bryson were babies. It was a meal they relished. There were even times when the grandkids would stay over for longer periods due to holidays, and Ms. Kelly would cook breakfast two and sometimes three times in a day. Even if the grandkids or Dalton weren't at grandmama's house, Ms. Kelly would prepare the same breakfast for Harrison every Saturday.

Bryson and Andrea were on Spring break for the rest of the week, and they decided they would stay with Grandmama the entire week to be by her side to comfort her. Dalton's immediate supervisor suggested he take the rest of the week off also, and it was indeed a great comfort to Ms. Kelly that she found herself surrounded by family. This was the first time that Harrison was not present for one of Ms. Kelly's delicious breakfasts, and the mood that morning was somber, to say the least.

Unbeknownst to anyone, Ms. Kelly prepared a fifth plate, covered it and placed it in the microwave for safe keeping. She had to think positively.

After they completed breakfast, Andrea and Grandmama decided to take a walk around the neighborhood. Dalton and Bryson stayed at the house. Dalton and Bryson traded stories about Harrison, with each trying to outdo the other. Each story got exaggerated, but they didn't care as they brought back wonderful memories. An hour later, Grandmama and Andrea returned, announcing they wanted to watch a scary movie. Dalton and Bryson wanted no part of that, especially since it was only eight o'clock in the morning. Nobody watches scary movies unless it is dark outside, they thought.

Grandmama turned on Netflix, and after scanning through the horror movie category, found one she liked and hit play. Dalton and Bryson looked at each other, then turned towards Andrea and winked at her with silly grins on their faces. They all knew that within fifteen minutes, grandmama would be fast asleep in her favorite chair and would miss the entire movie. Andrea settled into her Paw Paw's recliner, took the remote away from grandmama, and waited. Sure enough, fifteen minutes later, grandmama was fast asleep snoring up a storm, so Andrea stopped the movie on Netflix and switched to a National Geographic documentary about the plight of hunted African elephants.

Dalton and Bryson weren't particularly interested in the documentary, so they walked down the hallway, opened the door, and entered Harrison's office. They wanted to continue with their respective stories and being in Harrison's office seemed to be the best place to do so to avoid the constant snoring of Ms. Kelly. Harrison's office was an eclectic collection of four computer monitors, books, trophies, fishing rods and reels, tools, files, hats, and a variety of pictures showing Harrison's finer moments in life. When outside visitors would enter Harrison's office, they would stand there in amazement, gazing upon the ridiculous number of ball caps he had hung on the wall. Seeing some eighty ball caps neatly arranged around the perimeter of his office was a sight to behold, and to some, a very strange sight to see. Everything was in its place, nice and neat to perfection.

Harrison was proud of his office, and always kept it immaculate. One of Harrison's most cherished items was a framed newspaper article with two photographs from the *Star News,* about the story of his two hole in ones made one month before Dalton was born.

Dalton sat in his Dad's chair, leaning on the desk, while Bryson sat on the floor next to the closet door, admiring his Paw Paw's bass fishing rods. Paw Paw had four G-Loomis IMX custom made medium heavy rods, each outfitted with Shimano Calcutta 151 reels that he bought from Tex's Tackle five years after Dalton was born.

While working for the Sherwin-Williams floor covering division, Harrison had received a large bonus check due to an outstanding quarter of sales providing carpet to hundreds of condos at Carolina Beach that got ravaged by Hurricane Bertha in July 1996 and Hurricane Fran in September of the same year. He used the money to buy the rod and reels, but also his first Lowe Jon boat. When he received another large bonus check due to Hurricane Floyd in 1999, he used that money to take Mom, Dalton, and two neighbors on an all-expense paid two-day trip to the Charlotte Motor Speedway. Although Harrison was known to be a tightwad, at times he could be gracious and generous with his money.

Dalton and Bryson sat there just looking around the museum as they called it, and both began to cry. They really missed him. How many times had they come into this office to visit, to discuss their problems in life, or just come in to see Harrison hard at work, and now he wasn't there? They both felt the huge void in their lives, and it was crushing them.

Why was Paw Paw's office so torn apart? What do you think happened?" Bryson asked Dalton with tears still in his eyes.

"I can't figure that out. It just doesn't make sense. You know and I know that your Paw Paw wasn't a fighter. He hated violence, so he didn't do it."

"What was this person or people looking for?"

"I just don't know. After the cops left and Mom settled down some, I came in here and started to clean up. I did my best to put everything back in place just like your Paw Paw had it. You know your Paw Paw just like I do, EVERYTHING must be in its proper place."

Bryson laughed and said, "Oh yeah, God forbid you didn't put something back in its place. Paw Paw would get so mad." They both laughed through their tears.

Bryson got up from his spot next to the closet door and asked, "Are you sure you put everything back in its place when you cleaned up? Maybe we ought to double check, huh?"

Dalton and Bryson scanned the office once again, and both concluded that everything was in order. Andrea, bored with the documentary she was watching, entered the office asking the guys what they were up to.

"We're just making sure everything is perfect, that everything is in its spot, that's all," Dalton responded.

Andrea was standing at the door, and while looking around, she spotted Paw Paw's gray lightweight sweatshirt draped over something to the left of his office chair in the corner next to his printer. Paw Paw would never leave a coat or jacket just lying around, she thought.

"Hey, look, you best put that sweat jacket in Paw Paw's closet. It doesn't belong there," Andrea said, pointing to the area next to Harrison's printer.

Stunned that they overlooked that, Bryson then reached over and grabbed the jacket and pulled it away from the items it was covering and started to take it to the closet to hang up.

"Holy shit!" Dalton yelled out. "Dad's new metal detector is missing. What the hell?"

"What are you talking about?"

"Look, Dad wrote that book about finding treasure, and in the book, he said he used a brand-new Fisher metal detector, remember? Well, the Fisher company was so pleased about the publicity, they sent dad a brand-new detector. Didn't he tell y'all?"

"No," Andrea replied.

"Yeah, they sent him a brand-new fancy one, a real high-tech model, with golden headphones. And it's not here."

"Why would it be missing?" Bryson asked.

"It makes no sense, no sense at all."

"Do you think we should tell someone about this?" Bryson asked.

"Yeah, I'll call Detective Decker right now."

Dalton called Decker, who in turn passed on the information about the missing detector to Nicole. It was now Tuesday, and everyone knew they were running out of time, and any new clue needed to be thoroughly analyzed. Decker told Dalton not to touch anything, and that he would be there shortly. Decker called Gretchen, who answered on the second ring.

"Why are you calling me at this hour?" Gretchen growled with a sigh.

"Dalton just called and informed me that one of his dad's metal detectors is missing from his office. Maybe it's another clue we need to look at."

"Yeah, you could be right. Call everyone and get our team over there right away,"

"Oh, and tell my assistant to grab the folder sitting on my desk that has all the still photographs we've copied. I'm pretty sure I saw a few with Mr. Thomas clutching a metal detector."

Gretchen jumped out of bed and pulled down the sheet exposing the well-toned naked body of Agent Vickors.

"We gotta go, baby. Get up and get dressed. They found something at Harrison's house we need to investigate," Gretchen said, leaning over grabbing Vickors by his arm.

Twenty minutes later, Harrison's driveway was full of police vehicles. Nicole had spent the night with her parents Earnie and Tammy when the call came in. Sprinting from the house, Nicole, Patrick, and her parents scrambled into Nicole's car, just when their neighbor Lilly approached, wanting to tell them all about her recent trip to Mexico.

"Hey, what's going on? Did somebody get hurt?" Lilly asked.

"We're heading over to Harrison's. We've got a clue," Nicole explained.

"What do you mean, a clue? What the hell are you talking about?"

"While you were in Mexico, Harrison got kidnapped."

"Oh shit, let me come with you."

While Nicole's team was placing Harrison's gray jacket in the evidence bag, Gretchen took the folder of the dozen photographs from her assistant and spread them all over the top of the L-shaped bar desperately looking for that one photo she remembered that clearly showed him with a metal detector in hand.

While Gretchen was filtering through the photos, both Agent Vickors and Detective Decker sat down next to Dalton sitting on the fireplace hearth and asked him about the missing metal detector.

"Hold on a second, I'll be right back," Dalton said, getting up and heading towards his dad's office.

Harrison had a filing cabinet in his office where Dalton knew he kept information pertaining to the metal detector. Harrison maintained a file for everything he purchased in alphabetical order that would contain pamphlets or brochures along with the original sales receipt always stapled to the front of the file folder. A minute later, Dalton returned with the metal detector file folder and pulled out the colored brochure, then handed it to Decker.

"Is this the exact one your dad had? This CZ-21 model?"

"Yeah, it sure is. Dad even had a pair of gold-colored headphones that matched the gold Fisher insignia on the side of the detector casing."

Everybody else milled around the bar, gazing at the photos Gretchen had laid out. Lilly picked up one of the photos and stood at the end of the bar with a stunned look on her face.

"Who took this picture of Luke?"

The room fell totally silent.

"What?" Gretchen yelled out. "You know this guy?"

"Yeah, I sure do. He's my idiot cousin. Why do you have a photograph of him?"

"Dalton found his dad's wallet in a dumpster, and your cousin, we think, put it in there. We think he may have had something to do with Harrison's kidnapping."

For the next fifteen minutes Gretchen and Agent Vickors explained to Lilly the details of Harrison's kidnapping, while she sat at the bar totally befuddled. Gretchen set a tape recorder on the bar while the other team members surrounded Lilly. They felt positive they had found yet another clue, and they needed to pull out as much information from her as they could.

"Tell us everything about your cousin Luke, and give us all the details," Detective Decker asked politely.

"Well, about two years Luke and Jaxson called me...", Lilly didn't even finish her statement.

"Wait, Luke and who?" Decker asked, as the room fell deadly silent once again.

"My two cousins, Luke Clemmons, and Jaxson Cook, called me about two years ago looking for work. The Feds closed their oystering areas down in South Carolina and they wanted to come up here and either fish or work for me, doing some landscaping."

Nicole came forward and opened her laptop and played the video for Lilly, showing two men leaving Diamonds and getting into a beat-up pickup truck.

"Do you recognize the two men and the truck?"

"Yeah, that's them,"

"So, what happened next?" Agent Vickors asked, pushing aside the laptop so he could lean in closer to Lilly.

"I sure as hell didn't want them living with me, so I found them a trailer up in Hampstead...," again Lilly couldn't finish her sentence as Gretchen leaned in and grabbed Lilly's shoulder, spinning her around to face her directly.

"You know the address?"

"I can't remember the street address on Factory Road, but I know where the trailer is."

Nicole leaned in and, with a few clicks on the keyboard of her laptop, she had the Google map site up on the screen showing the Hampstead area in the satellite mode.

"See this large, wooded area about halfway down Factory Road on the left? Well, an old friend of mine used to have a small nursery there and I leased it from her to grow some of my plants and bushes. There's an old dilapidated mobile home in the back that had been vacant for years and my friend was willing to rent it out to my cousins."

After Lilly gave the team a description and directions to the trailer, Gretchen sent a screenshot of the location to her assistant at the office with specific instructions to secure the address, then get a court order for a search warrant. Detective Decker was already out the door headed to Hampstead, calling for backup while in route. Nicole's team would follow but hold their position in the BP gas station until Decker had cleared the trailer.

The whole investigation team was electrified with the information obtained from Lilly. They now felt for certain they would solve the kidnapping crime in a matter of hours. Gretchen and Agent Vickors hammered Lilly, seeking more information for the next hour, waiting to hear back from the court. The pieces of the puzzle were coming together, and Gretchen was going to solve this once and for all. This was a huge break in the case, and Gretchen was going to use every bit of it to her advantage.

Agent Vickors stepped off to the side and called his colleague in Myrtle Beach, anxious to give him the two names of the kidnappers and to see if any information was obtained from the register of deeds search, he requested earlier. Agent Lewis didn't answer his cell phone, so Vickors left him a detailed voicemail, telling him to call him as soon as possible.

Agent Vickors turned and stood mesmerized once again, staring at the medical dissertation contained within the brass frame. He still couldn't get over what he was looking at, and just as perplexing was the word Harrison's brother Rich used at dinner the other evening to describe his brother's personality.

Curiosity got the best of him, and Agent Vickors stepped outside and dialed Rich's cell number. Rich answered on the third ring.

"Rich, this is Agent Vickors. Have you got a minute?"

"Sure do. What's up?"

"What was that word you used the other night that some people use to describe your brother? Sounded like Shannagan or something like that?"

"Yeah, it's Shalogan,"

"What the hell does it mean?"

"Well, you see, my brother and I grew up in Wilmington Delaware, and we spent most of our holidays up in Queens, New York visiting with our mom's family. They were all full-blooded Irish, and a few of the old timers spoke the old Gaelic language. I can remember whenever we would get ready to leave and head back home, some of those older folks would come up and hug everybody and always tell mom in broken English to "watch over that Shalogan boy of yours." I heard that word so many times it just stuck in my head, so I used it a lot to describe him...kind of like a nickname."

"I still don't understand why your relatives used that word."

"Look, my brother was hell on wheels and was wide open from the minute he got up until he went to bed. He was a daredevil who feared nothing, and he took a lot of chances, showing off his athletic abilities like jumping off a two-story house landing in a nearby tree some ten feet away. He was always experimenting and trying to make things better, like tearing down a bicycle and changing out the gears to make it faster."

"Oh, I see now, Shalogan is just a catch-all name to describe someone as if they were a combination of an Evel Knievel and a Steve Jobs."

"Man, you got that right," Rich laughed.

CHAPTER 20

While the paperwork for the court order was being processed, Detective Decker arrived in Hampstead and parked his unmarked car on the shoulder of Factory Road. He was approximately a quarter of a mile from the driveway entrance to the trailer, waiting for backup. In the meantime, he had so much adrenaline running through his body, he had to exit his vehicle and relieve himself before his bladder spilled its contents all over his front seat. Eyeing a large pine tree just five or six yards away in the nearby woods, he jumped across the small drainage ditch, then leaned up against the tree and relieved himself, taking aim at a large spider web next to his feet.

Relieved, Decker turned to head back to his vehicle when he saw a blue and white Hampstead patrol car pull up behind his vehicle. Assuming this was his backup, he held up his badge as he jumped back over the drainage ditch and quickly walked over to the patrol car. The windows of the car were heavily tinted where he could barely see inside. The officer in the car was giving him a thumbs up sign while unlocking the passenger door.

Opening the door, Decker immediately noticed four or five empty protein cartons scattered on the floorboard along with a few empty boxes of sun maid raisins. Sliding into the passenger seat, he turned and leaned over to greet his fellow officer with his right hand extended. He leaned back abruptly and froze.

Officer Opal Turner was a muscular woman in her late twenties, weighing close to one hundred and fifty pounds, with every muscle on her body bulging through her tan shirt and black slacks. Her jet-black hair was pulled tightly back in a bun, with the bottom two inches of her hairline closely shaved, highlighted with three cross crossing edge up lines. Wearing a short sleeve standard beige uniform shirt with the top two buttons undone and with the sleeves rolled up, Decker noticed her ripped biceps that had to be at least four times larger than his. Her thigh and calf muscles filled every square inch of her black cargo slacks. No doubt in his mind she was a bodybuilder, but in a strange way she was rather sexy, Decker thought to himself.

"I'm Opal, Sergeant Turner if you will," she spoke with a slight Asian accent.

"Detective Decker with the New Hanover County Sheriff's Office," he replied, stumbling over his words gazing upon Sergeant Turner's gorgeous face. Her naturally long eyelashes were highlighted by a hint of light blue eye shadow and her voluptuous lips were enhanced with just a touch of pink lip gloss. If he had to describe her looks to someone, he would use the word sultry with a luscious body.

While waiting for the call about the court order, Decker brought Sergeant Turner up to speed. He suggested she load up her Mossberg shotgun that was holstered between them next to her mounted computer. Sergeant Turner explained to him she was aware of the location of the trailer. She further noted that just up the road, on the left side about one hundred yards there was a narrow-wooded trail that also led to the trailer, that would provide them sufficient cover.

Sergeant Turner, with her shotgun in hand, stepped out first, and before Decker could even close his door, she was already fifteen yards down the road, waving to him to follow her. He tried to catch up with her as best he could, amazed at her speed and

198

agility. Decker finally caught up with her and two minutes later, they reached the entrance to the small, wooded trail. Both slowed their advance and after a short hike, they had the trailer in sight. The old trailer was only twenty yards in front of them. Crouching together behind a cluster of wax myrtle bushes with weapons drawn, they sat motionless, anxiously waiting for the call to proceed legally via the search warrant.

Decker and Sergeant Turner were hunched down, shoulder to shoulder, where Decker could smell her perfume. Sergeant Turner could hear Decker slowly breathe in through his nose, so she turned, giving him a broad smile showing off her perfect brilliant white teeth. Looking over at her golden light brown complexion and physique, Decker, for a moment forgot what he was doing and started to get aroused. Not missing a beat, Opal turned just a few inches to her right, then leaned over just a tad allowing Decker to get a full view down her shirt.

Back at Harrison's house, Agent Vickors and Gretchen continued to push Lilly for more information. The clues were coming together, and the adrenaline rush was kicking in amongst the team members. Agent Vickor's intuition told him he was close to solving the case.

"When was the last time you saw or spoke to your cousins?" asked Agent Vickors.

"I think it was last Friday afternoon, maybe around five or six o'clock, at my house. I was getting ready to head out to the airport when they knocked on my door."

"What did they want?" asked Gretchen.

"Oh my God, they did it!" Lilly uttered, dropping her head on the bar.

"What do you mean they did it? Did what?" Vickors said, shaking her arm.

"Look, they were both so angry. They had just come in from oystering and were unloading their boat at Mason's Marina and apparently ran into Harrison. He was trying to offload his boat, I guess at the same time. They must have gotten into some sort of altercation, 'cause they bad mouthed the hell out of him and wanted to know if I knew him," Lilly explained, with tears running down her cheeks now.

"So, what exactly happened at the dock?" Gretchen asked.

"They really didn't say anything about that, they said stuff like... "He thinks he owns the damn place" ... "What an arrogant asshole" .... "His fancy boat" ... "He looked like a clown, stuff like that.""

"So, no physical fight broke out, no punches thrown?" asked Agent Vickors.

"No, I don't think so. They just wanted to find out who Harrison was. They sure were upset and jealous."

"Did you tell them you knew Harrison?" Gretchen asked.

Lilly was feeling guilty and could not continue speaking, once again laying her head on the bar sobbing. After a few minutes, with her voice a bit shaky, she continued with her recollection of what took place.

"Oh God, I messed up. I told them about how Harrison wrote a novel and got rich from it."

"Okay, what happened next?" asked Agent Vickors.

"I went to my den and got the book to give it to them to read, but they rejected it since they don't know how to read very well. So, I gave them a brief, I guess you would say, book report on the novel. I remember their reaction was not very positive. They thought the story content was plain junk and just not believable at all." She caught her breath then continued. "Jaxson, to my surprise, took the book with him anyway when they left."

"Did you at any time tell them where Harrison lived?"

"Oh God, oh God, I did. I didn't know the address, so I told them he lived around the corner on Marlin Court, in the only house on the street with the green front door. Oh God, what have I done?" she stammered, choking on her words.

"All right, calm down, and tell us what happened next," Gretchen spoke up, resting her hand on Lilly's shoulder.

"I remember them saying they were going to sell the oysters they had in the boat to some local customers in the Sound and then head up to Diamonds before heading back to Hampstead. They stunk so bad, I told them to take a shower before they left, which they did. They changed into some fresh T-shirts my son had in the house after showering, then they left, and about twenty minutes later, I left for the airport. I was on my way to Mexico to see how the repair work was going with my condo in Puerto Escondido."

Gretchen went over to the bar and picked up several blown-up photographs taken by the video camera in the Diamonds parking lot and placed them in front of Lilly.

"Are you absolutely sure this is the truck they were driving when they left your house?" Gretchen asked.

"Yep, that's it, they were upset when they left. I mean they had blood in their eyes. Their anger was scary."

"Do they have any weapons that you know of?" Agent Vickors asked.

"Oh, hell ya. They've got an arsenal of guns..." Lilly didn't even finish her statement when Gretchen held out her hand, instructing her to stop talking, and immediately dialed Decker's cell phone.

"They're packing man, be damn careful," Gretchen told Decker.

"Got it, What about the court order? We are ready to go."

Gretchen and Agent Vickors escorted Lilly out of the kitchen, directing her into Harrison's office to interrogate her more in private. They knew the first set of questions would not reveal everything, so they wanted to probe more away from the family. Lilly was subject to question after question, to the point she felt she might be a suspect, and it really made her angry.

"Hey, fuck you, assholes," Lilly bellowed, bringing out her New York brogue. "Do you really think I had anything to do with this shit?" Lilly sternly asked.

"Possibly," answered Gretchen.

"For Christ's sake, I was out of town, and I've got proof," Lilly said, slamming her fist on the desk.

Nicole, not missing the opportunity, stepped out into the hallway and called her assistant at the office, instructing her to research Lilly's plane ticket purchases and confirm her travel itinerary. Within minutes, it came back, verifying everything she had explained to the tee. Ten minutes later, Nicole came back into the office and nodded to Gretchen, letting her know that Lilly was telling the truth. But Gretchen still had her suspicions that maybe Lilly planned the whole thing and was using the Mexico trip as a cover.

Agent Vickors' cell phone rang, bringing him the much-anticipated news on the status of the search warrant. The judge had just signed it and copies were being sent to everyone's cellphones and Nicole's laptop.

"It's a go Gretchen," Agent Vickors yelled out, rolling his hand in a circular motion. "Move, move now."

Gretchen dialed Decker's cell phone and relayed the information.

"Be careful, remember these guys are heavily armed."

Decker removed his jacket, not wanting his sports coat to impede his movements, and nodded to Sergeant Turner. Tense and nervous, this was Decker's first search and potential seizure of a potentially armed individual. He released the safety on his Glock. Both prepared to storm the trailer. Opal leaned in towards Decker and gently placed her lips against Decker's ear while placing her right hand on his thigh.

"Let's get jiggy with it, big boy," Opal whispered, rubbing her lips softly against his ear.

They agreed that Decker would take down the front door first, while Turner would take her position guarding the back door. Decker, hunched down with his Glock racked and chambered, moved quickly towards the trailer. He stepped onto the front deck, approached the front door, and gently pushed away the broken screen door, and with one swift kick, slammed the front door open.

"Police, don't move," he shouted standing about five feet into the living room. Sergeant Turner followed in through the back door and stood in the kitchen facing him. Both were flooded with adrenaline and sweat gathered on their foreheads. They cleared each room, shouting out to each other.

"Clear here, clear here."

Within three minutes, the trailer was clear, and no suspects were found. Lowering their weapons, Decker called Gretchen and told her no one was in the trailer.

Gretchen called Nicole to send her team to the trailer with instructions to scope out the entire area. She then called Decker on his cell phone.

"Search that damn trailer from top to bottom and then scope out the property for any clues and let me know if you come across anything."

Decker and Sergeant Turner combed the trailer, starting with the back master bedroom. They turned over the bed, pulled out all the drawers and dropped the contents on the floor, and pulled down the items hanging in the closet. With nothing found, they moved on to the next bedroom and executed the same procedure. Once again, they found nothing. Moving on into the living room, the results were the same. The last area to scope out was the small kitchen. On the table was Harrison's book with several pages torn out, a bottle of bourbon and an old AAA road map.

"Holy shit, look at this," Decker said, resting his index finger on the map.

"What is it?" Turner asked.

"Look, this small island, it has been circled three or four times with a pen."

"So what, these guys are oyster junkies and maybe they're marking a new spot to fish at."

"Maybe, maybe not. I just don't know that for sure. Why are there pages torn out of this book? Let's check outside and scope out the property and see what we find," Decker said as he hurried out the back door, followed by Turner.

The backyard looked like a dump with beer cans scattered all around an old fire barrel and two green and white lawn chairs that looked like something popular back in the 1950s. In the back corner of the lot, engulfed with vines and branches from a massive bayberry tree, they noticed a shed at least twenty feet by twenty feet, with half the roof missing. The double door was not locked, so Decker grabbed one side and Turner grabbed the other. It took a little effort, but eventually they got the doors to swing open, letting the sunlight in.

A large object was covered with an old brown tarp. Decker grabbed the edge and removed the tarp with one pull.

"Well, lookie here."

"What is it?" Opal asked.

"I am almost positive it is the truck we got on video the night before Harrison got kidnapped. If it is, we know these guys brought Harrison here."

Decker sent the photos to Gretchen, Nicole, and Agent Vickors. Within minutes he got his confirmation.

Decker and Turner continued their walk around in the backyard, and not finding anything, decided to quit their search.

"Appreciate your help, Opal, but there is no sense in you sticking around. Our forensic team is on the way, and they'll take over from here. I'll wait till they get here; you go on."

"Are you sure you don't want me to stick around?" Sergeant Turner asked in a seemingly provocative manner.

As much as he would enjoy taking the opportunity to spend some time to get to know Opal, he needed to stay on task and do his job.

"Nah, you go on, I'll call ya later."

"Oh, by the way, what is your cell number?"

Sergeant Turner reached into her top pocket and pulled out one of her business cards and handed it to Decker, giving him a slight wink. He placed the card in his wallet, trying to decide if her little wink was a come-on signal or not. Watching Opal head back down the trail, Decker envisioned a romp in the sack with her where she would probably twist him up like a pretzel.

As soon as the Sergeant was out of sight, Decker went back inside the trailer and headed straight for the kitchen. He knew that he was about to do something that could get him fired, but he would cross that bridge later as he gathered up the tattered book and the old map. He needed to get this information to

Gretchen and Agent Vickors right away, regardless of the consequences.

Decker, daydreaming about Opal, walked back down the small gravel trail leading to Factory Road, and nearly got run over by a car when he failed to stop at the paved road. The near hit brought him back to earth and he safely crossed over the road when he saw Nicole and her team in their unmarked van heading his way. He flagged them down.

"You better wear masks when you go in there, it stinks to high heaven. I saw signs of someone's blood in the living room and kitchen, so I hope you brought along your luminol."

"Any sign of Harrison?" Nicole asked.

"No, no sign of him or the other guys."

"I'm going to call in the K9 unit just in case and see if we get a hit on Harrison," Nicole said while reaching for her cell phone.

"Oh cool, so you are going to bring in Rin Tin Tin, huh? Great idea, I must say. Let me know what you find out. I'm headed back to Harrison's," Decker said, tapping on the side of the van and pointing to the gravel driveway.

Nicole and her team looked at Decker like he was crazy.

"Decker, who is Rin Tin Tin?"

"Oh, you kids missed some of the greatest shows ever broadcast on television. You might want to Google *The Adventures of Rin Tin Tin, The Rifleman, Wagon Train or Bonanza* and watch a few episodes to see what you missed. Put down your silly video games that teach you nothing and watch some good stuff."

He watched the van turn onto the gravel driveway and once out of sight, jumped in his car, and headed back towards Middle Sound. He was perplexed and struggled to put all the pieces together. All the clues and leads gathered so far had brought him to the trailer, but nobody was there and still no sign of his buddy Harrison.

Decker arrived back at Harrison's house within fifteen minutes, more confused than ever. Sitting in the car with the AC running wide open, he took out his notepad and started to list the pertinent information he had in chronological order. He had a gut feeling they were all so close to solving the kidnapping, but he was lacking that one key component: Why?

CHAPTER 21

While Director Nicole and her team were scouring over the contents of the trailer and the dilapidated shed, Detective Decker gathered up his notes and headed inside Harrison's house. He found everyone gathered in the living room. Gretchen and Agent Vickors had spread out all the evidence gathered so far and placed the packets of information, in chronological order, on the living room floor in front of the fireplace. Seeing his opportunity, Decker walked over to the last pile on the right, reached in his jacket and pulled out the stolen evidence, and placed it on the floor. Gretchen and Agent Vickors looked at each other completely stunned and then turned towards Decker with their eyes wide open. They immediately knew this was stolen evidence that should have been left on site for the forensic people to deal with. This wasn't the time or place to scold the rookie detective, so both kept their thoughts and comments to themselves for the time being.

"I want each of you separately to start here at the beginning and proceed to the end," Gretchen said, standing over the first pile.

"Look at everything carefully and when you're done, we want to hear your thoughts and comments," Agent Vickors added.

While the family members and friends, one by one, viewed the evidence on the floor, Gretchen angrily motioned to Decker and Agent Vickors to follow her into Harrison's office. Decker knew what was coming, and he was prepared for it.

"You damn idiot!" Gretchen grunted, clenching her teeth together.

Vickors stepped forward but was abruptly stopped by Gretchen's outstretched arm.

"Thank God there isn't a lawyer out there in that room. We'd be crucified. Are you deliberately trying to sabotage my investigation by taking evidence from a possible crime scene? You have broken all the rules here, and you're going to pay for it," Gretchen added, looking over at Agent Vickors for backup.

"Look, did you really want Nicole to get her hands on that and have it tied up for days in her labs? Did you really want her to have this significant evidence and solve this before you do?"

Decker knew this would calm Gretchen down but dealing with Agent Vickors might be a different story. He was strictly a by the book law enforcement officer, and one word from him to his superiors could end his career. Agent Vickors stepped closer to Decker and was about to speak up when Gretchen grabbed his elbow and ushered him out into the hallway whispering something in his ear. Decker couldn't hear her words, but for now he knew his superiors wouldn't be notified. Decker also remembered and found some comfort, visualizing another phrase he saw pinned to Harrison's office wall "*The young man knows the rules, but the old man knows the exceptions.*" Agent Vickors could just go *chinga* himself.

A few minutes later, they joined the others in the living room and were anxiously awaiting any response from the family members. To her dismay, they were fumbling all over each other, making a total mess of the evidence that was placed in front of them. The group did as they were told, but Gretchen was not satisfied, as no one brought forth any new information or relevant conclusions. She was convinced in her mind that someone in that room knew something that would provide a clue. No one was to be trusted.

When Gretchen's cell phone rang, she held up her right hand, indicating to everyone to be quiet. They stopped what they were doing and focused all their attention on Gretchen.

"Go ahead," was all Gretchen said as she nervously paced around in a small circle.

"What do you mean, it's dead?" shrieked Gretchen into her phone.

Several pots and dishes crashed to the floor in the kitchen when Ms. Kelly briefly fainted and collapsed on top of them. Andrea rushed over and knelt beside her grandmama, demanding that someone needed to hand her a bottle of water and a cold rag. A few minutes later, with the help of Dalton and Bryson, they had Ms. Kelly sitting up, resting her back against the kitchen cabinets.

"Oh God, he's dead," wailed Ms. Kelly as everyone stood around confused at her statement.

"What are you talking about, grandmama?" Andrea asked with a bewildered look on her face.

"I heard what officer Gretchen said. She said he was dead, right?"

Gretchen pushed through the small group, and sat next to Ms. Kelly. She placed her hand on her shoulder in a comforting gesture.

"Ma'am, I said, it's dead, not he's dead. I was referring to the information given to me by Nicole that the K9 dogs lost the scent, and it was dead, in the sense that they had reached a dead end. You must have misinterpreted me, I'm so sorry for that."

"Okay folks, we've got some new information, so let's focus and move on. According to Officer Nicole, the dogs got a solid hit on Harrison's scent inside the trailer.

"We definitely know he was there at some point, but obviously they have moved on somewhere else," Gretchen explained, ushering everyone back into the living room.

"Come on people, let's do this again," she ordered, raising her voice an octave. "Take your time and tell me what your thoughts are."

Gretchen bent down and knelt before the pile of evidence in the first row and signaled to each person to come examine the evidence. She guided each one individually, from one pile to the other, asking each one if they noticed anything that would help solve the kidnapping. When nobody came forward with any new ideas or thoughts, Gretchen walked outside onto the back porch, shaking her head in defeat. She knew there had to be a clue, and she knew from her training that all crimes revealed a key clue at some point that led to the resolution of the crime committed.

Agent Vickors joined Gretchen on the back porch and offered a suggestion.

"Let's mix up the evidence on the floor and not put it in logical order. Instead of laying things out A to Z, let's throw them a total curve ball and see what happens. Go in there and really mix things up. You must realize these folks don't think the way we do. You're trying to get them to follow our methodical train of thought, which to them is not a normal way of thinking."

In desperation, Gretchen returned to the living room, and as Agent Vickors suggested, she shuffled all the evidence into multiple piles that followed no sense of chronological order at all. In her mind, she had just presented the group a hodgepodge of hieroglyphics that they surely would not comprehend.

"Okay folks, sorry to do this, but I need y'all to look at this one more time."

At first the family members rejected Gretchen's request, but, to everyone's surprise, Ms. Kelly stepped forward and took the initiative to follow Gretchen's lead. Soon after, the other family members joined in with newfound intensity.

To her amazement, the group, in a totally different approach, started to review the evidence with keen enthusiasm. Moving pieces of paper around to form their own piles to support their theory. Their shared conversations amongst themselves indicated to Gretchen and Agent Vickors that maybe this curve ball was working. The group continued their examination of the evidence. Soon arguments and shouting matches erupted as each one had a different theory about the kidnapping. Gretchen needed to take control of the situation before things got out of hand.

"All right, hold on a minute. Come into the kitchen and tell me, one at a time, what you think. Keep it simple and to the point."

One by one, each expressed their opinion to Gretchen on how and why the kidnapping took place. After listening to each one and without saying anything, Gretchen dismissed all the theories presented. None of them made any sense, but she thanked everyone.

Gretchen returned to the living room and found Agent Vickors staring at the picture frame once again. Even though he was given a full explanation of its origin earlier, he just couldn't believe someone would take the time to do this. Over his twenty-three-year career as a law enforcement officer, he met many strange people. He was able to solve all the cases he worked on, but this chart was pure insanity beyond his comprehension. If they found Harrison alive, his first conversation with him would be to understand the reason for such a strange writing.

"Is this actually real, or a gag?" Agent Vickors asked, turning to face Gretchen.

Gretchen paid no attention to Vickors, as she had noticed the only person that did not join her in the kitchen was Bryson, Harrison's grandson. He was still in the living room on his hands and knees, moving papers around making his own piles. He would stand up, move to the side to grab a piece of paper, then fall back onto his knees, and place a piece of paper on a pile; stand back up to pick up another piece of paper and once again kneel on his knees placing the evidence on another pile. Bryson was humming to himself, orchestrating his moves. The humming caught the attention of everyone standing in the kitchen, and they fell silent, watching in awe as Bryson was surely on to something. The humming continued and got even louder. Over the next five minutes Bryson accelerated his organizing movements almost into a frenzy. The entire time he held Decker's stolen evidence in his left hand.

Bryson suddenly drew himself up to his full height and bellowed, "I know where Paw Paw is. I know exactly where he is!"

"What the hell does this seventeen-year-old kid think he knows," Gretchen thought to herself. "No way I will be outdone by some young punk."

Agent Vickors quickly turned his attention away from the picture frame and approached Bryson. He bent down on one knee, then placed his hand on Bryson's shoulder. He could feel the young man was trembling.

"Okay son, stay calm and tell me what you've got. What do you see here?"

Even Gretchen could see that Bryson was struggling to speak, and she thought about consoling him herself, but before she could, Dalton pushed by her and sat down next to Bryson. Dalton motioned to Agent Vickors to stand back and extended his palm outward, stopping the rest of the folks from coming in too close. Dalton reached over and patted Bryson on the back, telling him to relax and take a deep breath.

"Okay, how do you know where your Paw Paw is at?" Dalton softly asked.

The living room was deathly silent, and nobody moved a muscle. With his back facing toward the fireplace and still kneeling, Bryson took a deep breath, then cleared his throat.

"Okay, follow along with me," Bryson said as he then motioned everyone to come closer. With a slight tremor to his voice, he began his presentation by showing everybody his assembled piles, laid out in chronological order. He labeled the piles from one to nine in bright red ink. Bryson picked up the pile labeled one and began.

"One, Beth said the cousins were really angry, right?" Everyone nodded in agreement.

"Two, we know they were at Diamonds driving that red truck the night before the book signing, right?" Again, all nods.

"Three, they had to know about the book signing and the time because there were notices plastered all over the place at Diamonds, right?" Silence.

"Four, Paw Paw's wallet is found in Hampstead and his detector is missing." More nods.

"Five, Lilly then told us where the cousins' trailer is at."

Everybody nodded yes.

"Six, Detective Decker brings us a copy of Paw Paw's book with pages torn out found at the cousin's trailer. Those pages were the next-to-last chapter of the book in which Paw Paw explained in detail all the treasure he found that made him rich. Pounds and pounds of gold and silver coins, jewelry, etc. Remember?"

A few nods of agreement followed.

"Seven, Paw Paw never revealed in the book the location of his find, did he? He told me, while writing the story, that he did not want to reveal the location, but keep it a secret, and let people try to guess where it was at." A few "Ohs" could be heard.

"Eight, Now look at this map with the circles on it," Bryson said, handing the old AAA map to Earnie.

"Nine, it's our camping site isn't it?" Bryson asked, raising his eyebrows.

"Holy shit, he's right, it *is* our camping site," Earnie bellowed, handing the map to his buddy Patrick. He took one look and nodded in agreement, while slipping the map into his back pocket and covering it with his T-shirt.

"So, you're saying that your Paw Paw is on some island? It doesn't make any sense?" Agent Vickors asked, stepping closer to Bryson.

Bryson then stood up and paced back and forth in front of the fireplace. He stopped and turned his attention directly toward Detective Decker.

"When you were at the trailer, did you see any boats in the yard?"

"None."

"Exactly, just as I thought. Listen, it makes a lot of sense. There is no doubt in my mind that these two idiots believed that Paw Paw did, in fact, find some kind of treasure somewhere and sometime in the past. They believed Paw Paw's novel was a true story of him finding treasure while metal detecting, not some fictitious story. They really thought Paw Paw has treasure or money stashed in his house or somewhere nearby. So, they kidnapped him and all along Paw Paw has been leaving us clues."

"Hold on. I'm still a bit confused with..." Agent Vickors couldn't finish his question when Dalton leaned in and told him to shut up and let Bryson finish. Decker smiled to himself.

"These guys tore up the house looking for something, right?" Bryson asked, looking around at everyone. "They obviously didn't find anything and no doubt in my mind, Paw Paw tricked them into getting out of the house. And then he left us the biggest clue he could think of that would lead us straight to his location."

Everybody just stood there looking at each other, trying to figure out what the hell Bryson was referring to. His whole story wasn't making any sense.

"Grandmama, what was the one thing Paw Paw *always* brought with him when we went camping on the island?'

"His white Russians," Kelly answered. Everyone laughed at her response.

"No, not that, the other thing. He always took his metal detector with him, right?"

"Yeah, you're right," Ms. Kelly exclaimed, clearly understanding where Bryson was going with his explanation.

"Look, Paw Paw always told us that he had a feeling, a notion that something valuable was on that island. That's why he always brought his detector with him. He was obsessed with that notion and was determined to find something. That's the big clue he left behind for us to find. It all makes perfect sense now. With the missing metal detector, the circles on that map, and no boat in the yard, I know they've got him in a boat, heading for the island, and we need to get there quickly."

Everybody stood there stunned, realizing that the logical conclusion Bryson had just laid out to them made absolute sense. They were amazed at how such a young kid was so methodical in his approach to solve the kidnapping, which had totally outsmarted the professionals. Grandmama Kelly, with tears in her eyes, walked over and hugged her grandson and soon everybody gathered around Bryson, offering their own warm congratulations.

"Okay, I'll call the Coast Guard and Marine Patrol and have them check out this island, and we'll get our helicopter out there also," said Agent Vickors.

"Hell no, don't do that," Earnie interjected. "It'll spook 'em and they might take Harrison down. Are you out of your mind? I've got a better idea."

Agent Vickors and Gretchen looked at each other puzzled. They shrugged their shoulders and asked Earnie to explain his plan.

"First, let's make sure Harrison really is there, in another way, that won't scare these clowns. My son is on his way to the airport right now getting ready to take his second solo flight, so hold on. Let me call him to get him to change his flight plan to fly directly over the island. If he spots any activity, he'll call us."

Earnie winked at his buddy Patrick, and both men headed for the front door without saying a word. They knew each other so well after serving in the Army for some twenty-seven years together that words were not needed. They knew that Bryson was right, and it was time to take matters into their own hands to help their buddy Harrison, who no doubt was in deep trouble.

"Where the hell do you think you're going?" Gretchen asked, stepping toward the front door. Her gut was telling her these guys were up to no good, and she wasn't about to have her investigation tampered with again.

Detective Decker had spent many hours listening to Earnie and Patrick's war stories, to know exactly what they were thinking and what they were about to do. He needed to accompany them to provide some sort of police presence as all hell was about to be unleashed on that island. Decker walked over to Gretchen and whispered something in her ear, patting her on the shoulder. He headed out the front door, catching up with Earnie and Patrick, who were about to jump into Earnie's truck parked across the street.

"So, we're really gonna do this, huh?" Decker inquired, asking both men.

"Damn right, and don't get in our way," responded Patrick with a stern look as the three men piled into Earnie's truck.

"So, what did you say to that bitch when we were leaving?" asked Earnie.

"I kinda told her the truth that you guys might try and "go Army" and I would keep y'all in check and report back to her."

"HOOAH"

CHAPTER 22

Nightfall on the island was utterly miserable for the three men. There was not a breath of air on the sandy knoll to ward off the constant attack of the gnats and the relentless onslaught kept everyone awake for hours. Throughout the night, Luke and Jaxson alternated throwing green palm leaves on the fire, trying to smoke them out, but their efforts provided no relief whatsoever. In fact, it made it worse as the heavy dew captured the smoke, holding it near the ground, making breathing difficult. Finally, around three thirty in the morning, a gentle breeze from the north swept over the island. It began to disrupt the invasion and pushed the smoke off into the trees. By about four o'clock a.m., the breeze got strong enough for all three to drift off in much needed sleep.

If the men thought the night before was bad fighting off the pesky gnats, they were in for a rude awakening, as the sun began to rise over the ocean, casting a gorgeous orange glow over the island. Another air force, what some locals called May flies and others called just biting black flies, set their sights on the unprotected slumbering men on the sandy knoll. The invasion did not come like the multitude of the gnats that would show up by the thousands. Oh no, these cunning kamikaze insects were solo and totally silent in their attack mode, not buzzing or flipping all over the place, but totally stealth in their search for blood. It was as if their tiny feet were covered in mini-Novocaine pads, because you would never feel them land on you.

Their favorite target were ankles, and if those were covered with socks, they would move on to their next favorite target, which was the backside of one's elbow. If the unassuming victim happened to be wearing a long sleeve shirt and socks, the attack would take place on the back side of one's ear. Many a fishermen came home deaf from slapping their ears so hard reacting to the vicious bite. Even if you did happen to pop one with a perfect slap, sending the wounded fly to the ground, it would still be flapping its wings spinning around like a top. And when you then stomped on its ass, you'd see your blood splatter all over the place. There was not a single bug spray known to man that would repel these mini vampires.

Crippled with fatigue, Harrison struggled to open his eyes. Staring into the darkness, he tried to lift his head, but the movement sent shockwaves of pain throughout his body. He let his head fall back down. Sheer panic rattled his mind when he realized his head was not on his own pillow, but something that felt like sand. Crazy and horrible images flashed in his brain making no sense at all. The panic escalated causing him to hyperventilate, and he lost consciousness.

Suddenly, Harrison felt himself being lifted off the ground into a standing position. There was just enough early morning light for him to instantly take a panoramic view of his surroundings. He had no idea where he was. Scared, he urinated all over himself. But his earlier panic turned into raging anger when he recognized the man gripping his shoulders. It was him, the devil himself.

The beast of a man turned and walked away. More images and memories filled Harrison's brain. Another man appeared creating an image of a garden hose. He was yelling at Harrison to start digging.

"Yo, Luke, bring that asshole over here," Harrison heard in the distance.

"Hey Jaxs, where did you put that bottle of bug spray at?"

As if turning on a light switch, at that moment, the memory of the last few days became crystal clear. He was on the island, fearing for his life, but he had a plan.

Just a few hours ago, before the deep fatigue carried him off to sleep, Harrison had laid on his back and let the oncoming gentle breeze ease his mind. Staring into the heavens, he felt as though the magnificent distant specs of flickering light were whispering to him. They were within arm's reach. Venus stroked his forehead and he succumbed to her gentle caress. She told him he was going to live. Orion appeared and strangely spoke to him in old Gaelic; *"Oh, how I pray that dragon will turn 'round so that I may smite it."* It was crystal clear now.

He knew why he was on the island. He knew why he brought these men to this location. The secret of the island would soon rear its ugly head. He would use the terrifying secret to survive. Just before falling into a deep sleep, Harrison envisioned his plan step by step.

During the night, Harrison dreamed that he was awakened in the morning with FBI agents standing over him, as they were handcuffing the two cousins. He had been found and would soon be reunited with his family. Dejected that it was only just a dream, Harrison now had to face reality knowing in just a few hours the cousins would realize he had been lying to them all along.

Did his dream foretell that someone was coming for him? How were these two men going to react once they knew they had been lied to? Would they, in a fit of anger, just kill him? Harrison had to fight hard to erase the negative thoughts that were once again creeping into his mind. Stick with the plan, it will work.

Harrison could hear seagulls screeching off in the distance. Down at the bay where they beached the boat, he could see the two men wrestling with the gill net at the end of their boat. Apparently, there were a few dead fish still caught in the net and throwing them out into the water caught the attention of a dozen hungry seagulls. The black flies were relentless in their attack on the two cousins, and Harrison found it quite comical watching them slap themselves repeatedly, while cursing up a storm.

Luke fired up the motor, put the boat in reverse, then pulled away from the shoreline and headed out through the narrow creek towards the waterway. About twenty yards out from the mouth of the creek, Harrison could see Luke setting the gill net across the entrance into the creek. With half a dozen empty white Clorox bottles tied to the top edge of the net, anyone familiar with the local waters could see that the entrance was blocked by a fishing net. Obviously, their intent was to block off and completely ward off any intruders from entering the creek.

Harrison desperately needed some coffee. He was developing a massive headache from the lack of caffeine. He normally drank three or four cups every morning as part of his routine to activate the Metamucil he took the night before. The pounding headache was clogging his ability to think clearly, and he needed a clear head to execute his plan. He was going to escape from the clutches of these two men. Failure was not an option. Although his mobility was severely hampered, and he had no weapon to defend himself, he would survive.

Fueled with thoughts of his family and friends Harrison found new vigor and confidence in his planned escape. A newfound strength was swelling through his battered body. He could see himself sitting at the breakfast table with his grandkids devouring Grandmama's delicious bacon and eggs. He envisioned a fishing trip with his son Dalton pulling in a big, speckled trout.

Jaxson remained standing on the bank of the small bay while Luke stretched the gill net out well over fifty yards, completely blocking the entrance into the creek. Jaxson gave Luke a thumbs up, then headed back up to the campsite to check on Harrison.

Luke anchored the gill net then headed back up the small channel where he beached the boat adjacent to the sandy trail. He gathered up the shovels, along with the metal detector and walked up the trail to join his cousin who was sitting by the fire.

"Okay, slick, time for you to get to work. Fire up that machine of yours and let's get digging," Jaxson ordered.

"You've got to untie my hands. I need my hands free to work the detector."

Jaxson and Luke looked at each other, trying to decide what to do. Luke shrugged his shoulders and Jaxson nodded, indicating to each other that it was a reasonable request. Jaxson placed his shotgun against a small tree stump and approached Harrison cautiously while flipping open his six-inch Buck knife. Jaxson glared into Harrison's eyes for a moment, then reached out and cut Harrison's hands free with a short flick of his wrist. He placed the tip of his knife blade directly into Harrison's right nostril, and gave it a slight turn, drawing blood.

"Don't you dare think about doing anything stupid asshole, or I'll cut your balls off," Jaxson said, now resting the blade against Harrison's right testicle.

It took a few minutes for the full feeling to come back into Harrison's hands so he could handle the detector. Strapping the cup handle to his forearm with the attached Velcro straps, he looked down at the four knobs on his Fisher detector screen and right then and there, an idea popped into his head that possibly could buy him some more time. He knew these guys would have no idea how to operate the detector and he knew how to adjust the knobs so that they would create a constant high pitched beeping sound blaring out of the speakers. After a few turns and twists, the detector responded with a series of short beeps, a pause, and then another set of high-pitched beeps.

"What the hell is that noise?" Luke asked.

"The friggin' batteries must be dead. It takes four 9 Volt batteries. Have you got some in the boat?"

"Hell, no. What do you mean the batteries are dead? Let me see that thing," Jaxson ordered.

Jaxson snatched the detector away from Harrison and opened the battery compartment casing and after seeing that one of the batteries was missing, he backhanded Harrison across his face, sending Harrison to the ground.

"Where did you hide the battery, asshole?" Jaxson demanded, standing over Harrison ready to strike his captive another vicious blow.

"I always take one out after using it just in case I accidentally leave it in the on position. I forgot about that when we were leaving the house."

Jaxson grabbed Harrison by the neck and pulled him up close, face to face. The rage in Jaxson's eyes foretold that another beating was about to be unleashed, but Luke grabbed Jaxson's shoulder and pulled him back.

"Wait a minute," Luke uttered. "We don't need this damn thing, anyway."

Turning towards Harrison, Luke's nostrils flared wide open, and Harrison could see he had pure evil in his eyes. Seeing his pupils glaze over and turn completely black, void of any color, Harrison shook with fear and uncontrollably wet his pants again. Luke curled his upper lip, contorting his face into a sneer that looked just like that of Sir Anthony Hopkins in the movie *The Silence of the Lambs*. Luke reached out and squeezed Harrison's swollen eyebrow squirting blood onto Luke's hand. Harrison stood in horror watching the demented man lick the blood off his hand.

"You know exactly where to start digging, don't you? You don't need this contraption. Quit stalling and pick up that shovel and start digging now," Luke ordered, spewing spittle laced with blood all over Harrison's face.

Now or never, it was time. What he envisioned earlier was about to become reality. His goal was to dig a wide hole, get down about three feet, and then stall the digging by asking for some water. If both men turned away for just a split second, he would drive the shovel straight down, cutting through the zip ties and set his ankles free. Just one perfectly placed strike would at least make him mobile enough to maneuver. If that succeeded, he would tell one of them to head out and get the keys to the safe deposit box. Should one of them do so, Harrison knew the playing field would shift strongly in his favor. There would only be two people left on the island. Giving him a better opportunity to escape.

It was during the second camping trip that Harrison took with the neighborhood group, where a frightening incident took place that nearly cost the life of Earnie's son. After their campsite was set up, the men decided to explore the adjacent tiny island while the women were busy preparing the afternoon lunch. On the north side of the bay leading out into the marsh, Wyatt had noticed a small shallow creek with a sandy bottom which he thought to be a prime area for clamming. There was also some sort of radio beacon or transmitter mounted on a pole, about fifteen yards up in the creek, that he wanted to go check out.

The men crossed the small bay and beached the boat just on the edge of the small creek. Wyatt removed his sneakers, slid overboard, and began to wade out into the creek, inching his toes along the bottom feeling for clams usually found just a few inches below the surface. He moved slowly up the creek, about ten yards from the anchored boat, when, in a split second, the bottom dropped out from under him, and he was completely stuck in the sand up to his waistline and sinking and sinking fast.

In sheer panic, Wyatt screamed for his Dad. Harrison stood there in total amazement as Earnie, Patrick, and Earnie's other son Clint jumped into action without saying a word. They formed a human chain to pull him out of the muck. No doubt the training all three men received while in the Army, especially with Clint being an Army Ranger, saved Wyatt's life that day. While returning to the campsite, they all agreed not to tell the ladies what had happened. They knew they would never hear the end of it.

Harrison knew the gruesome outcome should anyone try to retrieve the hidden keys. Any attempt to save someone would end in disaster. He hoped it would be Luke. Maybe both men would get stuck in the quicksand. Either way, it would give him the opportunity to escape. No doubt in his mind, as injured as he was, he could swim across the waterway to safety.

Limping to the picnic table, Harrison pulled the plywood off the stump and dragged it close to the red-hot burn barrel. He reluctantly began digging around the base of the barrel, while

Jaxson stood over him with the shotgun cradled in his arms. Harrison saw stars when he attempted to lift the first shovel full, but he didn't pass out. More determined than ever, he would not accept defeat. "God give me the strength to continue just a little longer." With his cracked ribs, Harrison struggled working at a snail's pace. He could tell both men were getting irritated at his progress.

"For Christ's sake, how long is this going to take, asshole?" Luke asked.

"I don't know, maybe forty-five minutes or so."

"Well, hurry the hell up, these damn bugs are killing me," Luke said, turning around in circles, trying to avoid the constant onslaught.

Harrison dug out around the barrel, placing the sand on top of the plywood. The bottom of the barrel came into view, and with a few more shovel loads, the barrel leaned over on its side. Luke came over with a towel wrapped around his hands and pushed the barrel up and out of the way for Harrison to continue his digging. Inch by inch, he dug wider and deeper. Harrison wanted to clean out an area of about three feet wide and three feet deep, so he would be standing knee high in his hole. Thirty minutes later, he finally got the hole dug out to his liking.

He could barely place any weight on his right leg. Each breath was like sucking in fire. His whole body was trembling from exhaustion, and he was drenched in sweat.

It was time.

"Guys, I need to take a break for a minute, and I need some water please," Harrison said, standing in the middle of the three-foot-deep hole.

"Yo, Luke, go get this prick some water. It's in the boat," Jaxson ordered, still staring at Harrison with keen interest.

Luke walked down the sandy knoll and, about halfway down, Jaxson turned his head and said, "Hey bring back that damn bug spray while you at it."

Within that split second, when Jaxson had turned his head, Harrison drove his shovel straight down perfectly between his ankles and cut through the plastic twist ties. His legs were free, and it was time to set his next move into action. He didn't move, not wanting to bring any attention to himself, with Jaxson standing close by with a shotgun in his hands. He waited for Luke to return, hoping neither one would look down into the hole.

Before Luke got within ten feet of the hole, Harrison set his plan into high gear.

"Hey look, with a little more digging, I'll be hitting the safe deposit box, probably in five or ten minutes. One of ya needs to go get the keys so I can open it. The keys are up underneath that radio beacon that is mounted on that black pole right across from where we docked. Go straight out with the boat and you'll see a little creek that leads to the pole. Just walk up the creek about fifteen yards or so."

"Screw that, you're gonna go get it, Luke said.

Harrison froze in fear, as his plan was unraveling right before his eyes. Dammit, he thought, how was he going to get out of this? He was running out of time and anger welled up deep inside him.

"Piss on you guys, I'm exhausted. I can barely move, let alone walk, for Christ's sake."

Harrison lifted his shovel straight in the air and drove it down as hard as he could to convey his anger. The blade hit something that sounded like a plink at the bottom of the pit. He momentarily looked down, but everything went black. Jaxson, who would not tolerate anyone giving him any back talk, had swung around and leveled the butt of his shotgun directly into Harrison's temple. Harrison's legs gave out and he crumpled, laying half in and half out of the hole. He was out cold with a steady stream of blood pouring out of his forehead.

"Screw it," Jaxson said. "Just go get that damn key, we don't need this clown anymore," Jaxson yelled at Luke.

"In just a few more feet, we'll have our gold, and we'll just bury this asshole right here."

Luke headed off down the path towards the boat, while Jaxson unwrapped one of the sandwiches. He grabbed the whiskey bottle and sat down underneath one of the nearby scrub oak trees, shading himself from the blazing morning sun. Keeping his back facing toward the ocean, Jaxson could see down the pathway with a clear view of the waterway. Relaxed, he crammed the entire sandwich in his mouth and washed it down with a large gulp of whiskey.

He could hear Luke starting the motor and then watched him slowly drive the boat out of the small bay towards the waterway. Looking north along the waterway, Jaxson didn't hear or see another boat anywhere, but suddenly he thought he heard a slight thrumming sound way off in the distance coming from the south. Jaxson sat up and turned his head to see what was making that strange sound, but the dense tree line blocked his view. Since it didn't sound like a boat approaching, he eased back down and took another shot of whiskey.

The thrumming sound continued to get louder and closer as Jaxson watched his cousin cross over the small bay. He headed for the narrow creek that led to the black pole set back deep in the marsh grass. Jaxson was getting edgy, with tiny beads of sweat forming on his forehead. Whether it was the baloney and whiskey combination or something else, Jaxson's stomach swelled up bringing with it some God awful lower intestinal pain. Frantically unbuckling his belt, he just barely pulled down his trousers in time, when an anal rocket flew out of his butt and splattered all over the tree behind him.

The cousins completely forgot to pack toilet paper on the boat, so Jaxson had to tear off pieces of his tee shirt to clean himself off. Even though his butt was now exposed to the elements, the biting black flies had their attention on something better. Walking away from his mess, Jaxson decided to finish off the digging himself and approached the hole where Harrison lay, still unconscious. That thrumming noise he heard earlier was now directly to his west and he could see a small plane slowly heading up the waterway as he laid his shotgun off to the side. He didn't pay attention to the low flying plane. Still suffering from a few lingering cramps, he gently bent down and picked up the shovel. He was about to step into the hole to start digging, when he heard Luke yell out a blood-curdling scream. It made the hair on the back of his neck stand straight up. He heard it again.

"*JAXS*"

CHAPTER 23

Earnie called his son as he pulled into the flight school parking lot. He explained in detail what needed to be done according to his plan and emphasized not to reveal to anyone the true reason for the change in his flight plan.

Wyatt was able to change his flight plan without any objections or questions from his flight instructor. Shortly after he registered his new flight plan, he called his dad letting him know he would be taking off on runway 17 at ILM in about twenty minutes and would climb to about twelve hundred feet heading straight to Wrightsville Beach before heading NNE along the waterway towards the island. He estimated he would be near the island within forty-five minutes. Earnie told his son to be on the lookout for his boat coming out of Pages Creek, heading north toward the island.

"Dad, you know if I drop down to nine hundred feet anywhere over the waterway, I'll get in so much trouble I might not get my license."

"Don't worry about that, I'll make sure Agent Vickors handles that."

"Okay, I've completed my preflight inspection and I'll be heading out to do my run up in probably five to ten minutes and then I'll taxi out to runway 17. I should be airborne in twenty minutes."

"Listen, once you reach Wrightsville Beach and start heading NNE, start your slow descent once you reach the middle of Shell

Island. Bring her down nice and easy maintaining your airspeed just above 42 knots so you won't stall."

"Dad, you know the control tower is going to radio me as soon as I descend that low. What should I tell them?"

"Don't declare an emergency. Just tell them you have a temporary power issue and that you are initiating an engine failure checklist and to standby. That should give you enough time to easily fly by the island. Continue at nine hundred feet until you hit Rich's Inlet, then begin to climb back up to twelve hundred feet. Call the tower and tell them the power issue is resolved, but you want clearance to return."

In the meantime, the three men arrived back to Earnie's house. They had forty-five minutes to prepare. Patrick gathered his ensemble of firearms out of his truck and placed them all on the pool table in Earnie's garage. Earnie went to his gun safe and retrieved everything he had. He too laid everything out on the pool table, including three radio headsets. Detective Decker eyed the Marlin 30 30 rifle with its attached high-powered scope and not a single word was spoken as the three men proceeded to get locked and loaded.

The weapons were secured in a large black duffle bag and placed in the covered bed of Earnie's truck. While Detective Decker and Patrick were doing radio checks with the headsets, Earnie went to his office computer, pulled up Google Earth and printed off three color copies of the island. Before returning to the garage, Earnie grabbed three dark green T-shirts from his bedroom dresser, three black ball caps and a small can of black shoe polish.

All three men piled into Earnie's truck and headed for Mason's Marina, less than two miles away. Earnie's boat was docked at a wet slip, ready for a quick launch. Detective Decker couldn't help but notice how amped up the two men were. Their facial expressions completely changed. Their jaw muscles were rigid, their noses flared wide, and their steely eyes were becoming bloodshot. Although it was a scary sight, he felt a sense of comfort since there were two highly trained combat veterans by his side. Also, they had an arsenal capable of taking down a ton of people, if need be. He knew what he was doing would most likely get him fired, but he didn't care. He had to rescue his dear friend.

Earnie called Ms. Kelly, putting her on speakerphone, and asked her what Harrison was going to wear to the book signing.

"Oh my God, he was going to wear that bright fluorescent orange fishing shirt, ya know, the one that looks like he works for your brother on the side of the road directing traffic. The man has no fashion sense at all. And I'm sure he was wearing his khaki fishing shorts. Jesus, they still had fish blood on them."

"Anything else? You know he never goes anywhere without wearing a ball cap, right?"

"Oh yeah, you're right. I think it would be one of his white hats, but which one I really don't know,"

"Okay, you're sure it was the orange-colored shirt?"

"Oh yeah, it's his favorite shirt to wear out in public."

Earnie pulled his truck into the marina parking lot and without saying a word, the three men walked down to the end of the dock. They boarded Earnie's twenty-two-foot Bayliner with all their gear. Earnie fired up the three hundred and fifty horse powered outboard engine and Patrick released the two dock lines. Normally a no-wake zone, Earnie had no time to waste, and throttled down, creating a three-foot wake which crashed into the finger docks. The other fifteen or so boats moored there rolled up and down and smashed into the dock, making one hell of a racket. Earnie knew he would have some explaining to do with the owners once he returned.

The Bayliner ran out of Pages Creek wide open reaching a speed close to forty knots. Upon reaching the waterway, Earnie made a wide turn heading north towards the Figure 8 Island bridge. Their island destination was only another quarter of a mile north of the bridge. Reaching the bridge just a minute later, Earnie eased back on the throttle and put the motor into neutral, then slipped underneath the bridge and waited. A few minutes later, Wyatt called his dad.

"I can see you now. I am going to ease up and drop down to about nine hundred feet. When I get close to the island, I'll let you know what I see."

"Okay, keep on the line, don't hang up. Look for somebody wearing a bright orange shirt. I want you to video your flyby with your phone."

Two minutes later, the Cessna 152 flew over Earnie's boat heading north directly over the center of the waterway. Earnie eased down on the throttle and brought the boat up to twenty knots. At this speed, they would reach the island in less than five minutes.

"I see a Jon boat with one person crossing the bay Pops, and holy shit, there's somebody wearing an orange shirt up on the hill."

"Do you want me to turn around and take another look?"

"No, don't fly over the island anymore. Thanks."

"Just head back to the airport. Hey, how many people are in the Jon boat, and did you see any movement with orange shirt?"

"One person in the Jon boat, and the person wearing the orange shirt is not moving."

"Anybody else?"

"No."

Target identified; all systems go. One minute from reaching the island, Earnie took the motor out of gear and handed Patrick and Decker each a copy of the colored prints of the island.

"Listen up, gather around," Earnie ordered, crouching down so the wind wouldn't rustle his maps. He carefully laid out the colored map he printed off at home, on the boat's deck. He positioned the map perfectly to reflect the true direction they were heading.

"Position check, we are here, check?"

"Roger," Patrick and Detective Decker replied at the same time.

"This black dot is where we pull the boat into the marsh grass at the center of the west side of the island, so no one can see us. Campsite is due east seventy-five yards. I am going to enter on the left flank, red dot E, Okay? Patrick, red dot DA is you entering on the right from the south. Decker, red dot DE is you coming straight in. All of us should be within twenty yards of the open sand pit and we should have a visual of Harrison within five to eight minutes after beaching the boat in the marsh grass. Understood?"

Decker and Patrick both nodded.

"Take no shot until we have visual confirmation."

The thought of having to shoot someone was unsettling to Decker. He had never pulled the trigger to shoot anyone during his short career. In fact, he had never even drawn his weapon while on duty. He had witnessed all the pain and suffering one of his fellow officers went through after shooting and killing a juvenile after a simple traffic stop. So many people were affected by that incident and the officer eventually committed suicide a year later.

Patrick retrieved the duffle bag while Earnie and Decker stayed topside and synchronized their watches. Within seconds, Patrick unzipped the duffle bag and handed each man a Kevlar vest. Earnie strapped on his double shoulder holster with two Glock 17s and his side holster carrying his favorite Glock 19 along with two grenades and one smoke bomb.

Patrick stuffed his side holster with his Beretta 92 and slung his Smith & Wesson AR-15 over his shoulder, also clipping two grenades to his vest. Both Patrick and Earnie carried seven additional clips per pistol in their side pockets. Decker made his final adjustments to the high-powered scope, setting the range at twenty yards with zero wind factor.

Earnie pushed the throttle forward easing the boat up to about fifteen miles an hour. Fifty yards from the designated landing spot, he eased back on the throttle. Maintaining a slow but steady speed of about five knots, he hugged the east side of the waterway, making sure the boat didn't create any wake. Earnie reached into his shirt pocket and handed Patrick the small can of shoe polish. Patrick quickly applied the make do camouflage onto Decker's and Earnie's faces and Decker, in turn, applied the same to Patrick's face. With the sun blaring out of the east about twenty degrees above the horizon and with no cloud cover at all, Earnie knew they could be sighted easily. He gave stern instructions to his team to make sure they stayed low and close to the ground during their approach.

After a final radio check and gear check, Earnie eased his boat into the marsh grass, tilting his motor up until the boat hit the muddy bottom bringing it to a complete stop. With the tide running out, there was no need to set out the anchor. Earnie retrieved his binoculars and bug spray from the glove box and handed them to Patrick. After the three were adequately covered with bug spray, they slowly eased over the stern and started walking towards the bow of the boat. Earnie led, followed by Patrick, with Decker in the rear.

Earnie stopped abruptly with his right closed fist in the air, bringing the three to a halt. Earnie turned around and with two fingers, he pointed to his eyes, then pointed to the north with his index finger. He signaled to Patrick to come forward with his binoculars and signaled to Decker to hand him the Marlin rifle so he could use the high-powered scope. Two hundred yards to their left, Earnie and Patrick could see someone walking up the small creek directly across from the camping ground. Earnie and Patrick looked at each other, and both understood the situation, with Patrick sliding his index finger across his neck in a sideways motion. They both knew now that they only needed to worry about just one person, but that one person could cause serious problems.

Quietly, the threesome waded through the three-foot-high marsh grass, trying to reach solid ground where they could move faster. Decker, heading straight in, hit solid ground first and easily traversed the small hill covered in cordgrass dotted with large scrub oak trees mixed in with small wax myrtle bushes. The vegetation gave him plenty of cover.

Patrick coming in from the south side, eased through the marsh grass with no problem, but slowed when he reached a thicket of thorny bushes which tore at his clothes. He managed to position himself twenty yards away with a clear view of the campsite. Earnie's route coming in on the north side of the island contained the same ground cover as Decker's and he took up his position behind a wax myrtle bush just on the edge of the bay. Earnie could see the man across the bay walking up the small creek, but he could not clearly see the campsite from his position.

Earnie crawled on his belly, inching forward for about twenty-five feet until he had a visual of the campsite.

Within eight minutes, all three men were in position, each with a clear line of sight into the campsite. Earnie turned to look over his shoulder when he heard a blood curdling scream that echoed throughout the island coming from across the small bay. Looking over towards the direction of the scream, he instantly knew why.

"That's one down," Earnie whispered into his headset.

"Check, have a visual on the man at campsite," Patrick responded.

"Check, have a visual" Decker echoed.

"Jaxs!" screamed Luke for the second time.

"Oh, shit I'm stuck, oh god I'm stuck, help, help!" screamed Luke.

Leaving his shotgun behind, Jaxson bolted from the top of the sandy knoll, where Harrison lay unconscious, and ran down the sandy path towards the bay. Earnie saw Jaxson heading straight towards him and froze. He thought about taking a shot and dropping the man dead in his tracks. Instead, he nestled himself deep into the wax myrtle bush as Jaxson rushed past him. Earnie wanted to just beat the hell out of this guy and make him suffer for messing with his buddy.

"What the hell are you doing?" Jaxson yelled out to Luke.

"It's quicksand, and I can't feel the bottom. You've got to help me!"

"That son of a bitch knew about this. Kill that bastard, bury that son of a bitch! Get me out of here!"

Greed, blinding greed, will make a person do strange and awful things. Jaxson contemplated swimming across the bay to help his cousin, but the thought of not having to share his pending wealth overtook all rational thinking. He slowly turned his back, listening to the last gurgling sounds of his cousin sinking to his death.

With gnats ripping into his face and hands, and small hermit crabs feasting on his ankles, the sight on Earnie's Glock didn't move from Jaxson's head. It took everything in his soul not to just shoot him dead. Not only did he hurt his buddy Harrison, but this slimeball let that man die. God, let me shoot him where he stands, Earnie thought, but he just couldn't do it. This isn't Iraq. You must stand down, he thought to himself, and he did not have a visual on his buddy yet.

Unaware of the three men closely watching him Jaxson headed back up the small hill to where Harrison was still laid out unconscious. With his cousin now gone, it was time to take it all and get rid of Harrison once and for all. Leave no witnesses.

"Target moving up hill to camp," Earnie radioed to Decker and Patrick.

"Copy that."

"I'm following," Earnie said.

From his position, Patrick had one single tree, fifteen yards in, blocking his line of sight directly into the campsite. Using the scope on his AR 15, he turned his attention to Jaxson, who was now jogging up the hill. He heard the faint sound of a twig snapping off to his left, and turning his scope in that direction, he could see Decker positioning himself behind a live oak tree.

The tree had a split in its trunk about three feet from its base, forming a perfect V. Patrick could see the rifle barrel of the Marlin 30 30 protruding from the split pointing directly into the campsite. Decker was at a slightly higher elevation and a few yards closer than his other two team members, where he could see clearly down into the campsite. Using the rifle scope, Decker scanned the area and finally found what he was looking for. Decker tapped his headset and whispered to Patrick and Earnie that he had a visual on an orange shirt, but no facial of Harrison.

"Any movement from orange?" Earnie asked, cupping his earpiece.

Decker zeroed in on the orange-colored shirt and, seeing no movement continued to scan the campsite first to the left and then to the right. Leaning up against a small tree just to the right of the old burn barrel, Decker could clearly see what had to be Harrison's metal detector. Although he couldn't see the lettering on the outside of the casing, sitting on top of the handle was a pair of golden headphones.

"Visual on metal detector, it's Harrison's," Decker said, tapping his earpiece.

"All eyes on target," Earnie spoke up.

Seconds later, Jaxson reached the sand pit fully enraged and spat on Harrison, who was laying there lifeless in the sand.

"You son of a bitch, I'm done with you."

Jaxson bent down and grabbed the shovel Harrison was using with both hands. Standing directly over Harrison, Jaxson breathed in deeply while he arched the shovel high in the air, then stood up on his toes, and with both hands firmly grasping the handle, started his deadly swing downward.

The hollow point bullet smashed through Jaxson's right shoulder, blowing out his shoulder blade and half of his collarbone. He violently spun around, and face planted into the sand. Surprisingly he was still moving, trying to crawl over to the picnic table just a few feet away to retrieve his shotgun. The shot echoed and all three men bolted towards the campsite. Earnie arrived first, finding Jaxson sprawled out in the sand face down.

With lightning speed, Earnie rolled Jaxson over while slamming his knee into the man's chest. Blood gushed out and splattered all over both men. Earnie reached over with his left hand placing his thumb just inside the man's cheek while jamming his middle finger into the man's ear. Tightening his grip, Earnie crammed his Glock into the man's throat, chipping off two teeth. He pushed until he heard the man gag.

"You're done. You tangled with the wrong person. Now you're done." Earnie screamed while placing his finger on the trigger.

"Earn, NO, this isn't going to happen. We must get Harrison to the hospital right away," Patrick said, reaching over and pulling Earnie's pistol away from Jaxson's mouth.

Patrick couldn't resist and landed a solid kick into Jaxson's ribs with his boot, with the full intent of breaking a few ribs. Hearing a crack and an anguished scream from Jaxson, he knew he had succeeded. Earnie followed suit by slamming his boot into the man's groin.

"He killed my cousin, that piece of shit killed him," Jaxson roared.

The wide-eyed stare on Jaxson's face was ungodly. Earnie and Patrick were looking straight into the depths of hell. Jaxson motioned with his index finger for them to come closer.

"I'm gonna kill all you. Your day is coming."

Patrick laid him out with the butt of his rifle.

While Decker was handcuffing Jaxson and zip tying his feet, Earnie and Patrick carefully pulled Harrison out of the hole and rolled him over on his back. Even the two combat veterans were shocked to see the horrific condition of their friend. They had seen a lot of wounded and mangled soldiers in their day, and now they feared the worst.

His face was so battered and swollen; he was unrecognizable. No doubt he would be left with multiple scars and some deformity. While Patrick unbuttoned Harrison's shirt to further access his condition, Earnie lifted Harrison's eyelids to examine his eyes. The left eye was rolled back, and the right eye was just a clump of blood. Kneeling next to their buddy, both men looked at each other in total shock. Noticing severe bruising on their buddy's chest, Patrick gently rolled him over just a few inches revealing a massive bruise covering his entire side. Not wanting to possibly cause any further injury, he removed his glove and eased his hand along Harrison's side then towards his kidney. The area was swollen and felt warm to the touch. Patrick knew that was a sign of a severe hematoma. At the same time, Earnie was examining the site where Jaxson head butted Harrison with the shotgun. An area about the size of a tennis ball was slightly caved in about two to three centimeters.

Both men turned their attention to the wooden splint on Harrison's leg, calling for Decker's assistance. They cut the duct tape loose then carefully removed the blood-soaked towel. The odor made them sick. Had this occurred in the battlefield, no doubt a medic would have to amputate. Decker turned away and vomited.

"Decker," Earnie screamed, "Call in for an emergency airlift now!"

Decker retrieved his radio from his belt, tuned in the emergency medical frequency, and calmly spoke, "Medical airlift requested, one injured at coordinates 34.28352 North 77.75011 West; I repeat 34.28352 North 77.75011 West."

"Copy, ETA twelve minutes," responded the operator. "Status of the injured?"

"Unconscious, in shock with heavy blunt force trauma to the head. No place to land, bring basket rescue stretcher, I repeat, bring basket."

"Copy. Trauma team alert initiated."

While waiting for the air rescue squad to arrive, all three men decided to fill the hole in the sand so no future campers would fall and injure themselves. Each bent down and grabbed the plywood full of sand and, using all their strength were able to turn over the plywood and partially fill the hole. Patrick grabbed the shovel nearby and finished filling the hole within about two feet, while Decker was setting the plywood back on the stump. Earnie rolled the burn barrel and set it in the two-foot hole and Patrick finished filling in the hole.

"Gretchen, we've got 'em, and a medical airlift is on the way for Harrison," Decker said, calling Gretchen on her radio.

"What's his condition?"

"He's alive, but just barely hanging on."

"Where the hell are you? Give me your coordinates and don't you dare move or touch any evidence until we get there."

After Decker gave Gretchen the GPS coordinates to the island, he helped Earnie prepare Harrison for the medical basket. Patrick took up a hidden position at the edge of the campsite in full view of the small trail leading up from the bay. Should anybody come up that trail, they would be quickly subdued, and find themselves with the barrel of an AR 15 resting against their front teeth.

When Decker could hear the whirling sound of the helicopter approaching, he got on his radio, directing the pilot to the best pickup location, which was the center of the sandy knoll campsite, allowing plenty of clearance to lower the basket. Within minutes, the basket was lowered with an EMT on board.

Earnie and Decker followed the EMT's directions and placed Harrison into the basket. Two minutes later, the helicopter sped off, heading west for the hospital some ten minutes out.

In the meantime, Gretchen and Agent Vickors were met by the Coast Guard at the concrete ramp of the old Johnson's Marina in Middle Sound. Gretchen handed the captain the coordinates for the island and after he punched in the numbers on his GPS, Captain Bud Hastings knew exactly where it was. He slammed the throttle forward, engaging the twin 250's that sent Agent Vickors flying to the back of the boat. At the furious speed the boat was traveling at, Agent Vickors couldn't even stand up. He just sat there dazed.

When Gretchen arrived at the campsite, she was met by three men armed to the teeth, she instinctively placed her hand on her pistol. Camouflaged, she didn't recognize them at all.

"Stand down bitch," Patrick said, stepping forward, aiming his AR 15 directly at center mass.

"Who the hell do you think you're talking to buddy? I'm the law!"

"I'm not your friggin' buddy so take your hand off of that gun," Patrick ordered, sneering at Gretchen. No one was coming near him or his buddies.

Gretchen hesitated just for a moment, but gently spread out her fingers and lifted her hand from her gun. This was not the time or place to pick a fight as she realized she was outnumbered and totally outgunned.

With her arms stretched outward, Gretchen walked over to where Jaxson was lying in the sand. She was shocked at what she saw. Fragments of bone and flesh protruded from his gunshot wound and he looked to be in shock.

"Jesus Christ, who did this? And why wasn't he airlifted out of here also?"

"Screw him," Earnie said.

"He's yours now," as all three men turned and started their trek back to Earnie's boat.

Gretchen could not recognize two of the men, but seeing the bushy black hair, she knew it was Decker.

"Decker, get your ass back here. You've got a lot of explaining to do," Gretchen yelled, furious at the scene in front of her.

"Yeah, well, I don't answer to you. Piss off. I'll have my report on the boss's desk by nine o'clock tomorrow morning."

Decker's veins were surging with adrenaline, and he didn't know how long the rush would last, but he wanted to take advantage of his raging masculinity. Once back on-board Earnie's boat, he retrieved his wallet, pulled out Sergeant Turner's business card, and dialed her number.

"Yeah, Sergeant Turner speaking," Opal said, answering on the second ring.

"Hey, it's Decker, are you busy?"

"Nope, I just got off work and I am cooking some lunch. Are you hungry?"

"Oh yeah, it's been a rough day, and I'm starving. Text me your address."

No doubt it was time to get jiggy and if anybody was going to end up looking like a pretzel, it wasn't going to be him.

CHAPTER 24

Harrison spent the next three months at the Novant Health Regional Hospital recovering from his injuries. He underwent two operations on his battered leg, along with two eye operations. One to repair his shattered orbital eye socket in his right eye and the other to repair a detached retina. Although the initial X-rays revealed that his skull had been fractured in two places, all neurological tests indicated there was no apparent brain damage. The MRI results of the two broken ribs showed one had slightly punctured Harrison's right lung, but not enough to cause severe internal bleeding.

Within hours after being airlifted to the hospital, the on-call orthopedic surgeons performed emergency surgery on his right leg just to stabilize the shattered bone, knowing a second operation would be required to repair the torn ligaments and tendons. Unfortunately, the second operation performed several weeks later was not successful, and Harrison also found himself in the ICU fighting off sepsis.

After spending nearly twenty-four hours in the ICU, the medications administered were stopping the spread of the infection enough that the doctors instructed the hospital staff to move Harrison back to his room on the fifth floor, where he could have visitors. Once Harrison had been cleaned up and all the IVs were changed out, Ms. Kelly was allowed to come into the room. A group of three surgeons met her at her husband's bed.

"Mrs. Thomas, I am Dr. Franklin, head of the orthopedic trauma team here at the hospital, and my two assistants are Dr. Pierce and Dr. Jenkins. Please have a seat."

"It's a miracle your husband is alive today, but he has another issue at hand we need to discuss with you. It is our medical opinion that once the infection is eradicated completely, we have no other choice but to amputate his leg just below the knee."

Ms. Kelly, totally devastated by the news, couldn't even lift her head up to watch the three doctors leave the room. After a few minutes, she walked over to Harrison's bedside, climbed into the bed and both wept in silence, holding each other tightly. Suddenly, Harrison pushed Ms. Kelly off the bed and started ripping the IVs out of his hands attempting to get out of bed.

"Get me Alex Smith, find Alex Smith," said Harrison screaming at the top of his lungs.

Harrison went berserk continuing his ranting and raving, yelling out the name Alex Smith repeatedly. The nurses had to sedate him before he hurt himself. Over the next few days, each time the sedatives would wear off, Harrison continued screaming the name Alex Smith. Ms. Kelly could tell that the devastating news was plunging Harrison into such a deep depression that she asked the hospital to put him on a twenty-four-hour suicide watch.

At first, Ms. Kelly didn't tell anyone about the possible amputation or Harrison's deepening depression, but late one evening, three days after receiving the doctor's opinion, she decided to visit Tammy and Earnie and reveal to them the whole situation. As soon as Ms. Kelly finished telling Earnie and Tammy what was occurring with Harrison and what was about to happen, Earnie jumped into action. He was determined. He was on a mission to find members of the highly specialized orthopedic team in Germany who treated injured soldiers during Desert Storm.

Earnie explained to Ms. Kelly, that while he was flying missions in Iraq and Afghanistan, he had flown severely wounded soldiers from the battlefield to the Landstuhl Medical Army Hospital in Germany, where a special team of orthopedic surgeons performed miracles on soldiers' extremities which had been severely mutilated. On several occasions, he had the pleasure of flying some of those same soldiers back stateside, and marveled that they were still alive, and many walking without any means of support.

"If I can just find one of those surgeons, and get him here, I promise you everything will be fine," Earnie said, hugging Ms. Kelly.

"He's in bad shape, Earnie, I don't think he's going to pull through."

"When are the docs going to operate?"

"Once the infection is gone, they intend on proceeding with the operation the next day. I think they told me in about five days."

"No problem. That gives me plenty of time. Now go home and get some rest, I'll keep you posted."

"Earnie, I need to ask you something."

"What's that, hon?"

"Who is this Alex Smith guy Harrison keeps yelling about?"

"Go home and google Alex Smith NFL quarterback and you'll read an interesting story about the horrific injury that guy suffered while playing football. He almost lost his leg, but after a dozen or so surgeries, he amazingly played football again. Read the story, it will give you a sense of hope"

He kissed Ms. Kelly on the cheek as she left.

After a dozen phone calls and several emails, two days later Earnie located one of the Army surgeons from the highly specialized team in Germany. He was retired, but still consulting part time at the Veteran's hospital in Fayetteville, North Carolina. Not wasting any time, Earnie jumped into his truck and sped off to Fayetteville. While en route, Earnie called his buddy Patrick, who lived in Fayetteville, and filled him in on the dire situation Harrison was facing and how he had found one of the surgeons.

"Yo bud, I need for you to call over to the Vet hospital and get hold of Dr. Reynolds and tell him we are coming to see him today."

"You got it, call ya back soon. Hey, how is brother man doing?'"

"Not good. He's barely hanging on. They got him so full of drugs he talks gibberish and nonsense when he's awake."

Earnie arrived at Patrick's house an hour and a half later, and the two drove the short distance to the Veterans hospital. Patrick had located Dr. Reynolds and set up a two o'clock meeting for that afternoon. It had been only two hours since his departure from Wilmington, and now Earnie was sitting in the staff lounge on the second floor of the east wing, facing Dr. Reynolds.

Earnie explained, as best he could, Harrison's dilemma and bluntly asked Dr. Reynold for his help. Although Harrison never served in the armed forces, it didn't matter to Dr. Reynolds. His fellow brothers needed his help, and he agreed to rearrange his schedule and travel to Wilmington early the next morning.

The day Harrison was admitted to the hospital, the Barnes and Noble bookstore set up a "Go Fund Me" account to help pay for Harrison's hospitalization and those rehab costs that Medicare didn't cover. Leaving Fayetteville after his visit with Dr.

Reynolds, Earnie called the manager of the Barnes and Noble bookstore requesting that she contact the administrator of the fund and submit a request to pay for Dr. Reynold's services, his transportation to and from Fayetteville, and his lodging while in Wilmington. Twenty-five minutes later, the manager returned Earnie's call letting him know that the fund executor agreed to release the monies, and within just forty-eight hours, Dr. Reynolds was operating on Harrison's leg.

The operation was a success. Harrison was faced with months of grueling rehabilitation that required hours and hours of boring bed rest with his leg elevated in a harness that was specially designed by Dr. Reynolds.

As he lay there hooked up to his harness after each rehab session, Harrison replayed in his mind the last few moments he could remember on the island before Jaxson butted him with the shotgun. Did he really see a gold coin at the bottom of the pit, or was it just a dream? No, it wasn't a dream. He was certain he saw that coin, but how did it get there? He needed help. Harrison dialed his granddaughter's cell number.

"Andrea, do you still have that laptop I gave you when you were in high school?"

"I sure do. What's up?"

"Can I borrow it for a while? I need to catch up with the news and send out a few emails."

"Oh, sure, I'll bring it by before I go to work."

Harrison needed the computer to research gold coins. He was on a mission to confirm what he saw at the bottom of that pit. Strolling along the beach and finding a coin laying on the sand was one thing. Finding a coin a few inches in the sand with a detector was another. He couldn't fathom spotting a coin four feet in the ground on a barrier island, especially a gold one. He would keep his research findings to himself. Not a soul would know about his last moments on the island.

Andrea came by several hours later and dropped off the laptop, but much to Harrison's dismay, the battery was dead and needed re-charging. His research had to wait just a little longer. It didn't matter anyway, as the medicine dispenser hanging on the wall injected its concoction and he was fast asleep.

He woke up in a semi-fog several hours later, with the laptop on his chest now fully charged. It was time to get to work. He needed to draft a short outline to keep his research on point and in focus, as the medicines being injected into his veins kept him in a fog most of the time. Taking a piece of paper, Harrison jotted down:

*Who would bury gold on an island?
*Why would someone do that?
*Research gold coins.

To answer his first question, Harrison researched all the known pirates that wreaked havoc along the North Carolina coast during the 1600s. During his search, he stumbled upon a fascinating book entitled *Legends of Old Wilmington* by John Hirchak. Multiple pirates did frequent the Cape Fear region. Harrison was familiar with them. Among those were Captain William Kidd, Stede Bonnet, Charles Vane, possibly Jack Rackman and, of course, the most famous of them all, Edward Teach, known as Blackbeard.

The story of Captain Kidd and Money Island caught Harrison's attention. As folklore had it, in 1699 Captain Kidd buried two iron chests full of gold and silver on a tiny island just off the mouth of Bradley Creek just outside Wilmington. Traveling south along the Intracoastal Waterway, the island, just south of Bradley Creek, can still be seen today, but it has been mostly destroyed by hurricanes since Captain Kidd supposedly left his mark there.

Bonnet apparently was in Virginia at one time and traveled south past Wrightsville Beach where he was captured at the mouth of the Cape Fear River in 1718. There are no written records of him burying gold coins anywhere.

Charles Vane, from some accounts, did travel from Nassau to Ocracoke to meet up with Blackbeard passing by this area. Again, no records of him burying treasure either. Blackbeard, who met his demise in 1718, kept close to Bath, North Carolina, and from all accounts, never ventured near the Wrightsville Beach area.

In the end, Harrison concluded that treasure chests laden with gold hidden by pirates with an *X* on a map was nothing but Hollywood make believe.

He turned his attention to the gold coins that had been found over the years by divers or metal detecting enthusiasts along the Florida coast. He learned the latest find was at Wabasso Beach, Florida, where the coins were from a Spanish galleon fleet dating back to 1715. The coin that Harrison saw at the bottom of the pit he dug looked nothing like those found at Wabasso Beach. It dawned on him that the coin he saw was not from some pirate burying his loot in the sand.

If the coin was not from a pirate, who else would bury gold in the sand? While he was working at the Sutton Council Furniture company back in the early eighties, he remembered Mr. Sutton telling stories about riding on horseback on the barrier island, now Figure 8 Island, as a member of the Coast Guard scouting for German U-Boats during World War II. On one occasion in 1943, there were reports from Kure Beach that a U-Boat fired upon a chemical plant a few miles inland. Rumors floated around Wilmington at that time, that German soldiers had landed and supposedly camped on some of the barrier islands. Harrison considered the possibility of German soldiers burying gold coins out there, but quickly dismissed that option.

Although he was coming up empty, Harrison was determined to push on with his research, making sure he didn't reveal the true reason for his inquiries to anyone. The medicine dispenser above his hospital bed started to beep. He knew his research would be taking a break.

Since he was a young boy, Harrison was blessed with a photographic memory, and if he could just see a gold coin that matched what he saw in the pit, he could conclude his research. He had to clear his mind, so he hit the nurse call button and waited. Two minutes later, his attending nurse and physical therapist, Ruby, knocked on the door and walked in, with her ever present warm smile on her face.

Ruby, a well-toned and shapely, tall woman just short of six feet, was of Jamaican descent. She had the most beautiful complexion Harrison had ever seen, which was enriched by her long straight black hair always pulled back in a bun. She was a pleasant woman in her late forties. Harrison became fond of Ruby during his recuperation, and he especially enjoyed her company whenever she would come sit with him after her shift was over telling him stories of her childhood in Jamaica. Harrison came to admire Ruby, learning that she was not only raising her thirteen-year-old daughter from her first marriage, but was also supporting her mom, who lived back in Jamaica. When her husband up and left one day some four years ago, she struggled each month to pay the mortgage and her other living expenses. When Harrison found out that Ruby was responsible for hundreds of book sales by encouraging all her colleagues and friends at the hospital to purchase the book, he contacted his attorneys at Baker and Baker and had them set up a draw of ten percent of the book's monthly sales to be given to her each month.

"Hello dear, what can I help you with today?"

"Can you ask the doc if we can stop these injections for a while?"

"What is your pain level right now? One for no pain and ten for extreme, unbearable pain. What would you say?"

"I think I can do without for a while, but I do need a laxative big time."

Ruby headed for her nurse's station to contact the attending physician. Ten minutes later, she came back into the room holding a small plastic bottle containing a clear liquid that had a long tube attached to it in her hand. She had a silly grin on her face.

"I want you to relax, don't be embarrassed, I've done this thousands of times," Ruby said, pulling back the bed blanket, then lowering Harrison's leg back onto the bed.

"Oh God, really?"

"Roll over honey, this won't take but a second. You wanted a laxative, so here comes your wish. Say hello to Mr. Fleet."

Three hours later, Harrison, now wide awake, got back to his research drowning himself with prescribed Pedialyte and Gatorade. The doctor agreed to lessen his medication but wanted to wean Harrison off the powerful pain meds, not just stop them abruptly.

He picked up where he left off, viewing gold coins, mostly those minted in the United States. Each page he viewed always had side links off to the side, and one such link caught his eye: "Confederate Spy drowns with $2,000 worth of Gold." This spy, Rose Greenhow, was traveling on The Condor, a British blockade runner, that ran aground at the mouth of the Cape Fear River on October 1, 1864. Apparently, Ms. Greenhow fled the grounded ship in a rowboat which later capsized, and she drowned. Those who retrieved her body from the river found that she had sewn pockets of gold inside her underclothes worth $2,000 back then.

More and more links popped up relating to the Civil War. Harrison got a tad sidetracked and found himself immersed with stories about how brutal the Union soldiers treated the southerners whenever they invaded a city. He found out that whenever the residents were forewarned of the invading Yankees, they took great effort in hiding whatever valuables they had. Some placed their fortunes up inside chimneys, some gathered their fortune in a satchel, tied a rope to it, and lowered the bag into the belly of their outhouses. Harrison dug deeper into these stories and found that most of the southerners buried their fortunes deep into the woods or countryside and would retrieve their fortune and valuables once the union soldiers had left. It was assumed that, in some cases, the entire family was killed, and their fortune still lied buried in unknown locations today.

Harrison dug deeper and further into the possibility of people hiding their fortunes from the invading Union soldiers. Two fascinating stories caught his attention. He stumbled on an article written by J.A. Bolton in the *Anson Record* back in October 2017 entitled *Confederate Gold in The Sandhills* that clearly answered the second question of his outline.... "Why would someone do that?"

When Harrison came across the story about how Henry Grob and Theodore Jones found five thousand coins buried by the Knights of the Golden Circle under an old house in Baltimore, Maryland in 1934 worth some ten million dollars, Harrison knew he was on the right track. The Knights of the Golden Circle was a secret society founded in 1854 with an objective to create a new country where slavery would be legal. They held a convention from May 7-11, 1860, in Raleigh, North Carolina and it was known that members paid dues with gold coins which were hidden or buried for safe keeping.

Harrison was satisfied that his research answered his questions. He shut down the laptop and laid back to think. He formulated two scenarios. A wealthy resident of New Hanover County, who had some knowledge of the barrier islands, took the family fortune, and buried it, was a solid possibility. Or did a member of the Knights of the Golden Circle bury it? Each party doing so before the Union soldiers got to Wilmington. Did these people then fight in the last battle of the Civil War at Bell Forks Road and get killed? Did they die before telling anyone what they had done? His intuition told him to focus on the first scenario.

"Andrea, I need your help."

"Sure, Paw Paw, what is it?"

"Could you go to the library and bring me as many history books you can find that cover New Hanover County prior to the Civil War?"

Harrison now had to rely on his photographic memory to recall exactly what he saw at the bottom of that pit. His memories were always in vivid color, so he had to focus on the color only, and block everything else out of his memory. Harrison closed his eyes and began a slow but steady regiment of deep breathing, allowing his body to relax so he could concentrate deep into his memory bank.

Like a movie in slow motion, Harrison could see the shovel handle, then the metal blade of the shovel, and slowly the image of the coin came into view. Although somewhat blurry, he could see what he thought were pieces of ivy, or plant, and the number 3. That was it, no more memory beyond that and he was overcome with fatigue and drifted off to sleep.

Harrison slept until the next morning and had not moved a muscle during the night, but the pain level was hitting at a high seven, so he pushed the button, hoping to see Ruby come through the door. Apparently, Mr. Fleet must have paid a visit during the night, so Harrison's early morning was a rude awakening. Candice was the morning shift nurse and Harrison felt sorry for her, but she was the consummate professional and performed her duties without saying a word. Thirty minutes later, he was back in the bed with fresh clothes and was anxious to get back on the laptop and research the last fragments of his memory.

Harrison opened Google and typed in, "gold coin, ivy, 3" and didn't have to wait but a second, and a picture of the $3 Princess gold coin came into view. The blurry memory he had yesterday came into full focus and Harrison, totally stunned, laid back, placed his hands over his eyes and had to take a deep breath.

"Jesus, Mary, and Joseph, what have I stumbled upon?"

CHAPTER 25

R oughly three months had gone by, and Harrison was finally released from the hospital. With tears in her eyes, Ruby escorted her favorite patient out in a wheelchair decorated with a variety of helium balloons. Easing through the double doors of the patient discharge area, Ruby pushed the wheelchair up to the side of Dalton's truck and set the brake. While Dalton was helping his dad out of the wheelchair, Ruby stood close by with a set of crutches ready to assist Harrison. Overcome with emotion, Harrison pushed aside the crutches and hugged Ruby.

"If it wasn't for you, I would have never made it. I will never forget you and thank you for all your kindness."

Ruby eased away from Harrison's embrace and lovingly placed her hands on his cheeks, rubbing away the tears from his eyes with her thumbs.

"God be with you, and may you find peace in your heart," Ruby said, kissing Harrison on his forehead.

Harrison got situated in the passenger seat and rolled down the window to wave goodbye to Ruby and the other nurses that had taken the time to wish him well and say goodbye.

"Oh, wait, I almost forgot," Ruby said, reaching into the carry case attached to the back side of the wheelchair. "We all chipped in and wanted you to have this," she said, handing Harrison a small, gift-wrapped package a little smaller than a shoe box.

Harrison eased back in the seat with the window down, taking in the fresh air all the way home keeping his hand on his son's shoulder. He was looking forward to getting home to take a long shower, get into his sweatpants and T-shirt and relax in his favorite recliner.

"Hey buddy, would you mind stopping at the liquor store so I can get a pint of Kahlua and a pint of vodka?"

"No need to Pops, all your friends have stocked your liquor cabinet full. You've got gallons for your white Russians."

"Hey, what's in the box?" Dalton asked, pointing to the gift lying on the seat between them.

Harrison tore off the paper wrapping and unveiled a plain colored cardboard box with a Bass Pro Shops label on it. While in the hospital, Harrison told the nurses many stories about his past fishing adventures, and he was anxious to see what kind of fishing lure or gear the girls had bought him. He thought it was so touching and thoughtful of the girls to give him something useful for his favorite hobby.

He opened the lid and immediately broke out in a fit of laughter where he couldn't catch his breath and tears were streaming down his face.

"Jesus, Dad, what the hell?"

Laughing even harder, Harrison reached into the box and pulled out a large Fleet enema bottle, holding it up in front of Dalton and they both lost it. Dalton had to pull off to the side of the road. It took them a few minutes to stop laughing and Harrison went to place the bottle back in the box when he noticed at the bottom of the box there was a small gift card. Harrison opened the card and read the note inside, and almost choked from another fit of laughter.

"Oh my God, those girls are a hoot. Check this out," Harrison said, handing the card to Dalton.

Dalton too cracked up reading the note written in cursive in bright blue ink.

We enjoyed your fishing stories, but we know you are full of it.

Twenty minutes later, Dalton turned off Middle Sound Loop Road, heading for his dad's house. Only thirty yards from his house, Harrison could see that a crowd of well-wishers had gathered in his front yard, with all the family members and friends lining the driveway ready to welcome him home. Dalton eased to a stop as the crowd encircled the truck, anxiously waiting for Harrison to step out. Harrison's grandson Bryson was the first person to reach the truck opening the passenger door then helping his Paw Paw out of the truck to an eruption of cheers. Andrea joined her brother and with each on either side of their Paw Paw, they would not leave his side as he greeted everyone one by one while Grandmama Kelly stood on the front porch.

Taking his time to greet everyone, it took nearly fifteen minutes before Harrison reached the front porch to receive a loving long embrace from his wife. In the meantime, Dalton, Bryson, and Andrea slipped by and went inside the house to prepare their special welcome home package they had set up the night before. After a long embrace from his wife, Harrison waved goodbye.

He noticed a black four-door sedan pulling into his driveway. A tall thin man dressed in a dark blue business suit holding a legal sized piece of paper got out of the driver's side while another well-dressed man got out of the passenger side. Not one single person in the crowd noticed the two men approaching the front of the house until they started hearing both men spewing out orders.

"Stand aside, excuse us please," barked out the tall man pushing through the crowd with his associate close behind.

Earnie and Patrick, standing in front of the crowd closest to Harrison, heard the commotion behind them and sensed danger in the air. Both Earnie and Patrick turned around to confront the two men, with Patrick reaching for his concealed pistol. The approaching men pulled aside their jackets to reveal police badges and holstered pistols and Patrick noticed the first man had already drawn his pistol, pointing it directly at him. Patrick quickly held up all ten fingers and let the two men pass and walk up the three steps to the porch.

"Mr. Harrison Thomas, we have a warrant for your arrest. Put your hands behind your back."

"You are under arrest for the Voluntary Murder of Luke Jefferson," stated the second man while placing Harrison in handcuffs.

Everyone was stunned as the two men led Harrison to the black sedan and placed him in the back seat. Before they could close the door, Rex Calder ran over but was stopped by a quick open palm to his chest from the officer that had handcuffed Harrison. Although stopped dead in his tracks, Rex leaned to his side just enough where Harrison could see him.

"You hold tight, I'll have you out in no time."

"You know a guy, right?" Harrison said, smiling.

Rex Calder did what he said he would do, and within three hours he was driving Harrison home.

"Don't worry about anything. I've already got you the best attorney there is, and he is flying in the day after tomorrow to handle everything. And his name ain't Tom Hagen by the way,"

Rex's attorney, Jason Whitlock, was a high-powered attorney from New York City, who was also licensed in the state of North

Carolina. He had made a name for himself defending several known gangsters over the last twenty years with an impressive success rate. Even before he met with Harrison, Whitlock and his team conducted in-depth interviews with the entire investigative team. Separate interviews were held with Harrison's family members. The interviews with Earnie Cafaro, Patrick Armstrong, Detective Decker, and Earnie's son Wyatt proved to be most helpful. Whitlock's interviews took four days before he finally sat down at Harrison's house to interview him.

Harrison's own in-depth interview started at eight o'clock on a Tuesday morning and lasted until about three o'clock that afternoon. As with all the other people interviewed, Harrison felt like he was being interviewed for an upcoming episode of *60 Minutes*. The questions were grueling, and Harrison had to stop the process several times to gather his thoughts because he truly couldn't remember everything due to all the trauma he had suffered.

Once all the questioning was completed to Whitlock's satisfaction, he informed Harrison of his impressions. Harrison was totally exhausted but anxious to hear what Whitlock had to say.

"I'll try to keep this short, but bottom line, you have nothing to worry about. We'll have this cleared up in no time."

"Look, I'm so confused about all this mess. How in the hell can I be charged with murder, for God's sake?"

Harrison gulped down his drink in one gulp.

"While you were recovering at the hospital here in Wilmington, that Jaxson fella was recovering from his injuries at Chapel Hill. At the time, they wanted to keep you two separated and his injuries couldn't be handled by the surgeons here in Wilmington anyway."

"Wait, what injuries and what about the other guy, Luke?"

"Look, nobody was allowed to speak to you about the incident at the island where they found you half dead. According to your detective friend, Decker, he shot Jaxson as he was trying to cut off your head with a shovel. While Jaxson was recovering, he got hold of some overzealous prosecutor out of Durham and told his version of what happened. That punk-assed prosecutor took it upon himself to present a case in the grand jury against you for killing Luke. As we all know a grand jury would indict a ham sandwich. Anyway, after the indictment was issued, he was able to persuade a dirtbag judge to put a gag order on everyone involved in the initial investigations. Once you were released from the hospital, the arrest warrant was executed."

"This is total nonsense. I never touched either one of them or killed Luke."

"Jaxson's story is full of holes. His crazy version is that you assaulted them at the boat ramp one day, in front of witnesses, and shortly after that you took them out on a fishing trip as a way of apologizing to them for being so abusive at the boat ramp. He claims you purposely sent Luke into the creek to get some clams where you knew he was going to drown in quicksand. He claims that after you sent Luke into the creek, you shot Jaxson in the shoulder, he fell overboard and swam over to the island while you took off in the boat."

"Jesus Christ, really? My actions were in self-defense, wouldn't you say?"

"Exactly, my friend. Once I get through this, we'll request the DA to charge Jaxson with attempted murder and turn this whole affair around. In the end, I'm gonna get that prosecutor's license revoked as well. I'm going to bury that pencil-neck, so he'll never practice law anywhere in this country."

The case against Harrison never made it to trial. Whitlock moved to dismiss the case against Harrison in the interests of justice. He requested an *in camera* hearing where he made a proffer of evidence including witness statements, forensic evidence and Harrison's medical records all substantiating Harrison's account that he was brutally kidnapped by Jaxson and Luke. The short video that Wyatt Cafaro took while flying near the island proved that Jaxson was lying.

The bogus case against Harrison was exposed as, in the words of the presiding judge, "the biggest crock of B.S. this side of the Mason-Dixon line." The court referred the matter to the State Bar to consider the prosecutor's fitness to continue to practice law.

A few weeks later, Harrison was before a grand jury as the key witness against Jaxson. The District Attorney welcomed the assistance of Jason Whitlock. Jaxson testified that he was an unwitting dupe of Luke's. The grand jury adopted a Solomonic approach and charged Jaxon with aiding and abetting a kidnapping and assault with a deadly weapon.

Whitlock was furious. They should have thrown the book at this guy. Harrison didn't care. He had a more pressing matter to take care of. Jaxson was ultimately convicted and the judge handed down a meager ten-year sentence. He was sent to the Caledonia State Prison Farm, the oldest state prison in North Carolina.

CHAPTER 26

Harrison was troubled. He needed to go see his dear friend Earnie, itching to reveal a secret he had been keeping to himself for the last couple of months. He had planned to talk with Earnie once he got released from the hospital, but due to the court cases, he had to wait until those got resolved first. The time was right, so Harrison took off on his bike for the short ride over to Earnie's house.

When Harrison rolled up into Earnie's driveway, much to his surprise, Patrick was in town helping Earnie scrape away barnacles off the bottom of Earnie's boat. No sooner had he arrived, when lo and behold Detective Decker showed up. What perfect timing, Harrison thought to himself. This was the perfect time to reveal to them his secret.

Harrison ushered everyone into Earnie's garage and had them take a seat at the bar while closing the garage door and the door leading into the kitchen, making sure only they would hear what he was about to say.

"Guys, I've got to tell you something nobody knows about, and if I'm right, we all could be very rich soon."

"I'm all ears buddy, what's ya got?" Earnie asked, mixing Harrison a white Russian.

"Do you all know what a three-dollar gold princess coin is, or even know what it is worth today? Well, it's worth a shit ton of money, my friends."

"What the hell are you talking about?" Patrick inquired.

"Listen to me, shut up. The last thing I can remember before you guys apparently showed up to rescue me, was a gold coin I saw at the bottom of the pit I was digging. While I was in the hospital, I did a ton of research, and to cut this short, guys, there's a fortune sitting out there buried under that burn barrel."

"So, you saw one stinking coin and think we're all gonna get rich, huh?" Patrick questioned, shaking his head.

"Are you still on heavy medication, dude?" Decker interjected, laughing.

"Hey, even if it is just one coin, split four ways could be a thousand bucks each. But guys, I am convinced one hundred percent that there is a lot more out there than just one coin."

Over the next fifteen minutes, Harrison explained to his buddies the results of his hours of research while in the hospital citing to them numerous firsthand accounts on how families hid their valuables from the approaching Yankee soldiers during the Civil War. They all knew that Harrison tended to exaggerate his stories a bit, but his delivery that day was spot on and eventually everyone agreed that the possibility did in fact exist.

Once Harrison had their attention, he hit them with the *coup de grace*.

"Look guys, near the end of my stay in the hospital, I had a wild idea to write a book about my experience out there on the island. After I realized what kind of gold coin I saw, I did more in depth research. Do you know that prior to the Civil War there were some twenty peanut plantations spread out from Sneads Ferry to the north all the way down to Middle Sound? Some of those farmers were wealthy folks, generating in today's dollars close to $750,000 a year in revenue. The transactions back then were done with gold coins, not paper money or checks like today. One of those farmers was so wealthy he constructed a shipping wharf so schooners could load up the peanuts and ship them north to Philadelphia and New York City. He shared that wharf with all the other farmers in the area. And guess what guys, guess where that wharf was built near?"

"Holy shit, don't tell me, near the friggin' island where we found you?" Patrick spoke up.

"Yes, it was. Almost directly across from it. It was still visible up until about 1953 by the way."

"I need your help guys. I really want to write another book and I am trying to come up with an opening chapter, introduction or what some people call a prologue. I think after you read this, you'll be convinced as I am, that there's a shit load of gold out there just for the taking. Here, I've made ya'll some copies to read to see what you think. If I am wrong and there is no gold out there, maybe we can write this book together and make some money from it."

"Hold on a minute. Are you telling us you want to write another book after all the mess you just went through? And don't tell me it's about finding treasure?" Earnie questioned.

"Yeah, I do want to write another one, and yes it would be about treasure hunting."

"You've lost your friggin' mind," Decker said raising his arms up in disbelief.

"You don't understand. I've got serious debt issues at home. I must do something to raise cash. The first book did alright, but sales are dropping off quickly. So, I was thinking about a sequel to the first one. Look, just read this and let me know if it would grab you to buy a book?'

Harrison handed his buddies his rough draft:

The news that Atlanta, Georgia was captured by General Sherman's union army on September 2, 1864, sent shivers down the spines of many southern residents throughout North Carolina. There were many chilling and disturbing reports written in local newspapers at the time that detailed how renegade members of Sherman's army, called "bummers" roamed the countryside terrorizing and looting Confederate civilians.

When news that Fort Fisher was captured on January 15, 1865, and the union army was advancing north towards Wilmington, North Carolina, one wealthy peanut farmer, whose three-thousand-acre plantation was about ten miles northeast of Wilmington decided it was imperative that he protect his family. He feared that those so-called bummers would eventually set foot on his land, so late one night under the cover of darkness he slipped out of his manor house unnoticed and embarked on a short journey. He told no one of his plan to protect the family. The secret plan was his and only his.

As he rowed his tiny skiff across the large coastal bay that abutted his property, he encountered a driving rain that slowed his progress, but undaunted he persevered and half an hour later he beached the skiff on his intended destination. The tiny two-acre island was where he learned how to shoot a rifle as a young boy with his grandfather hunting for wild rabbits. Although covered in thick vegetation, he knew from memory how to reach the two enormous live oak trees in the middle of the island that were perched on top of a sandy knoll.

With the heavy saddle bags draped across his shoulders, a lantern in one hand and a shovel in the other, he pushed his way through the heavy brush reaching the base of the largest live oak tree in less than five minutes. Tired and soaking wet, he took shelter for a moment under the huge canopy the tree provided, to gather his strength. A violent coughing spell hit him suddenly and that delayed his digging for a few minutes.

For the next hour or so, he dug down four or five feet and made the hole just as wide, when the blade tip of his shovel hit something hard and broke off the very tip of his shovel. He reached out for his lantern to take a better look and found himself staring at what looked like a wooden box. He brushed away the remaining dirt to uncover the top of a wooden chest, a rounded structure and design he had never seen before. With one mighty blow, he drove his blunted shovel through the top of the chest, and it shattered into a hundred pieces. He stared down in total disbelief when the glitter of a hundred or more Spanish gold coins reflected off the dim light of his lantern.

"Well, well, I'll be damned. Blackbeard was here after all."

After digging some more, he retrieved what was left of the wooden box and all the coins and placed it all off to the side. He dug down even further, another three to four feet and placed the broken wooden box and the coins into the hole. After covering up the Spanish coins with three feet of dirt, he placed his saddle bags on top.

Rowing back to his house, the farmer felt confident his little journey would no doubt protect his family. Should the union soldiers happen to invade his house and hold his wife and children at gun point demanding that he tell where his fortune was hidden, he could tell them the location and not worry, as what lie below that was far more valuable than the contents of the saddle bags.

In the early morning hours, the next day, the fever the farmer developed over night spiked so high and so rapidly, he went into a

coma before anyone awoke in the household, and by noon he was
dead.

No one knew of his escapade the night before. The secret
journey killed him, and the secret remains.

"Dang bro, I think you might be on to something," Earnie
acknowledged. "That really could have happened."

"Oh, hell no, he had way too many drugs in the hospital and
he's suffering from major brain damage," Decker interjected
again, grabbing another beer.

"Hey wait a minute, did ya read what he wrote? Think about
it. What he described really could have happened back then,"
Earnie strongly countered.

"Well, we've got nothing else to do. Screw it, let's go find out."

After a few more drinks, the men decided to venture out to
the island that afternoon armed with several shovels, a bucket
full of beer, and a pre-mixed half gallon of white Russians.
Decker had his guitar with him, and on the way there he belted
out:

Yo ho, yo ho, a pirate's life for me.
We pillage plunder, we rifle and loot.
Drink up me 'earties, yo ho.
We kidnap and ravage and don't give a hoot.
Drink up me 'earties, yo ho.
Yo ho, yo ho, a pirate's life for me.

Thirty minutes later, the three intoxicated men landed on the
island. Since Decker was the youngest, he started digging a hole
under the old burn barrel while Patrick stood over him, spraying
him down with bug spray. None of them, other than Harrison,
believed they would find anything, but to appease their good
buddy, the digging continued for the next twenty minutes.

Decker lifted a shovel full of sand and haphazardly dumped it on the ground near Earnie's feet. Everybody froze in disbelief when five gold coins came into view, glistening brilliantly in the late afternoon sunlight.

"Holy mother of God," Decker shouted out. "Look at this."

Lying at the bottom of the four-foot-deep hole had to be at least a dozen more gold coins, all of them in pristine condition.

Earnie ran down to the hill to the boat and returned with the bucket and his cast net. Decker filled up his shovel and poured the contents on the cast net draped over the bucket, letting the sand fill into the bucket but catching the gold coins. Within twenty minutes, they realized they needed another bucket to hold all the coins Decker was finding.

Earnie and Patrick ran back to the boat searching for other buckets, but at first couldn't find any topside. Patrick remembered seeing a large fifty-four-quart Coleman cooler down below deck when he had retrieved the duffle bag full of guns, so he went below and found it still there, stored in the small shower stall.

The sun was beginning to set and already they had two five-gallon buckets full to the brim with about a quarter of the Coleman cooler full, when they decided to fill the hole back up, get the burn barrel back in place and head back to Earnie's house. They were all so stunned at what they were carrying, nobody said a word on the boat ride back to the dock. Silence continued on the ride to Earnie's house.

The four men unloaded the contents of the two buckets and the cooler on top of the pool table and stood back in amazement.

"I told ya. I just knew it. My God, look at it, boys," Harrison said while leaning over the table and hugging the pile of gold coins.

"What are we going to do with all this?" Decker asked, fingering through a pile of coins.

"The first thing we need to do is hide this and we all need to keep cool and not say a damn thing to anyone," Earnie spoke up.

The attic to Earnie's house was located above the garage area that was accessible by a key operated mini elevator capable of handling five hundred pounds per load. They decided to hide the coins in the attic until they could figure out a way to sell them or dispose of them in other ways. Earnie turned the key to engage the elevator, bringing it down to about three feet above the garage floor and then jumped on board. All the coins were placed in the cooler which Earnie labeled on top with a black magic marker, the words Poison-Do Not Touch. Earnie pushed the on-board red button and within seconds, he disappeared up into the attic. He returned in less than two minutes. Turning the wall key to the upright position, the elevator retracted back into the attic.

The next day, the four men went back to Earnie's Island and filled two more coolers full of gold and silver coins along with an assortment of fine jewelry pieces. The loot was stored in Earnie's attic. Once the honey hole, as the men called it, coughed up its last coin during their second visit, they had the task of determining the value of their find.

Harrison ordered four copies of *The Official Red Book-A Guidebook of United States Coins* and the men met in Earnie's garage twice a week, taking a detailed inventory of the coins. The men stationed themselves around the pool table covered with the coins, armed with a lamp, a magnifying glass, the Red Book, and an accountant's ledger sheet. Taking each coin one at a time they assigned each one a value per the guidelines in the Red Book. The process took a month. Once completed, each man handed Earnie their respective ledger sheets to let him make the final tabulation. From the very start, they had agreed not to total their individual sheets, but to wait for the final tabulation as a group.

Decker, Harrison, and Patrick went to the bar to mix themselves a drink while they watched Earnie sitting at the end of the pool table compiling the totals from each sheet. You could have cut the tension in the air with a knife as Earnie's fingers flew across his calculator and it became dead silent when he hit the final total key.

"That can't be right, hold on, I've got to recalculate this."

Earnie once again ran the numbers from each sheet and hit the total key. Earnie spun the calculator around so each person could see the bright blue numbers illuminated on the calculator screen.......

$$\$35,455,774.00$$

Decker choked on his beer and Harrison dropped his drink on the floor, while Patrick slumped in his bar stool, not able to mutter a word. Earnie wrote down the final number on a small yellow sticky note, stuck it to his forehead and stood up facing his friends.

"You did it, you son of a bitch, you did it," Earnie shouted out rushing toward Harrison with his arms extended.

Their jubilation didn't last too long when Patrick, in his typical monotone voice, spoke up. "What the hell are we going to do now?".

"I know a guy," Earnie replied.

"Whoa, hold on, ease up a little. We've got some serious legal issues to consider before we contact your guy," Decker said shaking his head back and forth.

"What's there to worry about?" Patrick questioned.

273

"We don't own that island, the state of North Carolina does and there are strict Treasure Trove laws in this state."

"What the hell are you talking about? Its finders' keepers in my mind," Earnie said.

"Not in North Carolina. Whatever is found on state land is owned by the state, period. You break those laws and you're facing a stint in jail my friend."

All the jubilation evaporated instantly. They each had stunned looks on their faces.

Stepping away from his buddies, Harrison reached for his cell phone and dialed a contact number already programmed into his phone.

"Have you got a backhoe available for half a day rent tomorrow?' Okay, what time do you open? Great, thanks."

What the hell dude, what are you doing?" Patrick asked.

"Hear me out. Y'all remember when hurricane Florence ripped through here and snapped off that gigantic hickory tree in my back yard? Well, that huge stump is still there. Earnie is going to A- to- Z rental tomorrow and rent a backhoe. As a gracious gift to me to help with my rehabilitation of my leg, he decided to build me a swimming pool, okay."

"The first thing he needs to do is pull up that huge stump. When he does, well guess what he finds? You got it, the gold coins." Harrison took a long sip of his white Russian.

"That gold my friends is mine, not the state's. We'll take a dozen or so of the coins and place them down in the cavity and take a few pictures of me pointing to the find. So, if anybody gets nosy and starts asking a bunch of questions, we'll just show them the pictures. Who's going to know other than the four of us standing right here? Problem solved, huh?"

"Hooah" could be heard throughout Middle Sound.

CHAPTER 27

The gentle rocking of the seventy-foot Hinckley Sou'wester sailboat woke Harrison up out of a dead sleep. It was rare for him to sleep through the night without having terrifying nightmares from his ordeal one year earlier. After being exonerated from the murder charges, he wanted to get as far away from North Carolina as he possibly could. It took a lot of persuading to convince Ms. Kelly that they needed to leave their home in Middle Sound and begin another life far, far away.

After saying his goodbyes to Jason Whitlock and his team in late September, Harrison fired up his computer, wasting no time in researching luxury sailboats that were for sale and possible exotic locations that featured spectacular sailing opportunities.

In 1980, Harrison had attended the Annapolis Boat Show and boarded a Hinckley 50 Sou'wester model and fell in love with the design and features, so he narrowed his search down to Hinckley sailboats. In just two hours, he stumbled upon an upcoming estate sale at the Rodeo Marina just south of Vallejo, California, that listed a seventy-foot Hinckley sailboat up for auction. A week later Harrison and Ms. Kelly were the proud owners of a 1998 seventy-foot Hinckley that was in pristine condition.

Ms. Kelly, with little knowledge of sailboats, let Harrison select the sailboat he wanted, but she made it abundantly clear that she would choose the location where the sailboat would be moored at. While signing the papers in the dockmaster's office at the Rodea Marina, the attorney for the estate introduced Ms.

Kelly and Harrison to the previous captain of the boat, Roger McBride. Based on Captain Roger's impeccable credentials and his witty sense of humor, Harrison and Ms. Kelly took an immediate liking to the seasoned forty-six-year-old sailor and hired him on the spot.

Once the papers were all signed, Ms. Kelly asked Captain Roger if he had any suggestions on where they should moor the boat. His response was immediate, and taking Captain Roger's advice, the three boarded a plane that evening and flew to Bora-Bora to tour what Captain Roger described as, "God's Retreat."

Harrison and Ms. Kelly absolutely fell in love with Bora-Bora and the decision was made for Captain Roger, along with his wife Regina, to sail the boat from California to Bora-Bora.

Captain Roger explained the trip would take about twenty-five days and that gave Harrison and Ms. Kelly plenty of time to settle their affairs back in Wilmington. They agreed not to sell their home in Middle Sound but allow Bryson and Andrea to house sit while they were gone. Ms. Kelly knew down deep that Harrison would eventually tire of the sailing community and would want to return to North Carolina. But right now, she realized that Harrison needed to be in a non-stressful environment so he could recuperate.

The day before Harrison and Ms. Kelly departed for Bora-Bora, Harrison drove to the hospital to say goodbye to his wonderful nurse Ruby. It was her tender care that got Harrison through all the grueling and painful rehab sessions. Knowing her plight as a single mom and the efforts she made to help support her mother back in Jamaica, Harrison wanted to reach out and help. He had to let her know how much he appreciated her warm friendship. Without her care and continuous encouragement, he probably would have never recovered as well as he did. He truly cherished their relationship.

Upon seeing Harrison walking down the hallway towards her nursing station, Ruby jumped up and ran into Harrison's open arms.

He explained to Ruby that he and Ms. Kelly were going away for a while and he wanted to make sure he said his goodbyes, especially to her, before he left. Ruby was touched by Harrison's gesture, and both broke out in tears, embracing each tightly. Harrison said his last goodbye and handed Ruby a plain white legal-sized envelope with a card inside that read, *"How's this for some bullshit?"* Harrison had a huge smile on his face leaving the hospital and he knew that Ruby would soon have an even bigger smile than his. Inside the card were two first class round-trip plane tickets to Jamaica and a check for one hundred thousand dollars.

Ms. Kelly was busy preparing breakfast in the galley, and the wonderful smell of bacon frying on the stove permeated throughout the boat. Harrison put on his swim trunks, walked into the galley, and patted his wife on the butt and kissed her cheek. He made himself a mimosa while loading the CD player with Third World's *Journey to Addis* and headed to the upper deck.

His friends had arrived around eleven o'clock the previous night and they didn't have much time to chat, since they were exhausted from the long flights into Bora-Bora. Harrison was so elated having his close friends on board. Sipping on their own mimosas, Harrison found Tammy and Irene basking in the warm sunlight nestled in their padded lounge chairs, soothed by the easy beat of "Cool Meditation."

"Good morning, ladies, welcome aboard another beautiful day on *Magic*."

"My God, it really is exquisite here Harrison. Thanks so much for inviting us," Tammy commented. "Are we going sailing today?"

"Not today, we'll wait for tomorrow as I've got a surprise for y'all."

"Really, what is that?" Irene asked, rising in her chair.

"Our dear buddy Decker is flying in later today around four o'clock and he told me he was bringing all of us, a big surprise,"

"Oh fantastic, I can't wait to see him," Tammy said, reaching for another mimosa. "I always wondered what happened to him after he got fired."

"So, we'll have a good dinner tonight and we'll put *Magic* into the wind tomorrow."

"Hey, by the way, how did you come up with the name *Magic*?" Irene asked.

"Well, let me tell you a story about one of my drunken adventures while a bachelor at Wrightsville Beach some six years before Ms. Kelly and I got married."

As the story went, Harrison named his new sailboat *Magic*, which was the same name of the 1978 twenty-two-foot Ranger sailboat he owned back in 1985. He purchased it from Captain Kenny who at the time was the captain for Walter Cronkite's sailboat. In July 1985, when Captain Kenny found out he was hired as Mr. Cronkite's captain, he had to sell *Magic* within a week since he had to move up north to Martha's Vineyard. After a hard night of drinking on a warm Saturday night with Captain Kenny at the King Neptune bar at Wrightsville Beach, Harrison explained he woke up the next morning staring at a promissory note he signed for five thousand dollars made out to Captain Kenny.

"Did you have five thousand dollars lying around at the time?" Tammy asked.

"Oh, hell no, but my word is my word, so I went to the bank on Monday morning and with the help of the girl I was dating at the bank, I got approved for a loan. That afternoon I handed Kenny five grand."

"Anyway, enough about that. Where's Earnie and Patrick?"

"Oh, they're out snorkeling for lobster," Tammy chimed in. "Those idiots probably don't even know what one looks like!"

"Bullshit," Irene interrupted. "I bet you, they're at some bar chasing mermaid tails."

Everyone broke out in laughter. It was going to be another glorious day, for sure. In a few hours, the old gang would be back together again, and everyone was eager to find out what this surprise Decker had up his sleeve.

Decker's flight was due to arrive at four o'clock that afternoon and everyone was eager to see him. It had been a long six months since they were all together, and they were dying to find out what this surprise was all about.

Six months earlier, Harrison flew everyone out to California and had gathered everybody for lunch at the Four Fools Winery on the eastside of San Pablo Bay. He then shuttled everyone over to the Rodea Marina to show off the new sailboat he just purchased. That was the last time the entire group was together and both Harrison and Ms. Kelly were homesick for their company. Although Harrison and Ms. Kelly made a few casual friends on the island, those relationships with the locals were somewhat timid. They treated Harrison and Ms. Kelly as mere transients. So having their true friends all together again was going to be pure heaven at God's retreat.

Kelly brought up a tray full of another round of mimosas and joined Tammy and Irene on deck. Harrison stood at the stern of the boat scanning the water with his high-powered binoculars, searching for his buddies. A few minutes later they came into view about two hundred yards out, and all aboard could hear off in the distance, HOOAH over and over.

"Oh my God, they are hammered."

He watched the two men approach in the twenty-foot skiff skippered by Captain Roger. Harrison and Ms. Kelly, once they arrived at Bora-Bora, realized they needed a means to shuttle themselves from the sailboat over to the mainland, so they rented a Carolina Skiff from a local marina on the island the day after they arrived.

"I told you they didn't go snorkeling, they went straight to the bar looking for those tight-assed mermaids," Irene said, approaching the stern of the boat.

Harrison stored his binoculars and retrieved a few deck lines while Irene lowered the steel steps down to the water's edge, mumbling cuss words under her breath. The closer they got, Harrison and Irene could see they were totally shit-faced and realized it would take all four of them on board to help the two veterans on board.

While Earnie and Patrick were helped to their quarters for a well-needed nap, Harrison boarded the skiff to inform Captain Roger about Decker's four o'clock arrival and instructed him to go by the liquor store and get a couple of bottles of Dom Perignon and return to *Magic* around three fifteen to pick everyone up.

It was only ten o'clock, so Earnie and Patrick had time to sleep it off and be halfway sober when Decker arrived. While the ladies were enjoying their mimosas and getting a little tipsy themselves, Harrison went down below, fired up his computer and logged into his TD Ameritrade account. He wanted to check on the results of a few trades that Captain Roger had recommended to him the day before. The profit results were gratifying enough that Harrison sold his positions. Captain Roger's stock picks were spot on and paying off nicely.

It was soon after they arrived at Bora-Bora, that Harrison learned that Captain Roger once worked for one of the leading hedge fund firms in New York City but tiring of the rat race and backstabbing shenanigans of his co-workers, he resigned at the age of thirty-one, banking a small fortune.

Looking for peace and solitude, he took a menial job as a first mate on a sixty-two-foot Beneteau sailboat moored at the Sagamore Yacht Club on Oyster Bay Harbor on Long Island, New York. After just one short day trip he found his new calling and decided to study for his captain's license which he obtained eight months later. A member at the Sagamore Yacht Club referred Captain Roger to a relative in California, and he found himself the captain of *Magic* in the fall of 1998. Captain Roger fell in love with Regina, the first mate, and they got married on board in the Spring of 1999 while in Bora-Bora.

Later that afternoon around three thirty, Tammy and Irene went below with a handful of ibuprofens and got their husbands dressed. Everybody piled into the skiff to take the ten-minute ride over to the airport. Earnie and Patrick had no idea what was going on, and no one said a word to them. After Decker arrived, the plan was to go eat at Harrison's favorite restaurant, the Otemanu.

One by one, the passengers got off the Air Tahiti ATR-72 600 twin-engine turboprop and walked straight out onto the tarmac.

Decker came into view holding the hand of a young, short, pretty woman wearing shorts, flip flops, and a low-cut T-shirt.

"Oh my God!" Tammy shouted. "That's Willow from Diamonds."

Willow had been their favorite waitress at Diamonds, and they would always see Decker flirting with her when he was there. He was simply googly eyed over her for years. This truly was a huge surprise to everyone. Earnie and Patrick just stood there stunned, wondering if they were dreaming. What they were witnessing wasn't possible. It was a well-known fact that Willow professed many times that she was gay, so there was no way she and Decker would be together.

After everyone hugged and kissed, they walked a short distance to the dock, piled the luggage into the skiff and headed out for the restaurant. Harrison had reserved one of the private dining rooms which featured a round table able to sit eight people comfortably, with a panoramic view of the ocean from any seat. The setting was angelic.

Although the scenery was breathtaking, Earnie and Patrick just could not fathom the sight of Decker and Willow holding hands and nuzzling up to each other. Earnie just bent down and shook his head when he saw Decker reach over and grab a white gardenia flower and gently place it in Willow's hair.

"Unbelievable," Earnie whispered to his wife. "Can you believe this shit?"

"No possible way, but let it be."

Willow was so elated to see everyone again that she broke down in tears of joy.

"You all just disappeared into thin air, and you never said goodbye. That really bothered me to no end, but I am so happy to see y'all now."

She got up and went around the table and gave everyone hugs and kisses, with tears streaming down her cheeks. It was a warm touching moment, and a few other tears were shed.

"I heard you were in the hospital for several weeks Harrison," Willow said, holding his hand. "Are you okay now?"

"Oh yeah, no problems. I've got a small limp, but it's not too bad."

"Well, what the hell happened and how the hell did you get all the way out here?"

Harrison looked around at each person, especially Decker, looking for nods of approval so he could tell Willow the story of what really happened. Should he share the story or not? Looking around the table, he could see no one objected.

"Let's eat first, and I'll tell you an incredible story you won't believe."

After a wonderful meal featuring all the island's tasty seafoods, Harrison ordered himself a shot of Grand Marnier and a round of buttery nipple shots for everyone else, with instructions to the waiter to keep them coming every fifteen minutes. Harrison leaned up on the table and motioned for Willow to come closer so he could lower his voice.

"I'm sure that Decker has already filled you in on all the shit that happened, right?"

"Yes, he did, it was awful."

"Well, I'll assume he didn't tell you everything. Just before that knucklehead Jaxson knocked me out with his shotgun, I had pushed the shovel into the ground one last time. I hit something other than sand, and when I looked down, I saw a gold coin. I quickly covered it so Jaxson wouldn't see it. So, after I recovered and didn't go to jail for trumped up murder charges, I went over to Earnie's house for a visit and told him what I saw. Patrick happened to be there also, and we were getting ready to jump in Earnie's golf cart when Decker showed up. We grabbed shovels from Earnie's shed, jumped in the golf cart, and headed to the marina.

"We got to the spot on the island where I was digging before, and we took turns shoveling. Maybe four to five feet down, we began to uncover coin after coin, to the point our pockets were full. Earnie had a five-gallon bucket on board his boat, and we filled that up within minutes. To make a long story short, it took us a few days to unearth all the coins and some other valuables. We made trip after trip, back and forth, loaded down with coins. All in all, we pulled out thousands and thousands of rare old gold coins, dating back to the early 1800s. Do you know we sold some of those coins for $7,000 each? Just three hundred coins at $7,000 each equals a cool two million dollars sweetheart."

The waiter arrived with another round and shots, and Harrison took a break from his story.

"Wait, how the hell did those coins get out there, and why didn't anybody find them before? I know guys that have taken their metal detectors out there, so why didn't they find anything?"

"Look, that burn barrel out there has been in that location for decades because it is the safest location to have a fire on the knoll. Although it probably has been replaced tons of times, it always gets placed in the same spot. Nobody goes near it with a metal detector, and nobody ever thought of moving it to scan underneath."

Harrison paused to take a sip of his drink, then continued.

"From what I learned while in the hospital, during the Civil War, whenever the Union soldiers were about to invade a southern town or city, many of the residents would bury their valuables and gold somewhere that they could retrieve it once the soldiers left. I think a wealthy family, or maybe a group of wealthy residents back in Wilmington, took all their wealth and buried it out on the island. Maybe they got killed, or killed each other, or just died and nobody knew about it. Who knows, but somebody buried it out there and it made all of us very rich people."

"Well, I guess that makes sense."

"Earnie contacted some guy with the JM Bullion Company who bought gold and silver in Dallas and set up a meeting in his office where we could show him a few of the coins we had. We sold off some of the jewelry to pay for our trip out there and it was well worth it. Our buddy here, good old ex-Detective Decker ran a background check on this guy to make sure he was a member of the American Numismatic Association and fully accredited with the Professional Coin Grading Service. Anyway, to make a long story short and not bore you to death, this guy managed everything for us, and I mean everything. He even flew into Wilmington from Dallas, loaded up all the coins in an unmarked armor truck, put it all on a special jet, and flew back to Dallas. We just sat back and watched our bank accounts swell up like a balloon."

The waiter arrived with another round.

"I don't know about the rest of them, but I kept a few of the more valuable coins and locked them away in a safe deposit box in a bank back in Wilmington. They'll be passed on to my son and grandchildren when I depart. They'll be set for life,"

"Well, what about you guys?" Willow asked, turning her attention to Earnie and Patrick.

Earnie then told his story about how he and Tammy moved to Ormond Beach, Florida and bought a channel front home in a small community called Tomoka Estates. They wanted to be close to their son Wyatt, who was attending college at the Embry-Riddle Aeronautical University located in Daytona Beach, which was just a short drive south on US 1.

Once Earnie finished his story, Patrick explained that he and Irene moved at about the same time Earnie and Tammy did. They had decided to spend the summer months up north in Patrick's hometown of Pittsburgh and bought a new home in the Cherry Valley Lakeview Estates community to be close to his family. They also purchased a nice Winnebago and rented a spot at the Sunshine Holiday Daytona RV Park, that was only a few miles from Earnie and Tammy's house. In that way, they could spend the winters in the warm weather and be close to their dearest friends.

"Oh, no wonder I didn't see y'all much. Wow, everybody just scattered, huh?"

Harrison grinned, stood up, raised his glass, and belted out, "A toast to the Good Life!"

The sun was setting, revealing a majestic blaze of colors that took everyone's breath away. The oranges, and the streaks of yellow mixing with vibrant purples radiating off the golden tipped clouds in the distance, portrayed a heavenly picture that touched the soul. Nature's beauty, God's portrait, was on full display and not a sound could be heard all over the entire island.

Harrison remained seated as the others left their seats and walked over to the large plate-glass window to gaze upon the phenomenal display. Wiping away the tears in his eyes, Harrison was overwhelmed with emotion as an immense sense of comfort and peace overcame him seeing and being with his closest friends once again. He loved them all dearly and at that moment, he felt he was no doubt the luckiest man alive.

He got up out of his seat, walked over to the window and stood between Earnie and Patrick, extending his arms around their shoulders. Earnie and Patrick reciprocated. Harrison leaned over and kissed each one on the cheek and all three men came to tears, hugging each other even closer. For the first time since the attack on him took place, Harrison felt safe.

Moments after the sun had set, and while the group were all headed back to their seats, Willow politely excused herself and told everyone she needed to call her mom to let her know she arrived safe and sound. She grabbed her pocketbook and left the dining room, heading for the main entrance.

Once outside, Willow spotted a small open floral garden about ten to fifteen yards away with a huge palm tree in the center. Willow walked into the empty garden and stood behind the palm tree, blocking her view back towards the restaurant. She paused and took one last look back towards the restaurant and seeing that nobody followed her, reached into her pocketbook, and pulled out her cell phone. Holding the phone slightly above her head, Willow checked to make sure she had a good signal. Satisfied with the four solid bars displayed on her screen, she dialed the number and waited.

"Caledonia Prison. Officer Brennan speaking."

"I want to leave a message for inmate C-8468, Jaxson Cook."

"What is your message?"

"I found them."

CAST OF CHARACTERS

Harrison Thomas – Paw Paw, author
Ms. Kelly Thomas – Harrison's wife, Grandmama
Dalton Thomas– Kelly and Harrison's son
Andrea – Harrison and Kelly's granddaughter
Bryson – Harrison and Kelly's grandson
Earnie Cafaro – Harrison's best friend
Tammy Cafaro – Earnie's wife, Kelly's best friend
Nicole Cafaro – Director of Forensics, Earnie's daughter
Wyatt Cafaro – Earnie and Tammy's son, the pilot
Patrick Armstrong – Earnie's 82nd Airborne buddy
Irene Armstrong- Patrick's wife
Jaxson Cook – Kidnapper
Luke Jefferson -Kidnapper
Detective Anthony Decker – Lead investigator
Gretchen Banks – Assistant Director of Forensics
Sebastian Vickors – SBI Agent
Rex Calder – Publisher
Lilly Maynard – Gardener, Aunt Lilly

ACKNOWLEDGMENTS

This novel could not be completed without the love of family and friends that were so instrumental in providing guidance, direction, and encouragement along the way.

Special thanks to my dear friends Earnie, Tammy, Paige, and Hunter Chance, along with Dan, and Todd for their input and sincere inspiration.

Enormous gratitude is given to Mrs. Robin Cunningham for her keen insights and writing talents.

Much gratitude is given to my editor, Frank Amoroso, for his guidance and patience.

To my grandkids, Andrea Mills and Bryson Mills, whom I adore and love very much. Thank you for all your ideas and support.

To my brother Rich Mathis . . . "luv ya bro" . . . . I need to say no more.

To Randy Ivey for the book cover photograph.

To my wife of 31 years...I am a lucky man. I love you dearly.

To my son Dalton, who inspired me to write my first novel. Thank you for the wonderful book cover design.

Made in the USA
Middletown, DE
21 March 2023